# Occhi Belli

by

## Tim McDonald

## Dedication

To Paul Tompkins, for his wisdom, his love, his forever support, and for never giving me a bad book

Prologue

His eyes opened again to the black hole of the hell he was in, stymied by a stagnant, impenetrable, indeterminate darkness, his mind as blank as what his eyes could see. He lay straight upon the muddied earth like a corpse seemingly sinking farther down with each passing moment and the cold, damp, stone walls enclosed around him offered no asylum—no windows, no light, only somewhere a dark door lay beyond within the shroud of blackness. He knew he was still alive: he could smell the stench of the grotesque earthly hole dug in the corner for what little fecal matter there was, feel the chapped insides of his mouth as he slowly roved his tongue over his teeth, the enamel beginning to wear away. Perhaps soon, the madman he would become— delirium, madness, and ultimately, death. His name, he told himself upon each waking moment lest he forget, was Luca Lucchesi.

He knew he was underground. Water trickling down the rock walls beckoned to him. As he peered into the dark void, his thoughts turned just as dark, to just let himself go by denying the body and the will to survive, but then he found himself propping his elbows up into the mud, then his knees, groping in the dark for the slimy wall and the trickling water. He thirstily licked the stones, tasting minerals and clay, perhaps *galestro*— perhaps, he was still in Tuscany.

It was difficult to know anything concretely. Knowing neither the time of day nor what day it was, he only knew he was in a hell of his own making. His diminishing life that existed in that cell had been forged from the fires of escapism and addiction. 'How did I get here,' he often philosophized, knowing full well that question was the victim crying out for an answer to the larger question, 'what is the meaning of it all.' He knew exactly how he found himself in that cell and moreover, why. *Occhi Belli*, the beautiful-eyed woman. But she was not the catalyst to the problem, but the answer. He knew his only purpose was to answer the question of how to escape and rescue her before madness inevitably settled in and forced her hand. With no recourse, she would have to deny him. Time was not on his side; and his captures knew that.

He heard faintly the soft steps of what must be some corporeal apparition coming for him just beyond the steel door. The delirium was upon him as he rubbed the tufts of newly grown hair on his head—he remembered that someone had at one point come in and shaved him, perhaps so that he could acutely feel the cold sensations of his underworld. He heard the jingling of keys and the clanking of the steel door unlocking. Perhaps he would eat that day—his mouth, dry and crusty, as the watery walls offered only a paucity of H2O molecules, his time, he knew, was imminent. He couldn't remember the last thing he had eaten and it seemed his stomach stopped growling eons ago. But as the door swung aside, his insides gave out a gurgling cry and suddenly a light so bright lit upon Luca that he instinctually shrank back into the cell and cowered up against the wall. The light burned into his eyes like the sun radiating down upon an exposed body on an island rock in the middle of the sea and he couldn't see who or what was there. He put his hand out in front of the beam and saw the shadow of a person. Then he heard a deep, gruff voice, a cacophony of cruelty in that darkness.

"Bene?" Luca recognized the voice. It was the bald man with cruel, sociopathic eyes.

"*Che schifo. Lui non significa niente per me.*" A woman's voice rang callously into the cell. *Disgusting. He means nothing to me.* Luca tried to look into the light and find her, but the light was gone, the door closed, and he heard the footsteps hurry away. He found in front of him cold, half eaten *lasagne*, which he began to shovel into his mouth in great heaps.

It was impossible that it was her, his *Occhi Belli.* Luca sat against the wall holding the *lasagne* in his hands, his eyes shifting left to right, thinking, trying to think. *Disgusting. He means nothing to me.* No, there was no way it was her. But he couldn't think anything with certainty. He could only imagine what she saw in that cell, could only imagine the effluvium that was there. It was her; it had to be her; the purpose was all too clear. It was over. Everything was over. She was finished with him.

Luca threw what was left of the *lasagne* into the corner and bowed his head into his grimy hands and tried to weep. She was all he was holding out for. The cell grew darker than before, trapped him inside like a completed Rubik's Cube—it was finished and nothing more had to be done. Before he perished into the real darkness, he wanted to recount in his mind the story that made him, the beautifully imperfect story that brought him to this.

He first thought of his mother.

\*\*\*\*

Luca gazed out at the sun slowly inching up into the pale gray sky as his mother, Francesca, drove the car laden with ski gear out of the city. Out in the fields, dollops of dew descended down the wheat and corn stalks and Luca caught the tiny tears of glittery pearls before they merged with the earth. Luca's friend, Tony, slumbered next to him in the backseat without a care. Tony had spent the night and the boys had presumably gone to bed at a reasonable hour under Francesca's watchful eye, but as soon as the bedroom door closed and the footsteps were out of earshot, the boys turned on a bedside lamp and played video games with the sound down for another few hours. Luca yawned resentfully as Tony snuggled into his pillow against the car door. He caught his mother's eyes peering at him through the rearview mirror. "Eyes on the road, mom."

Bluewood Ski Area was just under two hours away—two hours of being in his own head without an escape. The road was long and straight and sleepy. Cold fields of alfalfa on the lefthand side, wheat and corn on the right, but at that time of year, only barren fields of shriveled stalks peeked out of the hard earth. The small towns they drove through were interesting because Luca was interested in old, junky things like box cars and dilapidated buildings, but they passed them by in a blip so Luca couldn't see if there were any vagabonds or storytellers hanging about like his dad always said there were in places like that.

Luca had just lost his father to lung disease; his mother, having just turned forty, had lost her husband of twenty years. Neither knew what to do next, but they both knew they needed each other close without saying so. It was just Luca and his mother now. The ski trip was his mother's idea, something new, something different, something to get their minds off of life for a while and to learn something together. Luca had never once thought about going skiing and his mother had never mentioned it. The idea was so absurd, so explosive like the big bang coming from nothing, that Luca instantly agreed with one caveat—that he could bring a friend, someone to fill the space between his mother and himself. That had been just two days prior and here they were, trying to act as if everything was peachy. Luca thanked his mother for that—he didn't want to think about his dad's death. Only twelve years old and fatherless: it was not right.

Francesca had made her coffee extra strong that morning and Luca instantly perked up as she opened the vacuum flask, the robust aroma wafting back toward him. He looked at his mother through the rearview mirror and saw himself in the backseat, saw his father, Mateo, as a young man. Perhaps that was how his mother saw him—the ghost of her youthful husband. She had known Mateo since they were children; they had grown up together, played childish games together against a rebuilding nation. Luca understood he had lost someone he had known for twelve years, but had only really known for a few, but his mother had lost someone she had known for almost forty years. Luca couldn't imagine how it would feel to lose someone so close to oneself, who had become a part of oneself.

"You're eyeing my coffee, and I can see your nose wrinkling up," Francesca said. "I suppose you want some." Francesca looked like a diminutive child behind the steering wheel, barely high enough to see out the front windshield. Luca thought his mother was beautiful and all his friends told him she looked like his older sister, young and pretty. She hadn't the gray hairs like other moms her age or the lines on her face. She always said she stayed youthful because she grew up in Italy drinking olive oil like water and wine like olive oil.

"I can't sleep like lug head Tony here," Luca said. "So, yeah, can I?"

"Only a little," she said, passing the vacuum flask back. "You don't want to stunt your growth."

Luca blew on the coffee and took a small sip as he watched the flat, brown and green fields pass by like checkered flags carefully quilted together. He thought of how the land looked so different from one place to the next. His parents constantly talked about their hometown in Italy—Lucca—where a new hill crested after every other hill with vibrant trees of all kinds—oaks, chestnuts, olives, sometimes figs and cypresses—nothing like where they lived in eastern Washington State where the hills were filled with brush and brush. Luca knew his mother missed Italy, more so now than when she first came to the country, when her English was so bad that she woke up with a headache every morning knowing she would have to talk to people—there weren't many Italians in the area.

Suddenly, Luca's mother began to speak and break into his thoughts. "I like these drives, going through small town America. It reminds me of the drives I went on with my father as a little girl through Tuscany. Simpler people live out here. They follow God and they love their country. Never go against God, Luca: or your country. I don't understand people who go against their own country, no matter what politics are going on. A country is made up of people and a patriot always supports their own people. That's how the Italians are; Italians will always support Italy."

"But what about Italy during the war?" Luca asked.

"The people are not the government, Luca," Francesca said. "Always support the people because that's the real country. The fascists were very few, but they had the power. But Italy was still the people. Always the people."

They had driven through Dayton and taken the road up the mountain. The weathered trees took on frost as the vehicle climbed higher and higher. Mounds of snow clumped to the sides of the road and Francesca gripped the steering wheel tightly as she slowly drove around the curves, a backup of traffic trailing behind her. Finally, the ski lodge could be seen coming up a long, wavy white road like a castle at the base of a mountain. Francesca parked the car just below the lodge and the sleepy Tony opened his eyes to a wonderland of snow. Luca shook his head as Tony yawned and stretched his arms.

They donned their mittens, jackets, and ski hoods and carried their rented skis, boots, and poles up to the lodge. Huffing and puffing, skiing already seemed like a lot of work and they hadn't even done anything yet. Francesca had packed lunches for them, but kept all the food and water in the car where it would remain chilled. They made their way into the lodge to first use the bathroom. Then Francesca bought three tickets and attached those to their jacket zippers.

"We almost seem like we know what we're doing." Francesca laughed.

The lodge was bustling with people. Luca looked around to see if anyone from school was there, but everyone was dressed head to toe in snowsuits and goggles. It was hot in their gear and Luca swore as he sweated trying to tighten his boots up. Tony looked at him and together they shook their heads. When was it supposed to become fun? Finally, outside with boots on, Luca attempted to attach them into the bindings on the skis. He immediately fell down and Tony laughed heartily, but that laughter was quickly diminished as Tony then tried the same thing and he fell too. Luca and Tony lay spread-eagle and exhausted and began flapping their arms and legs to do snow angels—the cold snow felt refreshing against their warm bodies. Francesca looked worried. She didn't think skiing would be that difficult, more like gliding through soft snow on well-greased sticks. But they couldn't even put their boots into the bindings. She waited until Luca and Tony got theirs in before she attempted her own.

"No laughing," Francesca said. "Here, hold me up while I do mine."

Luca and Tony each took ahold of one of her shoulder blades to steady her while she attempted to put her boots in—at twelve years old, Luca was already the same height as his mother. She got her left boot in first, but when she went to put her right boot in, she became off-balanced, falling against Luca and both falling over.

"Damnit, mom," Luca said. Tony was laughing again.

Francesca laughed too, which eventually got Luca to laugh. All three were laughing as she tried to roll herself up, but with the ski boot attached to the binding attached to the ski, she wasn't able to get up at all. She continued laughing until Luca had to get out of his bindings to help her get out of her one binding so she

8

could stand up again. Fifteen minutes later, all three were in their bindings and ready to get on the lift.

"I think that was the easy part," Tony said, eyeing the lift and the people pushing themselves forward with their skis and poles and then waiting to be whisked up into the tree line by a fast-moving air-exposed chair.

If getting into their bindings was a disaster, getting on the lift was Armageddon. When it was their turn to go, Francesca had trouble pushing herself forward so she tried to grab onto Luca's jacket so he could pull her, but he didn't know her plan so when he leaned back, he lost his balance and fell over and then Francesca fell over him and Tony kept going, but luckily, the lift operator knew amateurs when he saw them and stopped the lift, much to their chagrin as those waited impatiently behind them groaned and moaned. The operator helped them up and put them in place. Luca was happy that they were all wearing ski goggles and nobody could tell who they were.

"Don't say my name out loud today, mom," Luca said. "Call me…Mario."

Getting off the lift was hilarious if seen from the viewpoint of the crow that flew just overhead as they came to the top of the mountain. They were like pins at a bowling alley, a spare being picked up as they crashed together and fell together and rolled down the slope together, their skis popping off, their ankles twisting, their curses in Italian thrown into the wind. Other skiers simply skied around them, left them to their demise. The process of getting the skis back into the bindings began again in earnest and again and again for the entire day.

Luca and Tony got the hang of snowplowing rather quickly and as the day went on, their skis began to line up more and more parallel, their speed increasing. They were twelve-year-old boys, fearless and devout to the art of chasing danger. Tony wanted to push and push, but Luca said no, they must wait for Francesca always lagging.

"Go, go," Francesca screamed as she was being propelled down the hill against her will by the mountain's volition. She slipped and crashed and rolled down to where Luca and Tony were waiting. She was laughing and Luca could see the smile behind all that gear. "Go ahead. I might be here for a minute."

"C'mon, let's go," Tony said.

"No, I need a break anyway. All this falling is tiring."

All that day they fell down the mountainside together, their skis popping off, their screams and curses reverberating through the trees, but by the end of the day, they were aching and laughing in the lodge getting a much-needed hot chocolate before the long drive home.

After dropping Tony off at his house, Luca climbed up into the front seat with his mother. "That was really fun, mom," Luca said. "You know, not a lot of moms would do that."

"What? Take their son skiing?"

"I mean to learn how to ski at forty years old. I'm proud of you."

"Well, my body might not like me tomorrow, but I'm glad you had fun," Francesca said.

When they pulled into the driveway, Luca grabbed his bag and headed into the house. Francesca stayed back. Luca set his things by the door and looked sneakily out the curtain. His mother had her eyes closed as if in prayer. She had begun to cry, tears squeezing out and down the sides of her face like the dew down the stalks earlier that morning. Luca thought about going out there but decided against it. It had been a wonderful day and his mother had been strong. If she needed to cry, she could cry. He watched her make the cross across her body and then begin walking toward the house, head down, silent words whispered on the wind. He slipped away from the curtain and scrambled upstairs to change.

For years, Luca remembered the fearlessness his mother had shown in the face of his father's death. As he grew older, he realized too how much pain she must have been going through, losing her husband and trying to raise a boy during it all. Luca knew that his mother could have done it for as long as it would take, but he was thankful for when David entered into their lives—it gave his mother just the spark she needed—because it was Luca who eventually went away.

Chapter 1

Luca leaned against the bar and surveyed the dining room, relishing the soft tranquility of early morning. The rosy curtains still drawn, a soft pink light came through and lit up the front room, the table glasses reflecting a glowing reddish hue. He took a rock's glass and poured a heavy bourbon, the swashing coating the sides soporific in the sweet silence, and he sipped slowly while he lazily went about next making an espresso. He felt like whistling, but didn't as the silence was ephemeral. He ground the beans, filled the portafilter and turned it hard counterclockwise into the machine. A steady, slow drip coalesced into a lightly foamy short macchiato, the coffee aroma permeating the bar. He took in a deep breath before downing the espresso quickly, shaking his head from the burn—the burn was what broke the dilatory effects of the restaurant's morning bliss. Now he could get to work.

Luca perused the bar: the gins, vodkas, bourbons, rums, tequilas, the cordials, liquors, and the digestifs. All was arrayed orderly. He took down a coffee liquor, turned to the espresso machine and made a face, knowing that he should have thought of that in the first place. He went to work making another espresso. This time, he poured a dollop of the coffee liquor in with the black juice of restaurant kings. It was early morning, but time exists separately outside the physical world and within the black hole of the restaurant walls—morning, evening, night was the same. It's a dangerous and exciting, sublime and diabolical place—a happy restaurant is most dangerous as it sucks the soul slowly as if it were simply a newborn babe feeding on the celestial tit.

Luca took a sip of the espresso, feeling the milky liquor diffusing down his throat. Now, to work—it was a Tuesday, the slowest day of the week so there wasn't much to do. He paid a few bills, ordered some wine, and thought about what he would make for dinner that evening. Something simple, a slow *bolognese* perhaps or *vongole* since his wife, Lillian, loved clams. "If I do *vongole*, then I'll need a white. Let's try the whites, shall we?" Luca looked down into the small refrigerator underneath the bar—he had prosecco, arneis, chardonnay, sauvignon blanc, and caricante. He took out each bottle, took an empty wine glass and first poured a bit of the sauvignon blanc, finished that, tried the caricante and then on through the rest, finishing with the prosecco to cleanse his palate. "Okay, if we do clams, I'll take a bottle of Sicily's rather superb caricante. But what if I want to do *bolognese* instead?" Luca now whistled merrily as he took down another wine glass and lined up all the glass pour reds to taste. He tried a sangiovese, barbera, nebbiolo, and a primitivo, and then decided to text his wife as if she were already thinking about dinner that evening as he was.

—*Do you want clams or bolognese tonight*? —

Luca poured another bourbon and thought about the upcoming Halloween wine dinner with Giorgio Colutta, just three days away—also Luca's birthday and ten-year restaurant anniversary, a time for celebration. He looked at the list of those who had reserved spots for the dinner: seventy-five guests, the entire restaurant booked. Lana would be there, but Luca didn't think on that—Lillian would stymie any flirtatious advances. Ten years owning a restaurant and another eight as a server. Eighteen years given to the industry—his entire working life spent entertaining.

Time flowed differently in the restaurant and in the lives of restaurant people. There were two types: transients and lifers. Luca was the latter, but it had never been the overarching plan. The years kept flowing incomprehensibly, passing by so quickly, and only in those moments when Luca thought about time could he realize that the days, months, years flowed into each other—otherwise, time was an invisible clock increasingly adjusting for the years. The restaurant business seduced a person in with kisses and money, whole soul and everything. And the lifestyle was just grand enough to hold one in place.

Having graduated from university with a degree in English, Luca had not known what to do next—eventually going to graduate school was the foreseeable option, but taking a job as a server at an Italian restaurant made more sense at the time. And the nights were fun: the drinking, the flirting, the money, the schedule, the time off, the prestige. Servers believed they were the essential show—it's really an entertainment business—and they weren't often wrong. Luca learned that quickly, eighteen years ago. His degree and a nascent desire to be an actor quickly vanished once the easy money and the excitement of the restaurant world took hold of him.

He leaned against the bar, made of solid oak, just refinished: smooth and glossy and three inches thick. It was a small bar, just five stools, but the best people came and took up those seats and there was never any want of action. Bar people in an Italian restaurant were talkers and Luca loved hearing their stories. And they loved hearing his: many of which he borrowed from his father growing up in Lucca, the ones he could remember at least.

Luca's phone buzzed.

Lillian: —*Clams*—

Vongole it was then. Luca finished off his bourbon, the smell of sweet alcohol lifting his spirits and decided on having one more. He poured a heavy one just as the restaurant's front door opened. A large, bulbous man waddled in like an over-stuffed peacock; his head was huge with graying hair and a signature large red-rosy familial nose. He swung his fat, sausage-like hands side to side and his paunch suggested he was as wide as he was tall—this was Salvatore, the finest chef that Naples had brought to America (a title he bestowed upon himself).

"*Ciao bello,*" Salvatore bellowed. "*Come va?*"

"*Eh, va bene il mio amico*," Luca replied. "So, the wine dinner. We have seventy-five confirmed. Should be a good one."

"Okay, I'll order the food today," Salvatore said.

"*Grazie mille*. Okay, I'm out of here. *Ci vediamo domani.*"

"*A domani bello.*"

Luca downed his bourbon, took up his keys and headed outside into the mist. The fog had thickened since the morning and he looked south towards downtown; he could no longer see the Space Needle from his vantage point as thick, gray clouds had rolled in from the Puget

Sound. He was glad to be going home for the day; he got into his SUV and drove off into the hazy grayness. He decided to stop at the grocery store to pick up a few things on his way home: clams, some greens, a bottle of white wine since he forgot to bring one from the restaurant, and a loaf of sourdough bread because he forgot that too. First thing he was going to do at home was take a nap. The bourbon had started to settle in and his body felt loose and his eyes drowsy. The bright sun came through the windshield and Luca squinted his eyes to keep them on the road.

He first felt a bump then heard a loud crash and glass shattering: powerful smells of metal and gasoline filled his lungs. It was dreamlike, a nightmare when he opened his eyes to shattered glass and a destroyed hood, the surroundings strange, his bearings disoriented. He shook his head, but the pain in his neck was tremendous so he momentarily kept still, trying to focus. He looked at his hands, cut and bleeding; he shook them in case there was any glass embedded within the folds of his skin. He wiped his face and his hands came back bloodier. Luca looked out what was the front windshield and saw that he had hit a tree, a thin aspen, but it had been enough to cripple the front of the SUV and shatter his windshield. He was alive though, bleeding, but alive.

He slowly unbuckled his seatbelt and opened the screeching door. He got out, stretching his banged-up body, feeling for any broken bones. A vehicle pulled over, the driver rushing over asking if he was alright, already on the phone calling the police.

"God damn it Luca, you idiot. Why Luca? Why man?" Luca surveyed the crash and thought about running, but decided against it—where would he go?

The state patrol arrived shortly, and an officer approached, immediately looking for the signs. Luca could practically see the officer wrinkling his nose, sniffing like a blood hound. Luca couldn't deny being stupid; he couldn't deny anything. He was trapped.

"You okay, sir? Have you been drinking today, sir?"

"Just a couple," Luca said, cringing at the sound of it coming out of his mouth. How many times had a police officer heard that one?

"Would you submit to a field sobriety test?"

Luca knew what not to do. He had plenty of friends and associates who had gone through this rigamarole. He refused the sobriety test, refused the breathalyzer, and was subsequently placed in handcuffs and put in the back of the patrol car.

At least I hadn't bought the clams yet, he thought. Lillian was going to kill him. Luca found that the handcuffs were incredibly uncomfortable, boring into his bloody skin. He knew to be cordial if he was going to be comfortable—it was going to be a long night.

"Officer, is there any way we could loosen the cuffs a bit? They're tearing into me."

"Sure." The officer came around, opened the door and loosened the cuffs just a bit, then went over to survey the crash scene. Luca listened to the officer's music on the radio, something country, something he would normally despise, but at that moment, it was the nicest thing he could hear. Where he was going, it was a no music no fun kind of place. Luca hoped the officer couldn't see the tears coming down the sides of his face mixing in with the drying blood.

\*\*\*\*

Lillian opened the front door to the house and

walked in, setting her handbag down on the couch. She turned on a lamp. She took off her black jacket and hung it up in the closet, kicked off her shoes and placed them into a small basket by the front door. She slowly ascended the stairs, went into the bedroom and plopped down upon the bed.

There, she lay like that for a good fifteen minutes with her eyes closed. But she couldn't nap: work circled inside her head. She sat up, then stood up and took off her black slacks and white blouse. She went into the bathroom and turned the hot water on in the shower. Looking up into the mirror, she surveyed herself critically. She was a bit thin she thought, but not unhealthy. She easily spotted the four gray strands mingling within her pale blonde hair. She took off her bra; at least her breasts were still perky. She had a bruise on the outer thigh of her right leg and she tried to remember if she had bumped into something. She scrutinized her face, an intrinsically beautiful angular face, but all she saw was the beginning of a pimple vying to burst through to the left of her nose. Her pale skin couldn't hide that blotch.

She finished undressing in silent exhaustion and stepped into the shower. It didn't dawn on her that Luca wasn't home; she stopped asking about his comings and goings long ago.

The shower felt good, scalding, just how she liked it. She stood under the head unnaturally long, the water turning her skin a deep pink. Lillian looked at her toes, her feet, dainty but tough, calloused. She had danced ballet long ago. She had been the tallest girl in her class through middle school and always got the best roles. But she fought for them. That was another life though…

She turned off the water and took a towel down from the rack on the door, dried off and tied up her hair. She dressed in jeans and a light sweater as the house was always cold with nobody home until the evenings. Where was Luca? Even on his day off, he had to be somewhere else. She was hungry and would have to eat a snack if he wasn't home soon. She dialed his number; it went straight to voicemail. She texted:

*—ETA? I'm starving—*

Her message didn't register as delivered.

Lillian looked about the room. What to do next? She sighed and headed downstairs to do some more work. She opened her briefcase. She took out a binder and sat down at the dining room table, sifted through notes on various patients, and then decided she deserved a glass of wine if she was going to work while at home waiting for Luca.

She went out to the garage and opened the refrigerator. There was plenty of wine, too much. She rarely had more than a glass, but she saw a half-full bottle of pinot grigio, shrugged her shoulders, oscillated her head a bit back and forth, and went for the bottle. She took the folder out for a Daniel Clark: depression, low sex drive, family problems with his parents, and recently lost job as a bank clerk. Lillian took out a pen and began taking notes, but every few minutes she would return to her phone to see if any messages had come through. Nothing yet. She was too hungry to focus.

"Jesus Luca," she said, tossing her pen down. She got up, went to the kitchen refrigerator and took out some sliced prosciutto and mortadella, some chunks of parmesan, and then some crackers from the pantry. She placed them on a plate and began munching greedily at her makeshift mini sandwiches whilst returning to her work.

After an hour and her text message still not read, she tried calling Luca again. Voicemail right away. She hung up, dialed the number for the restaurant and got one of the servers on the phone.

"Hi Gabriele, it's Lillian. Is Luca there?"

"Don't call me Gabriele. That's my slave name. My name is Muhammad Jafar Islam and you've killed my people for too long—"

"Is he there or not?" Lillian interrupted.

"I haven't seen him all day. Let me ask Sal. Hey Sal, Luca come in today?"

Lillian heard Sal's booming voice in the background saying something about seeing him this morning and that's it.

"Sal said he left a long time ago. Maybe he had a meeting or something," Gabriele said.

Always covering for him, Lillian thought. "Yeah, okay, thanks Gabriele."

"Don't call me Gabriele, that's my—"

Lillian hung up the phone and thought for a moment. What to do? She looked at her phone: 7:59 in the evening already. She decided to prepare a simple pasta—no clams tonight. She put some water on to boil. She polished off the rest of the wine. She wasn't going to drive anywhere to pick him up if he did call her for a ride.

Finally, at 8:15, her phone rang. She didn't recognize the number, but she answered right away. "Hello, this is Lillian," she said, cautiously.

"Lillian, thank God," Luca screamed. "Look, I'm sorry, and I'll explain later, but I was at work doing a wine tasting and I was driving to the store and I got pulled over so now I'm at the King County jail. Look, I don't have—"

"What're you talking about? You got pulled over? For DUI then?"

"Yes, for suspicion of DUI," Luca said. "Look, I'm sorry. I didn't even have that much, but I was tired. Anyway, I fell asleep at the wheel and went off the road. I hit a tree. The car's pretty messed up, but—"

"Jesus Luca, are you okay?"

"Yes, I'm okay. A little banged up, but I'm okay."

"God, Luca," Lillian said. She put the phone down for a second and stared up at the ceiling, hearing his voice come through like a cartoon character squeaking and squawking.

"Luca," she began again. "What do you need?"

"I'm sorry Lillian, I really am. I just need you to bail me out tomorrow morning after my initial hearing."

"Fine, I'll be there. What time?"

"Nine in the morning," Luca said. "Listen, I'm done with this stuff. I've abused alcohol for way too long. It's finally caught up with me."

"You've said that a million times," Lillian said. "This time's no different."

"No seriously, I'm done with this stuff. It's a poison—"

Lillian hung up the phone, set it down on the counter. She sat down on the kitchen floor and the water boiled over the pot, sizzling as it hit the stove's counter. She cried until she couldn't cry anymore. She was amazed she had any tears left.

Finally, she got up and looked around the kitchen and dining room, at all their things: the painting of Florence they bought when they had gone there together a few years ago, the large white cabinet with their cookbooks, wine glasses, a cake holder, tins of rice and pastas and couscous, another cabinet with teas and cocoa, honey and mugs. They had pots and pans, a cookie jar with old wine corks, a calendar with important dates coming up, all these small things that made up a house, a home, a life together.

And now Luca had ruined it once and for all.

\*\*\*\*

The next morning, Luca awoke lying on the cell floor next to five fellow drunks that he had been processed with as-well-as two new ones that must have come in during the night. Hair disheveled, body aching, and with poisonous breath, Luca got up to await his day in court. That came around nine with a court appointed lawyer. With bail set at one thousand dollars, he was soon out as Lillian had looked up his case on the King County website, posted the bail, and was waiting for him outside of the downtown courthouse.

Luca opened the passenger door and flopped down into the seat. He peeked over abashedly at Lillian, but she sped off without a glance or a word.

"Look Lillian, I'm sorry. I messed up big time."

"I can't believe you. How many times? I always knew this was going to happen. Every night you come home drunk. Every freaking night. Jesus Luca, you're a freaking alcoholic. I can't…I just…don't talk to me right now. You stink and your breath is terrible. I'm shaking. I can barely drive."

They drove home the rest of the way in silence, each in their own thoughts. When they arrived at the house, Lillian couldn't get herself out of the car.

"You okay?" Luca asked.

"No, I'm not okay," she said, finally opening the door, getting out and slamming it shut. She strode quickly toward the house and opened the front door and went inside. Luca watched her, slowly got out, and followed like a bad dog. When he went inside, he saw what she had been doing all that previous night: putting things in boxes. The house looked as if they had just moved in and were sorting the boxes into their new respective places, but this time, quite the opposite.

Lillian stood in the kitchen, her hand covering her eyes.

"I'm done Luca. I'm done," she said.

"Lillian, I'm sorry. I won't let this happen again."

"Luca, you say that every time, every week we have this same fight. You're a broken record. I'm done. I told you last time I won't stand it anymore. What does this make me? An idiot? I'm thirty-six years old, Luca. Too old for a lot of things, but young enough to still have a life with someone who cares about me and doesn't want to fuck all of it up every night for some freaking alcohol. I'm done Luca, I'm done. You always choose alcohol over me."

"What do you want me to do? I'll do anything," Luca pleaded.

"You need help, Luca. Get help."

"Will you please stay if I get help?"

"If? No, you need to get help for yourself, not for me. It doesn't work that way. I've been living like this for too long. I don't want to live with you anymore; I don't want this life anymore. We're getting divorced, Luca."

Luca stood still, stung by the word—he understood the word divorce, but it was unfathomable. She couldn't mean it. They were Luca and Lillian—they came as a pair. "Look, I understand you need some time—"

"Luca, *you* don't understand. I needed some time *a long time ago*. You think I suddenly want out because of the DUI? I knew the DUI was inevitable. I've worked with many people just like you. No Luca, you need help, but you must do it. I'm done with this marriage. I'll find a place."

Luca couldn't think, not with any semblance of rational thought. He just needed some time; she would need some time to change her mind, to calm down. "You don't have to move out. I'll get my things and find a place. You stay in the house."

## Chapter 2

Luca double, triple checked the tables—all appeared consummate: white napkin folded neatly on top of white plate, centered, table fork to the left, salad fork to the left of table fork, steak knife to the right of the plate, butter knife to the right of steak knife, stemless water glass to the right of butter knife, three stemmed wine glasses above the plate—sparkling flute, riesling glass for whites, Bordeaux glass for reds. The silverware was polished, the glassware was polished, the chairs were wiped cleaned and perfectly aligned with each other. Afterward, he nimbly placed a printed-off menu of the night's wines and dishes below each plate.

Luca perused the tables and their settings, tinkering with a fork or knife or glass here and there. He checked the chandeliers, making sure all bulbs were functional, the internet connection clear, the fireplace in the center of the restaurant warm and cozy. All was pristine. The entire restaurant was booked for the wine dinner so the kitchen only had to focus on the main menu, which was a relief. What a birthday! A costumed wine dinner and ten-year anniversary with a hanging DUI and an imminent divorce.

He began opening bottles that were being served that night for the dinner. He tasted each in turn, thinking about the properties, thinking about what he would say in his initial address, introducing Giorgio, thanking all those who supported the restaurant. The opening aperitif would be a glass of prosecco as the guests came in, followed then by the whites with the first two courses, a friulano and a ribolla gialla. The party's reds were a refosco and then finally a pignolo: then, perhaps a digestif to cap off the night.

Luca poured himself a glass of friulano; he allowed himself a little wine on his birthday despite the circumstances. He peered out the rosy curtains at the empty space his SUV would usually occupy; it had been deemed totaled. No car, no problem—he was free for the night. The restaurant was set up; he had a few hours to dilly-dally. He sat at the bar sipping the wine. An arraignment date was imminent. Luca knew he was guilty. Why fight it? Take whatever punishment was dealt out. He deserved it anyway. He could have killed, maimed, paralyzed someone; those fates could have been his. He was lucky, beyond lucky. He gulped down the last bit of friulano and poured a glass of the ribolla gialla, a straw yellow wine with hints of minerals and acacia and at that moment, being in the restaurant alone, he felt good and was happy.

What a life! Ten years! He could almost do as he pleased, drink what he pleased. He met new people every day, worked the hours he wanted to work, did well financially. Was there anything better in America? Lillian was going to divorce him. Did that not mean he would be free? Free of concern, free of having to think and do best for another person. Would he not be his own lord once again? He would never be lonely; he had the restaurant. He would always have somewhere to go and people to see.

Luca stood up and paced the jagged tiles in the

silence of the morning, his favorite time. He had no idea what Lillian would ultimately decide, but he knew, deep down, that whatever she decided, it would be okay. She would be happier and that was the most important thing. He had already found a new apartment; luckily, a friend of his from the restaurant had a place he could rent for cheap. And, now that it was closer, he could walk or take a short train trip. He was in the position wherein he knew the right people at the right time. Things always seemed to work out. He did not want to anger the gods with his arrogance, but he smiled at the thought of the fortune he had built for himself. He remembered vaguely that someone he admired had once said you have to create your own luck.

A large figure suddenly coalesced outside the restaurant through the red curtains—the front door swung open and Salvatore's booming voice bellowed. "*Ciao bello, come hai fatto?*"

"What did I do? I was stupid. Drove home after drinking, am now charged with DUI."

"DUI is nothing. No big deal," Salvatore said, dismissing it with a wave of his arm. "Everyone has DUI. My friend Benito has five. What you do?"

"Plead guilty, take the punishment, move on with my life I guess," Luca said.

"Pay monies, do community service, that's it."

"Yeah, exactly. Anyway, we ready for tonight?"

"I've everything. Don't worry bello. Sal's here."

\*\*\*\*

Luca dressed as Danny Zuko, but without Lillian there as Sandy, he felt ridiculous and banal in black jeans, black shirt, a red and white sweater opened at the front with a large '17 emblazoned onto the breast, his thick hair slicked into a pompadour. But as prosaic as he felt, his dress was unimportant as he was more preoccupied with the conviviality of the evening. He wandered through and around the tables, checking that nothing had moved out of place, glass of wine in hand to calm the nerves. This would be the largest wine dinner the restaurant had ever put on.

"The phantom of Occhi Belli is here, inside your mind." Daniele charged in wearing a Phantom of the Opera mask and pulling a flimsy black cape around his protruding bulk, he headed immediately to the computer to clock in; not one second in the restaurant off the clock was one of his mottos. "Boss, what're we doing tonight?"

"The same thing we do every night," Luca said. "Try, to take over, the world. Or, at least the restaurant business."

"How many glasses you have so far?"

"Hey, hey, hey, hey," Luca said. "Calming the nerves. Calming the nerves."

The other staff came in together: Natasha, a tall Russian wearing white, black, and red smudged makeup that Luca guessed was supposed to be that of a zombie; Astrid the Norwegian who wore elven earrings and whose face sparkled with glitter; and lastly, Edgar, the busser wearing his usual red and black striped chef's coat.

"Ladies, love the costumes," Luca said. "Edgar? You're a busser, *si*?"

"*Si*, I'm the busser," Edgar said, confused.

Luca had the best staff in the city and together they had built Occhi Belli into the neighborhood gem that it had become. For Luca, the vision was simple—a great restaurant was made from great food and great characters—actual place, location, was what one made it. He had initially wanted to have a restaurant downtown, but spaces were not available and the rent was too high anyway. When he found the empty restaurant building in an atrabilious little neighborhood in north Seattle, he figured it was a terrible gambit. The streets were ruled by junkies, the apartment buildings ancient, the nightlife scarce. The houses in the neighborhood were worth something, but most had been bought thirty years prior so the owners weren't wealthy unless they sold and moved somewhere else. Luca knew the only way to make money was to win the heart of the neighborhood and let the word diffuse, which meant great food, great service at great prices. People would travel to a place worth traveling to.

Luca had said yes to himself when he saw the building—built in the early twentieth century as a general store, then converted into an old car garage, and finally into a restaurant in the early eighties—there was a large gas fireplace in the middle of the main room, the building was constructed of tough concrete that Luca painted a dark mustard and red-tiled eaves overlooked the patio space. Ivy grew incessantly but beautifully alongside the south side of the building and the patio was gated off by a fence made of oak wine barrels. Luca painted a mural on the north wall with two large luscious brown eyes and the words 'Occhi Belli.' The restaurant was born.

That was ten years ago. What a ride it had been, an undulated stream of emotional moments. He still loved it, but the sourness of an imminent divorce, the DUI charge, and all the time the restaurant took away from what could have been a different life, left a bitter nugget tucked away into the recesses of his mind. What had been missed because of time spent there, he wondered. No, can't think like that; that thinking led to places he didn't want to go.

When Giorgio Colutta arrived, Luca quickly poured some prosecco and nimbly placed the glass between the famous winemaker's outstretched fingers and while Luca explained the plan for the evening, Giorgio sipped the prosecco with pleasure, a creased smile peeked at the sides of his mouth as his mind seemingly flew from the room, cognizant of an immaterial remembrance. "This wine always takes me back to my younger days." Giorgio had been a pharmacist before getting into the ancient family business of wine making, a tradition his family had been doing for over a century. A well-dressed man in a lime suit, mid-fifties, and atypical Italian: born in Friuli, he had short silvery hair once blonde, a fit, runner's physique, and he spoke softly and humbly—he was the opposite of Salvatore in the kitchen.

"And how many for the dinner tonight?" Giorgio asked.

"Seventy-five," Luca answered, clinking his glass of prosecco with Giorgio's.

Giorgio frowned, nodding his head with raised eyebrows, obviously pleased. "All the people wear costumes for the Halloween?"

"Yes, for the most part, but don't worry, you look *fenomenale*. You're dressed as a fashionable winemaker."

Halloween night and the restaurant was about to come alive. Luca tore open the red eyelids of the façade and rain descended down the eyes like tears. Thunder boomed and shook the roof like an edacious stomach, but the bones were sturdy, strong and held off the storm. Vampires, Jesus, a jester, animals of all sorts, science fiction characters, fabled princesses all arrived and were greeted with prosecco and aromas of garlic, onion, freshly cooked pasta all coming from the restaurant's gaping maw. A red sea of wine, like blood, lay before them and the thirst drove the energy upward. Lana and her entourage arrived chirping loudly dressed as fairies wearing one-piece swimsuits, leotards, gauze wings, and elven ears. Despite Luca's insistent admonitions that there would be plenty of wine, Lana seemed especially ebullient.

She gave Luca's arm a tight squeeze.

"Well, good to see you. Prosecco?" Luca offered.

"Why thank you sir. You look debonair tonight." Lana, pint-sized with mousy freckles put on her winningest smile.

"I suppose you didn't even dress up. You wore your work clothes?" Luca asked. Lana was a pole dancing entertainer for the Dancing Scimitar acrobatic company.

"Oh, you're funny," she said.

"I mean, I just thought that's what short people wear anyway."

"You know short people live longer."

"Not if they drink too much."

"I'm young still. Unlike you." She smiled, her face radiating that pre-funk energy that captured rooms and audiences alike. Luca had seen one of her shows. It had been surreal watching her glide along that pole seemingly floating without care, smiling to the crowd despite being easily near death with one mistake. It was breathtaking—Luca turned away and served others

31

prosecco. She was twelve years younger than him and surrounded by incredibly talented and attractive people with the Dancing Scimitar so he couldn't fathom why she flirted incessantly with him. Perhaps it was all in his head and he was just a fool. He hoped so anyway. Luca topped her off and tried to look nonchalant, stupidly holding the bottle of prosecco and not knowing what to say.

"What're you supposed to be?" Lana asked.

"Danny Zuko, from Grease. Have you heard of it?"

"Oh, you're on a role," she said, sipping down half the Prosecco.

"Lillian was going to be Sandy, but she's not coming tonight. Or ever."

"What does that mean?"

"We're getting divorced."

"Oh, I'm sorry. That's no fun. But that means I get you all to myself tonight. That's dangerous."

"For who? You or me?"

"Don't play coy with me mister," Lana said. "You know fairies put spells on people, right? Maybe I'll put a spell on you. Maybe I already have."

"You know there are plenty of people here who'd want you to put a spell on them," Luca said.

Lana perused the room. "All I see are bears, vampires, and droids."

"I love it when you know what science fiction things are called." Luca put his hand over his heart.

"Which ones, vampires? My glass is empty mister. You're not doing your job."

"Yes. Right away," Luca said, filling the glass. "Just know we're serving quite a bit of wine tonight, just like all the other wine dinners."

"Good, planned on it," she said, winking.

Well into the party, the wine flowed like the salmon of Capistrano, and everyone was having a good time. Even Giorgio, who didn't normally partake too much, was a bit ruddy in the face.

"How're the wines? People like them?" Giorgio asked Luca.

"Quaffing them down like water," Luca said. "They love them."

"Perfect combinations. The food, it is wonderful, even from a *Napoletano*," he said, laughing.

Luca surveyed the room, his eyes half-glazed. The fairies were naturally a huge hit with the wolves, vampires, and droids and Luca purposefully sat them dead center in the restaurant. He held a contest for best female and male costume. A ninety-nine-year-old man who came dressed as George Washington won hands down best male costume and his caretaker, dressed as Lady Liberty won best female. The prize was two bottles of pignolo, but since they didn't drink much red wine, Luca gave them each a bottle of champagne instead.

By the end of the night, only the fairies, vampires and wolves were left drinking after dinner cocktails (not that anyone really needed anything). Giorgio had said goodbye and thanks and left soon after the dessert course, having another wine dinner at another restaurant that next night. Luca went to use the restroom and when he came out, Lana was there to corner him.

"Hey *bella*, my girls want to go out. You're coming with us."

Luca's head swarmed with alcohol and his cortex had cut off any ability to make rational decisions, but he knew one thing and that it was a terrible idea to go anywhere with Lana.

"I can't. I need to go home," Luca said. "I'm done for."

"You shouldn't drive," Lana said. "Nobody here should drive."

"I'll walk. I moved closer…it's been a heck of a week. Lana is…I mean Lillian…is at the house so, so, so, I moved."

"You said Lana first," Lana said, leaning into Luca on her tippy toes and whispering into his ear. "Have you been thinking about me?"

"I've always thought about you," Luca said, thinking he should just shut up.

"Let me come see your new place."

"Ah…"

"C'mon. I'll go with the girls and have a drink with them and then come over."

"It's not even furnished," Luca said.

"Does it have a couch?"

"Yeah."

"And a bed?"

"Yeah…"

"What's the address? Text it to me right now."

Luca did as he was told.

"Then I'll see you in an hour." Lana smiled.

When everyone had left and the servers had closed out their tips, Luca paced the restaurant, oscillating between his options. If he did let her come over, nothing had to happen. Nothing could happen. They have some wine, talk, that's it. She probably wouldn't come over anyway once she was out with her friends, especially looking like she did in that fairy costume. Luca checked his phone. He had all sorts of friends wishing him a happy birthday via social media and text, but nothing from Lillian. That was disappointing. Finally, he decided to take a bottle of wine home and try to do some reading—cap off his birthday with something wholesome.

****

Luca was just finishing his first glass of wine when he heard a knock at the front door. He took a deep breath, let it out slowly and tried to focus. When he opened the door, he stepped back suddenly and nearly fell over from shock. Lillian stood there dressed as Sandy in tight black spandex sharkskin pants, belt, low cut black shirt, and leather jacket. She wore large golden hooped earrings, something that Luca knew she would normally never do, and for her own flourish, a spiked red choker.

"Sorry for coming unannounced. I'm glad you're here. I was nearby and it's your birthday and I just wanted to come say happy birthday. So, happy birthday." Lillian looked past Luca into the apartment eyeing the empty glass of wine sitting on an end table next to the couch. "Still drinking. Even after all that's happened."

"I didn't drive anywhere, just an after-work glass of wine," Luca protested. "It's my birthday."

"And tonight, was your wine dinner and you didn't have anything there?"

"No, I was just hosting," Luca lied.

"I don't believe you," Lillian said. "I can smell alcohol all over you and your eyes are bloodshot. But I suppose it doesn't matter now. You can do whatever you want with your life. It's not…" Lillian paused when she felt another presence coming around the corner and into the light. She turned her head just as Lana started to stumble up the stairs. Lana didn't stop until she was almost upon Lillian.

"Oh, sorry, I didn't see you," Lana said.

Luca poked his head outside the apartment and closed his eyes hoping that when he opened them, Lana would have been a mirage, an apparition, but she was still there looking at both Lillian and Luca, from one to the other when he re-opened his eyes.

"I see," Lillian said. "Wow, three days Luca. This is your birthday present to yourself? Wine and women: the things you always wanted?"

"Lillian…"

"Go screw yourself, Luca—or her if that's what she's here for. Any remote chance we had to stay together was just lost." Lillian stormed down the stairs past Lana. "Good luck with him; he's all yours." She turned the corner and was gone.

"That's…Lillian?"

"Yeah, that's Lillian," Luca said.

"Well…"

"I need a glass of wine," Luca said, taking a deep breath. "You want one?"

"Are you sure?"

"Hell, why not?" Luca didn't know why or why not. He didn't know what he knew. His marriage was over. He didn't want to think. His life was unraveling and he simply wanted to drown it all out. So why not have a glass of wine with somebody who wasn't close to the mess he called his life?

Luca poured two large glasses and gave one to Lana. "*Salute bella*," Luca said.

"Cheers, *bella*."

"*Bello. Bello* is for men. *Bella* for women."

"I always wanted to learn Italian." Lana hiccupped.

"You should teach me."

"I stopped studying years ago. I've forgotten most of it."

They finished off the bottle and opened another. Both, hideously drunk by that time, were laughing and chattering about stupid things. Luca had forgotten all about his troubles with the law and Lillian, when Lana leapt into his arms and suddenly kissed him, and he couldn't stop and didn't want to stop.

"How do you say I want you in Italian?" Lana whispered.

"*Voglio scopparti en Italiano,*" Luca laughed.

"Why's that funny?"

"It's not. I'm stupid. Anyway, *voglio scopparti.*"

"*Voglio scopparti* too," Lana said, smiling that irresistible smile, her teeth stained from wine, her eyes twinkling and blurry.

Luca carried the beautiful fairy into his makeshift bedroom and laid her down on the bed. He closed the bedroom door out of habit and lay down next to her.

"Tell me again," Lana said, drowsily, smiling grandly up at the ceiling.

"*Voglio scopparti,*" Luca whispered.

"Italian sounds so nice," she whispered back, falling asleep instantly.

\*\*\*\*

Luca woke up with a monster headache and his stomach didn't feel great either. He sensed that there was somebody next to him. He rolled to his side and saw Lana wrapped up in a white sheet. His head was pounding so he got up, went to the kitchen, took some ibuprofen, and downed it with water. Horrendous breath wafted out and he almost gagged. He went into the bathroom and quickly brushed his teeth. He turned on the shower and climbed in, lying down in the tub. He tried to go to sleep with the water pouring down upon him.

He *must have* fallen asleep in there because the water had turned cold. Lana knocked at the door.

"Come in," Luca said. He peeked out from the curtain; Lana was wearing one of Luca's sweatshirts over her costume. She put the toilet seat down and sat on it.

"My head is pounding," she said, putting her head into her hands.

"Yeah, mine too," Luca said through the curtain.

"Hey…"

"Yeah?"

"Did we, do anything? I can't remember at all."

"We did not," Luca said. "We passed out just in time."

"Okay."

"Hey, it was a fun night."

"Yeah, it was. I'm sorry I got so drunk."

"Well, I did too so don't worry about it."

"Can I brush my teeth?"

"Yeah, you can use my toothbrush if you want."

Lana brushed her teeth and used the bathroom while Luca was drying off and getting dressed. She came back into the bedroom.

"Hey, sorry to ask, but can you give me a ride home?"

"I don't have my car right now. I crashed it into a tree."

"Damn, were you drinking?"

"Yeah," Luca said. "I was."

"DUI?"

"Will have one soon, I'm sure."

"Oh."

"You can wear any of my clothes, shorts, or whatever if you want to take the bus or call a car."

Chapter 3

The cemetery was lit by the high moon. Luca hid underneath a tree's shadow, still fearing the night watchman despite the courage from the bottle of Tennessee sour mash, the treasure he held tightly and securely, the one thing he could always hold onto. He steadied himself against the tree watching the grave as if waiting for his father's ghost to rise up and reveal truths of the realm of the dead. As roving inky dark clouds passed over the moon shielding the graveyard, Luca creeped toward the grave and peered in close to read the inscription: Mateo Lucchesi, B. 1957, D. 1997, "*Sempre e per sempre*".

"Always and forever," Luca whispered. "*Mi Manchi sempre*." Luca chugged the last of the sour mash and laid it to rest on top of the gravestone. He staggered into the street, steadying himself on the cold iron gate that barricaded the house of the dead. He let the streetlights guide him to the only place he knew where he could go at that hour. The bar was nearly empty when he swung open the door as does a weary traveler having been out in the storm; it was midnight and most had given up for the night. Two bikers were shooting pool with a big-bosom redheaded woman, probably playing cut throat, but that was the only action. Only the drifters and talkative drunks were left at the bar hoping to connect with a human being. The loners and misers haunted the dark corners left to their own contentious thoughts.

The bartender's name was Jake, a large man, once muscly, but now his blood ran with alcohol and cheeseburgers. He had a mustache tightened like the handlebars of his bike outside and a tattoo of a heart with an arrow that had the word 'Mom' inside—a symbol tired and trite Luca thought, but that was his whole persona. He didn't want to be noticed for anything other than what he strove to be: a biker bartender who liked to eat and drink and yet could still muscle someone around if needed.

Luca on the other hand was thin, almost wiry, a runner and he liked to drink cheap drinks in a cheap bar so he was no threat to anyone. He knew when to be flashy and when to keep his head down, except he couldn't hide those lingering flirtatious eyes that he looked over the red-headed woman with. But Luca was no foolish drunk, he could read a room. He turned away from the woman before being too conspicuous and eyed the man sitting closest to him at the bar—an old man with disheveled sandy hair and a rough beard; a man staring moodily into his pint of foul-smelling beer and in no mood to talk, just the way Luca wanted it. Each in their own contentious thoughts.

Jake sauntered over after a moment. He refused to approach anyone as they first sat down as a rule. He wanted a person to sit and squirm for a bit, to let them know that he, Jake, was in no hurry to serve them and he was only there because it was a job he happened to have at the moment. If he was listening to a story, he would wait to hear the end before serving anyone another round, he refused to make complicated martinis, and he openly scoffed at questions regarding alcohol percentages. He had seen Luca before, but Luca was no regular so he didn't bother to say hello—he simply nodded his head once and lifted his eyebrows, indicating Luca could now order something.

"Red label, on the rocks, splash of water, please," Luca said straight faced. He had to at least act like he wasn't already drunk, although Jake may not have cared anyway. The drink was there in a flash and Jake went back to leaning against the bar watching the results of local motocross races. Luca sipped the scotch, boring a tunneled gaze into the ice and thought of his mother.

****

Earlier that night after Luca came home from the restaurant, late as it was, he cooked up a simple pasta of *aglio olio* topped with loads of parmesan and drank sangiovese. He paced the apartment eating off his plate; he didn't really know what to do with himself.

Normally with Lillian home, they would drink wine, although she rarely drank to excess, would play dice games, word games, and the occasional game of rummy. They'd talk into the night sometimes, even after all the years—Luca was fascinated with her work as a psychologist as he considered his own work a psychology study. She wouldn't tell Luca her patients' names, but she would expound upon their difficulties. Luca dubbed pseudonyms to remember them by—there was Donkey, whose laughter resembled a *he-haw, he-haw* soft of guffaw, which he exuded often enough, but underneath that boisterousness, there was a severely depressed man who hated his job; there was Miso, short for misogynist, who had been divorced three times to American women who he thought were too entitled and demanding and was now trying to find an Asian wife online, but he was also severely depressed because of his incrcmental weight gain over the years and his balding; and then there was Trickster, who did not perform magic or anything like that, but would go out on expensive dates just to get laid and have a good meal, which inevitably was why she, too, was depressed because she never knew if she was the one not getting called back or vice-versa.

There were many others. Luca had his own list of characters from the restaurant, but he told Lillian their names and stories— "They're too good to make up," he told her. Those late-night talks were probably what he enjoyed most, the story swapping character game at night with some wine, cheese, and cards. It was the life he had dreamed of when he was in college. Luca meets girl, falls in love, late nights telling stories over wine, making love afterward, falling asleep to a good book. That was his fairy tale life, white picket fence excluded.

The restaurant had provided a sense of completeness, but now Luca felt as alone as he had ever felt, alone in a semi-furnished apartment, the sounds of the city dying down leaving only the silence. He heard the constant static of the silent mind, but he couldn't bear it. He tried reading, but found he couldn't focus. He checked his phone instead—perhaps he'd watch reels for two hours before nodding off. But that's when he noticed that he had missed a call from David, his step-dad; he had missed four separate calls over the last three hours. Luca sat up quickly, spilling some of the wine onto his shirt and biting down into his lower lip…it was Saturday night so David would have known he was at work— something must be wrong. Luca called David despite it being so late.

"David, everything okay? I saw you called quite a bit," Luca said.

"Luca, I'm sorry," David began slowly. "Francesca has taken a turn for the worse."

Luca moved the phone away from his ear, knowing instinctually what those words meant. "What does that mean?"

"I've had to take her to hospice. I'm here now. If you can, you really should come down right away." David's voice trailed off into that free space between phones and Luca could barely make heads or tails of what he was really trying to say, but he felt his heart pounding against his chest and he knew, he knew the time was inevitably coming to a close.

His mother was dying. Not someday, but now. Hospice was the end of all things.

"I'll leave tomorrow morning, first thing," Luca said.

"Drive safe," David said.

Luca set the phone down, but then immediately called Lillian. She didn't answer of course. He texted her instead.

Luca—*I'm sorry to bother you. Can I borrow your car tomorrow morning? I have to go see my mom. She's in hospice. She's dying. I've no way to get there. Please respond when you get this—*

\*\*\*\*

When her phone rang, Lillian peeked at the caller before silencing it: Luca.

"It's Luca of course. If you're here, who else would be calling me?" she said to her best friend, Sarah, who had come over for take-out Thai and riesling. Despite the rather pedestrian evening, Sarah wore black pumps, a black, knee-length skirt, and a sheer red blouse—Lillian was in gray sweats, sock-less, and a pink tank-top, braless. But they sat together on the off-white couch that had seen better days in the living room lit by a crackling fire sipping riesling and chatting away about their lives.

"Well, the *bastardo* can just squirm a bit and wonder what you're doing without him. He can be antsy for a change. God knows you've had your share waiting up for him, wondering if he would make it home in one piece. Anyway, he's probably drunk and missing you. Cheers sister." They clinked their wine glasses. "To a new life, a new Lillian."

"A new me," Lillian said. "First thing I'm going to do is get rid of this horrendous couch."

They both snickered, but then Lillian's phone dinged from an incoming text. She read it quickly. "Oh no."

"What is it?" Sarah said, suspiciously.

"Luca's mom has been put in hospice. Remember I told you she had stage four lung cancer. Luca needs to borrow my car tomorrow."

"That's sad. What're you going to do?"

"I guess let him borrow it. As long as he doesn't drink and drive," Lillian said.

"Honey, just don't let this change your path, please promise me," Sarah insisted.

"I promise. New Lillian. New me."

****

Luca had made the drive from Seattle to eastern Washington many times; he could almost do it in his sleep. When in college, he used to close his eyes for a few seconds to see how long he could go, but quit that when he was once saved by rumble strips. He drove that morning without care, passing the majestic trees, the volcanic boulders, the falling waterfalls without seeing them. He careered around slower vehicles on the right side, on the left side, it didn't matter—he wasn't waiting for them to get over. He hardly noticed driving over cracks in the interstate crust; he felt he wasn't in control of the wheel, but was flying. He wanted to be there already, to see his mom and laugh when she told him it was all a big joke. "Funny, funny," he'd say. "I needed a drive anyway." She'd be fine; the new pills would work their miraculous properties.

But she wasn't fine. It was unfair. She had smoked for a few years growing up in Italy and before she got pregnant, but quit as soon as Luca was more than an idea. He remembered occasionally seeing long, thin cigarettes lying around the house when he was younger, but his mother fervently denied ever smoking once God gave her Luca. But to go because of lung cancer for a few cigarettes? It was more than unfair.

His life was unraveling as he trepidatiously sped along I-90 through the trees and windy tunnels. It was a brisk Sunday morning and the deep gray clouds were moving in, positioning the troops for the inevitable November downpours. Let the rain come, Luca thought. But, a moment of clarity came over him suddenly and he slowed down, moved over to the right lane and took deep breaths. He was in Lillian's vehicle and the last thing he needed was to spin out of control and destroy her trust even more. And he needed to see his mom; that was paramount.

Luca stopped halfway in the city of Ellensburg to get a snack and fill up on gas. The attendants at the

Flying J looked at him menacingly, knowing he was not of their ilk—driving a compact crossover SUV and having long, wavy dark hair may have set them in that direction, but Luca didn't care that he had changed over time from a short-haired, pickup driving boy. He filled the gas quickly, paid quickly, and began the trek again quickly. Normally, he'd expound on a diatribe to Lillian about his eastern Washington ilk, but deep down he relished going 'home.' He relished the drive, the sea change of lush forest to arid high-desert, the descent out of Snoqualmie Pass into the beginnings of the fields glowing with golden wheat and spring hops. Stratum of sedimentary rock formations and the long, flowing deep blue Columbia River that had carved its way through that mass of land and rock one pebble at a time. When Luca began to pass the vineyards and wineries, he would begin to get thirsty as if he were Pavlov's dog, but this time was different. None of that was going through this mind: only faster, faster, faster, get there faster.

Passing Yakima, he thought only eighty miles more; passing Prosser, he thought only forty miles more; passing Benton City, he thought only ten miles more. An incoming text from David read that he was at the hospice house and that Luca should head straight there.

As Luca crested the hill just passed Benton City, Richland, and the whole of the Tri-Cities lay before him in a valley and he had fleeting thoughts of this as home. He tried to remember which friends of his were still living there and whether he wanted to see any of them. But mostly he thought that this was going to be the last time he would see his mother ever again and he had to get there soon—he hadn't thought about God in some time, but he prayed at that moment to let her live, just let her live.

The Tri-Cities Chaplaincy Hospice House was just off of highway 395 near Columbia Park. He found a spot in the lot and found a bodily paralysis stymieing him from going in—he was breathing too hard, too fast. Panicking, he bit his lip and tasted the blood—the blood of the living Christ, he thought. Is it still within us all? Within a short time, the life of the woman who brought him into this world would be gone, that soul would be flying off to the somewheres of myth, lore, and superstitious realms. And he would be left here, alone, living in the realm of the unknown, the unknowledgeable. But it's not about you, Luca; it's about your mother who gave her everything to teach you to become a good person. Was he a good person…or had the means to become good? He needed a sea change.

Luca opened the car door and put one foot outside of it, then both feet, and then he found he was walking toward the looming entrance to the house of death. He opened the front door and was greeted by a lovely middle-aged woman named Daisy or Dorothy or Doris—Luca didn't really hear what she said, but he felt that she was a good person. He knew he needed to know that only good people were here with his mother, even if only in felt-sense. He followed D. until they reached his mother's room; he first saw David standing over the bed with a worried or sad or agitated look, Luca couldn't tell. Then he saw his mother, sleeping, her thin face serene, breathing softly while lying in a blue nightgown. She was propped up and Luca saw she was connected to a plastic bag with yellow liquid in it. Her long, beautiful medusa hair was long gone, but she was radiant and Luca came up and caressed her soft cheek, kissed her pale forehead.

"She's sleeping now," David said as if he wanted Luca to know that she was indeed sleeping and not the scary alternative. David had been a professor at the community college (and in fact that's where he met Francesca in the first place when she signed up for an English literature class), but he retired once her lung cancer looked to be getting worse. So, the two of them took to traveling the world together for three years until they came to that point in the hospice house. David wore an Irish tweed driving cap that he got when Francesca and he went to Ireland the year before and his usual corduroy pants and navy-blue sweater. He looked as one would want an English professor to look.

Francesca had gotten into the English and American classics twenty-four years ago. She read everything from Dickens to Jane Austin to Jules Verne and she loved Emily Dickinson's poetry. She didn't like Shakespeare except live productions and she hated Samual Taylor Coleridge's Rhyme of the Ancient Mariner, which was Luca's favorite poem next to the Conqueror Worm by Poe. Luca had followed in David's footsteps and got a degree in English so naturally he became a restaurant owner he liked to joke. That joke seemed to have worked on Lillian those nine years ago, but after many uses, it had lost its luster.

David handed Luca a wrapped gift. "Happy birthday," he said. "Not what we wanted."

Luca opened the present, a book. "House of Leaves. Thanks, looks interesting."

"It's unique to say the least," David said, turning again to face his wife. "It's about love and emptiness."

Luca turned away from the salty tears streaming

down David's face and looked out the window at the world that continued to move along through time having no feeling or care that Francesca, his mother, was dying.

"I'm sorry, I just can't believe it's actually here," David said, straightening his shoulders up, wiping his tears. "Death, Luca. A wind blew out of a cloud, chilling my beautiful Annabel Lee so that her high-born kinsman came and bore her away from me. Sorry, Luca. I know you like Poe. Poetry is all we have in the end."

"David, I'm still here. I'm here."

"I know. Listen, she's on medication to numb the pain. She's in and out and sometimes can't form her words. The people here say they're usually best in the morning. I'm going to stay here tonight with her so you can sleep at the house."

"No David, it's okay. You were here last night. I'll stay here tonight. I want to."

David looked at his wife and seemed to think for an eternity a decision that was impossible to decide. "Okay, but call me if anything changes. Anything at all. Don't hesitate. Okay?"

"I promise. You hungry, you want some lunch? I'll take you out. What's good around here? I don't know this place anymore."

\*\*\*\*

David drove both out to the Red Mountain wineries to have lunch. They stopped at Animal Farm Winery first to taste and talk about what the next steps were. The sun had absconded away, and the clouds had quickly stridden in; it was a somber day for a somber time. Even the full-bodied malbec tasted astringent, sour and lacking fruit.

David dropped Luca off at the hospice house in the early evening. When he went into his mother's room, she was awake, staring out the window, looking at what he couldn't tell. Luca's eyes immediately watered up and he wiped the tears away before his mother could see them. He put his arms around her frail body and squeezed, smelling sharp wafts of iodine oozing out of her pores.

"Ow," she managed to get out.

Luca loosened his embrace but could not stop hugging her. "I love you, mom. I love you so much."

"I love you," she whispered back. "David?"

"He's at home. I'll be here tonight with you. But I can call him any time."

"Okay."

"Are you okay? Does it hurt?"

Francesca fluttered her eyes, drowsy from the medication. "No pain. Drugs."

"Momma, I love you. I'll always love you. I want you to know. Everything is good. Lillian is great. The restaurant is great. I'm happy and doing well, momma. I prayed to God."

"Good," Francesca whispered. "Happy…birthday."

"Yes, forty years old. I can't believe it. And the restaurant is ten years old now. Lillian couldn't be here, momma, she had work, but she loves you and…David loves you…are you scared, momma?"

"Not scared," she said. "Just disappointed."

The nurse came in and said it was time to administer more medication, so Luca got up and paced the corridors. He called Lillian and told her the situation.

"Are you okay?" she asked.

"As okay as I can be," Luca said. "I wish you were here."

"Call me if you need to," she said.

Luca went back to his mother's room; she was

already fast asleep. It seemed she had a smile on her face. He hoped that wasn't an omen of things to come—the serene smile just before the seraphim takes the soul and leaves the body for the sepulcher. He looked at his phone. It was only six. He would need some food and perhaps something to drink. He left the hospice and walked to a nearby grocery store, bought a pint of whiskey and a ready-made sandwich. He had forgotten to bring a book with him so instead he picked up a couple magazines.

When he came back to his mother's room, she was sleeping soundly as before. Luca opened the pint and took a big pull. He ate his sandwich, read some *Science Weekly* and then the *Cosmopolitan* and then when that wasn't doing the trick, he drank some more and surfed reels until he decided he would try and sleep.

He dreamed nightmares that night of dark black horses with flaring fiery nostrils appearing as apparitions in the night dragging an empty black carriage behind them. They were coming, coming to take someone away into that void of death. He heard a scratchy voice coming from the carriage: "Ssssssoon."

Luca woke up in a sweat. He took another pull from the whiskey and felt the silence and cold of the room, as if death had already been there. His mother slept peacefully in her bed.

****

The next morning, Luca's head felt fuzzy and when he opened his eyes and scanned the unfamiliar space, the bright light hurt, and he shielded his eyes with his hand. It took a second to realize he was in his mother's hospice room. Suddenly he sat up, found his mother in bed, still breathing. He sighed and went to her side. He stroked the cheek of her beautifully serene face and bent down to kiss her on the forehead. He looked at his phone; it was only six in the morning.

Luca used the restroom, found some coffee and texted David to see when he was going to head that way. David arrived within fifteen minutes and Luca said he'd give him some time with mom while he went to the grocery store to pick up some meager form of breakfast. Luca made a mental note to remember to get some toothpaste and a toothbrush.

He strolled around the store, picked up some prosciutto and cheese, a baguette, some butter, and hot coffee. He had just finished paying when his cell phone began ringing. It was David.

"Luca, come back right now. She's going fast."

Luca hung up, put the stuff in a bag, and ran out and across to the hospice house. He charged through the doors to his mother's room. David was there with a nurse.

David's face was wet with tears and he shook his head left and right, but he didn't, couldn't say anything as he held her hand. Luca just stood there, not knowing what to do. He watched as his mother's temperature dropped, her breathing got shallower, and her eyes fluttered softly as if she were watching, communicating with something from the great beyond.

And then she was gone.

No words, only silence.

They stood still, watching, waiting to see if something would happen, a healing, a miracle. But no, her body lay still and only the ticking of a clock broke into that deathly silence. She was gone; her spirit was gone. Only a body remained. Luca felt the room icy and cold with death, real death. He couldn't take his eyes off his mother as the hope slowly drained away from the deep insides of himself.

The nurse left the room. Luca went to David, hugged him. He looked at his mother, that beautiful soul of a woman. He couldn't believe that that was no longer his living mother. Where was she now, at that moment, at that exact moment? Was she simply gone? Was she away with God? Was she there in the room watching them begin that terrible process of grieving?

"Marriage—yes, it is the supreme felicity of life. I concede it. And it is also the supreme tragedy of life. The deeper the love, the surer the tragedy," David said, wiping his tears away with the sleeve of his shirt. "Mark Twain," he whispered.

"You loved each other so much," Luca said.

"She loved nobody greater than she loved you," David said. "I hope you know that."

"She is the embodiment of love," Luca whispered.

Chapter 4

A piercing light flitted its way through a window and around the room. Lillian stirred in sleep. She found herself strolling through a large garden, barefoot in blue jeans and a blouse, a white-water lily pierced through her hair. Rows of hedges zigzagged across manicured greens and lines of lettuce, cabbages, and carrots. The sky, overcast, drizzling rain slanting downward in a soft wind, whisking it all about—she found she enjoyed being there, that secret place. A thick forest waited on the outskirts of the garden, dark and forbidding, but inside its walls, it was safe, magical. She strolled along without purpose until coming to a fountain gushing with sapphire water. A crescentic stone wall revealed an opening leading to the dark forest; she ducked under and went through it. Just beyond, she saw a small raccoon eating away at a purple cabbage. Lillian knew instinctually that she wasn't exactly Lillian anymore, but rather Lillian transformed into a bunny so that she could understand. She hopped toward the raccoon who began to speak to her.

"I love morning cabbage," the raccoon said, munching greedily away on the vegetable. "You didn't do anything wrong." Munch, munch. "You had to leave."

"Yes. I did."

"Forgive him in time, for your own health," the raccoon said, tossing the end piece of the cabbage aside.

"He's unable to understand his life right now."

"I'll try."

"I'll miss you," the raccoon said and before Lillian could reply, it scurried away into the dark forest. Suddenly, thunder boomed and Lillian the Bunny frightfully jumped high up into the air.

The human Lillian sat up quickly in bed, breathing hard. The thunder had scared her. She looked out her window into the darkness as the rain pounded the pumpkin patch that ran amok in her own little garden, but it was resilient enough. She half expected to see a raccoon, but nothing was stirring out there. She turned her head to look at the shadowy figure in the elongated mirror on the wall across the room—a shapeless, faceless, creature stared back at her in the pale morning light.

****

Lillian was meeting Sarah that evening at a chic Italian restaurant downtown. As soon as she walked in, she knew what Sarah had in mind. A darkened subdued atmosphere ensconced the petite, close-knit tables along the walls of the restaurant save for silvery stools around a dimly-lit bar. Sarah, already sipping on a vodka martini wearing one of her black dresses, red six-inch high-heels, and a short black leather jacket. She had applied ample red lipstick and wore her long, curly dark hair down, flowing. Sarah was the bait; Lillian, subtly, would be the catch. A number of older gentlemen were anxiously awaiting the opportunity to approach Sarah, but she had stayed them off thus far. Lillian did not feel like a catch in simple black jeans and a light blue blouse, but she did attempt the no-bra trend.

"You little hussy," Sarah said, hugging her. "I know

a woman on the prowl when I see one."

"Are you talking about yourself?"

"I can see those nips," Sarah whispered.

"Really? I didn't think it was that obvious."

"Yes, and good. Don't think about it. You need a drink."

A slender, dusky skinned bartender dressed in slimming black asked Lillian what she would like.

"Besides you?" Sarah said.

"Sarah, you stop that right now. Gin martini, olives please." The bartender smiled, went to go concoct away.

"Now I know why you chose this place," Lillian said.

"I'm not trying to fool anyone. The bartender is young, attentive, and freaking hot."

"How young do you think he is?"

"Does it matter?"

"I'm thirty-six. If he's under thirty, he's definitely not interested in talking to an old lady," Lillian said.

"I hope to God he's not talking at all," Sarah said in a hush just as a martini appeared in front of Lillian.

"This one's on me tonight," he said. "I believe you're going through a tough time."

"I can't imagine how you could know that," Lillian said, giving Sarah a face.

"I have a gift for reading people. It's part of my job," he said. "And, your friend spilled everything."

\*\*\*\*

Luca lit a crackling fire to engage the apartment. He sat on the couch with a thick blanket, his new book, *House of Leaves,* and a heavy pour of scotch. He kept the bottle close. While Navidson explored the cavernous labyrinthine wayward walls within the *House of Leaves*, flickering shadows grew larger and larger against the white, bare walls of Luca's apartment. The room was silent and yet as the night wore on and the drowsiness creeped in, Luca's arms pickled with gooseflesh. A fleeting draft seemed to sift through the room, gushing in and around the windows, and then quickly absconding away. Luca decided it was time for bed. He got up, turned the gas off and the fire died down; he kept the lamp on as total darkness lingered uneasily in the apartment.

As he readied for sleep, he felt strange, as if someone were in the room or someone was watching him. He turned off the bedside lamp and closed his eyes and listened. Silence. He was about to roll over when he felt the end of the mattress sink down and crunch as if it were made of compacted snow. Luca kept his eyes closed, his arms still, his mind whirling from the scotch. He felt, he heard, the crunch, crunch, crunch as if the something was anxiously adjusting positions, finding its place. Luca frozen not from fear, but fear of losing the moment whispered, "Momma, I know that's you. I know you're here." Silence permeated the room; thud, thud, thud beat Luca's heart. There was a presence, an energy, something tangible Luca could feel. "I love you momma. I always will and I'll think about you every day. I want you to know that I'm going to get better, I'm going to be better. I'm going to do something that you'll be proud of. You always loved the restaurant, but you always knew the restaurant consumed me. And I've done bad things, momma. I really have. And I'm sorry. But I'm going to get help. I'm going to change. I love you, momma. You can go, momma. You can go wherever you go next."

The salty tears stung his eyes and Luca licked what

ran down the sides of his face. The mattress lifted and the incorporeal air whisked away. Luca lay there, wondering if truly he imagined it all, the scotch fuzzing his brain. But no, he felt her presence. She had been there. A final goodbye. Luca fell asleep, desiring to become something greater, to become the one thing that mattered in life: a good person.

\*\*\*\*

Lillian and Sarah laughingly left the restaurant arm in arm, feeling maudlin. "I guess thirty-six isn't too old for that insanely attractive younger man," Sarah said.

"He gave me his number, big deal," Lillian said. "He probably gives a bunch of women his number and sleeps with the ones who'll let him."

"And you're going to let him, right?"

"No, I'm not. I don't need…that," Lillian said, strolling Sarah along down the street.

"You do need *that,* Miss Priss. Where're we going? What about the ride?"

"Let's walk for a bit," Lillian said.

"It's a horrendous night," Sarah objected.

"Let's be wild," Lillian countered. "Let's be those young sprites of our youth."

"Oh boy, either the alcohol or that bartender has gotten into your heart and mind."

"I just, I needed this. You and me."

"Yeah, it's been rough with Luca. For a long time," Sarah said.

They walked until they came to a city park. "Let's sit in here for a while," Lillian said.

"Here? No way. I'm all for adventure, but not hanging out here at night. This is Seattle, remember?"

"That's true. You're such a good friend. I…" Lillian

stopped mid-sentence.

"What is it?" Sarah asked, turning around and following Lillian's gaze into the park. At the edge was a large tree and underneath the tree was a lone raccoon.

"A raccoon?" Sarah said. "You're under some spell?"

"Wait, look," Lillian said.

Just then a bunny popped out from behind the tree. The raccoon and the bunny stared at each other, but neither seemed intimidated. Then, just as suddenly, the raccoon climbed the tree and the bunny hopped away as if they had said what they needed to say to each other.

"Okay, that was a little strange. I thought the raccoon would tear that bunny apart," Sarah said.

"No, it's something else. I had a dream last night, a strange one," Lillian said. "In the dream, I was a bunny and a raccoon told me to forgive Luca. I felt like the raccoon was the spirit of Luca's mom."

"You're the psychologist," Sarah said, taking Lillian's arm and leading her down the street. "You'll have to decipher that one."

"Yeah, later, let's get out of here."

****

Luca was heading to the restaurant, the sunlight penetrating shinily through the train's windows and he shielded himself with the *House of Leaves*. It was the first time he had used the Link Light Rail and was surprised at how clean the train appeared to be aside from a few candy bar wrappers wisping here and there when the doors opened. It was fairly sparse save for some junkies with heads between knees, completely asleep or rocking up and down to the music in their heads. Luca tried to read, but he struggled to focus on the words entering the stymied cavern of understanding, words that were quick to disappear into the dark eddies of elusiveness.

Luca unlocked the front door to the restaurant. The day brought a different light. Dust came down upon his head from the chandelier above; his nose tingled and he sneezed. He turned on the lights and looked up into a haze of particles that tried to find new places to settle. There was a framed picture of a wine barrel in the little hallway that led to the front room with the name Antinori inscribed at the bottom. Marchesi Antinori, one of the oldest producing wine families in Italy, a family that had officially been making wine for over seven hundred years.

He gingerly walked into the front room unsure of what he'd find having been gone a couple of nights. He surveyed the bar, the tables and chairs, the furniture. It all seemed dirty, decrepit, and hostile. It was a façade, a dingy strip club in the morning, the girls with clothes on, makeup off, sticky floors from spilt soda pop, sticky tables from sweat, lighting showing off marked walls and scratched polls: an entertainment business that fed gluttony instead of debauchery.

Luca had decided to go to rehabilitation—a one-month reprieve in the countryside at Sundown Ranch. Some things needed to get done first. He stepped further into the bar, sorted through some papers. He paid the bills that needed to be paid for the next month. He had been thinking of doing a post-Thanksgiving wine dinner, but discarded that idea. He emailed his VIP guest list that he would be gone for the next month so not to cry foul in his absence. And then he turned to look at the bar shelves. The liquor stared back at him enticingly, whispering sirens on the sea. He would be a whole month without anything to drink and he could already feel his thirst as he unconsciously licked his lips. What to have first!

He poured himself a bourbon. He dropped in a couple ice cubes and went to work on it. He paced, the restaurant drink in hand, and tried to imagine what it would be like in his absence. Surely it would stay the same since he was bound to return. But he couldn't imagine the feel of the place without him there. The servers would do an amazing job, but these walls were his home and he was its caretaker. It would be, in a word, different. It would lose a bit of its zest for life, its vitality. But it was only one month. A restaurant cannot fall in one month.

****

The hilly country of Yakima glistened in the morning frost and Luca was reminded of the "Hills like White Elephants". Lillian turned onto a long road deep into the underbelly of a mountainside just outside of town, hidden away from the main highway.

"I never knew this was here," Luca said. "I've driven this way for years."

"Yeah, it's hidden out here," Lillian said.

"They keep people like us hidden," Luca said.

Lillian drove on until coming to a walled estate with long stretches of green grass and rows of oaks and quaking aspens. The ranch was nestled within a valley between hills and within the center of the compound was a large building resembling a school, behind it a gymnasium and basketball court. Lillian parked in front of the main building and held her breath, not understanding the fear of knowing the answer to her next question.

"Luca, that other night, did you—"

"Nothing happened. I promise you."

"It doesn't matter anyway if it did," Lillian said.

"It does matter," Luca said. "And nothing happened."

"Okay. I believe you."

Luca took a deep breath, opened the door. "I guess this is it."

"Luca, I need you to sign these before you go in." Lillian held some papers out.

Luca looked them over. "I guess this is it."

"Yeah…"

"You have a pen?" Lillian handed over a pen and Luca signed his name quickly. "Thanks for the ride," he said, shutting the door. He walked with his things toward the entrance of his new home thinking how easy it was to end something so important. A quick signature and his divorce was final. He didn't turn around until he knew Lillian had driven off. He looked into the glistening hills under the blue sky and shining sun, his face forlorn and downcast. A beautiful November day—the dissolution of his marriage—the beginnings of redemption.

When he stepped inside, he was surprised at just how school-like the interior was. There were classrooms, a cafeteria, a front office, and there were rooms to house the recipients of the opportunity—it was an opportunity Luca found out since he was told that many tried and failed to get into the program. Popular place, unfortunately.

He checked in and was shown to his room, which was double-sided with a shared bathroom and shower. There was a bed with a thin comforter and two pillows.

There was a desk, an end table with a lamp, an old dresser, a small refrigerator, and closet with loose hangers. A painting hung on the wall of some bucolic scene somewhere, could be anywhere, and a sliding-glass door with drawn curtains with faded flower prints opened to the back of the campus. His things were searched for any weapons or drug paraphernalia and he was told he'd meet his roommate shortly. The attendant left him.

He sat down on the edge of the bed, not knowing what to do with himself. He had made the decision to come, and now that he was there, the alienness of this new world felt cruel, like he had been captured and set out in the zoo for study. Luca bit down on his chapped lips and wiped the blood away. The air was thinner there, and dryer. In Seattle, at the restaurant, he felt like a king; he had a place, people, he knew all the ways, he knew the culture. This place felt as remote as Antarctica and yet it was in his own backyard, here all the time he was growing up, hidden from society. Taking a deep breath, he decided to put his things away. He hung up shirts in the closet, set books on the desk along with his empty journal, put jeans, underwear, socks, slacks (in case there was a Sunday service), and undershirts in the dresser drawers, and his dress shoes, tennis shoes, flip flops he aligned next to the dresser. He found a heater next to the bed and plugged that in to give the room some warmth.

That took all but five minutes. He didn't know if he could walk around the complex so instead, he plopped down at the desk, opened up the journal, which seemed to creak open like a closed casket, dust puffing out like an Egyptian mummy finding. His journaling days had ceased with the opening of the restaurant. He began to write.

\*\*\*\*

*November 10*

*I've arrived in my alien world I'll be calling home for a month. It's sort of like a school fully fitted with classrooms, a cafeteria, an office, the whole works. I don't know about this place. I don't know why I'm here. I'm having second thoughts already. Yes, I've struggled. Driving after drinking was stupid* ('but you've done it countless times' Luca thought). *I don't know who I am going to be when I emerge from this place, but I hope it's a better person. I feel that there is much that needs to change in my life if I'm going to be happy. Am I happy? For so long, I feel that I've been simply living day to day, working and going home. My life has been that restaurant for ten years. I am completely consumed by it. Every waking day, my thoughts gear toward something with the restaurant.*

*And in the meantime, I've lost Lillian (we just signed the papers), I've lost my mom…how much had I even seen her in the last ten years? And my new best friend, alcohol, a best friend that is trying to kill me. So yeah, maybe I should be here.*

\*\*\*\*

Luca put the pen down and stretched his fingers, atrophied from lack of use. He closed the journal just as a knock came at the door. He opened it and saw the attendant who showed him his room and another man in his late forties perhaps, a bit of gray stubble for a beard, but a head full of hair like a sack of cotton candy.

"I'm your roommate, Franklin," he said. "You can call me Frank, just don't call me Lynn. I hate that."

"Come in, please," Luca said. "It's your room too.

I'm Luca."

The attendant left and Franklin slid in the room, eyeing Luca as if determining if he were a dog that would genuflect or one that would bite the hand. Franklin looked upon Luca's desk, saw the stack of books and asked Luca if he had read any of them already.

"Not yet, hopefully I can get through some of them here," Luca said.

"*Anna Karenina*," Franklin said. "I've read that twice now. I'm an English teacher at a high school. I'm from Republic. Do you know where that is?"

"Northeast Washington. The one part of the state I've never been to actually."

"And good riddance. That's why I'm here. Only thing to do there is drink and fish. Unfortunately for me, I was doing it in the classroom. Drinking. Not during class, but in-between."

"Well, I can't judge. I drink at work all the time. I own an Italian restaurant."

Franklin explained how Sundown Ranch operated, explained the class schedule, what sorts of things they would have to read and write, how the food system worked, the nightly AA meetings in the auditorium, breaks—and the women situation.

"Can't talk to the girls," Franklin said. "No fraternizing at all. I've heard of people getting kicked out for slipping notes, like teenagers. They aren't playing around here."

"It's probably for the best," Luca said.

"Yeah, but they don't make it easy. Think about it. You have a bunch of young boys really, they have drug and alcohol problems, aren't good at controlling themselves, and then you put a bunch of females close to them and tell them not to talk to each other. It's a time bomb waiting to happen if you ask me."

"Yeah, that's true. And not just the young guys. So, what do we do now?"

"You'll start your classes first thing tomorrow. It's break time right now and then dinner. Then we have the AA meeting and then if you want, there is a movie to watch in the auditorium. Other than that, free time until night night."

****

Patients were separated into groups for their time at the ranch and Luca was placed with the Oldies but Goodies. He met some of the other members sitting at a round table in the cafeteria during dinner and he was just happy he wasn't the oldest person at the ranch. There were a good fifteen guys the same age or older than he was. He wasn't the ranch's only old screwup it seemed. Luca's group consisted of eight guys, coming from all walks of life. There was Franklin the teacher, an archeologist working for one of the tribes, a retired fisherman, an ex-police officer, a toothless junkie with a list of odd jobs he performed, a tech guru with a young wife and a newborn, and a mechanic. Luca the restauranteur made up the fateful eight. Only in America were people defined by their occupation, Luca thought.

"This place is aight," Chris, the junkie, said, rubbing his bald head. "Just do the work man, do the work. When I get out of here, I'm going to do some fucking work man. Get a job, get monies in the bank, get a honey. Done with the drugs man. Life's gonna be straight."

"When are you out of here?" Luca asked.

"Got one more week and it's killing me. I'm fucking ready."

"This is my second time here," Mike, the ex-police officer said. "I didn't do the work the first time and now I'm back. It's time to do the work."

"Yeah, don't end up like me," Chris said. "Or those other guys." Chris pointed behind him with his thumb at the younger kids acting like they were in a ghetto high school art class.

"These kids think they're in play time man. They'll learn the hard way life ain't playin'," Chris added.

Chuck, or Chuckles as he was dubbed, the retired fisherman who had a bum leg stretched out under the table looking like a stone mermaid, perked his hairy head up. "Those girls sure are pretty."

The table laughed.

"Yeah, you can look all you want, but no touch," Chris said. "Believe me. I've been here the longest and I've seen guys get kicked out. Girls too. I've six days left here. I'm not gonna fuck it up, but I've caught the eyes of a couple, and I know where to find them when I'm out. I'll be waiting. Need to get a job though. Need money, man. No money, no honey."

The women took dinner first and then the men, but there were always a few women stragglers who came late and overlapped with the guys. They'd wait in line and the guys acted like they were a covid patient, six feet away. The younger boys had to make a scene though, talking loudly, flexing their strengths, whatever. The girls just stared straight ahead, feeling the eyes on them. Sometimes they'd ask a simple question to nobody in particular are there chicken strips?", "has anyone seen Julie?", "what's the movie tonight?"—but never if a staff member was present. Some people just can't seem to follow rules from the astringent to the simplest, Luca thought—even in here, only for one month, the rules had to be tested.

After dinner and a short break, the guys prepared for the AA meeting. Luca never understood AA and especially the powerlessness part against alcohol, he being in the business of entertainment and alcohol being a part of it. It was his business to know about alcohol, entertain his guests and if sometimes he went overboard, that was collateral damage all for the good of the restaurant. He knew he needed to simply adjust his drinking, realize when it was time to stop, and make the decision to never drive afterward. It was that simple. Being here for a month would straighten him out, reset his equilibrium.

Luca walked with Franklin into the auditorium and sat near the back as more and more men filled the seats, usually sitting with their groups. Eventually an older gentlemen with a guitar came in and began with the credo. It was run just like any other AA meeting except at the end, the gentleman finished with a song on his guitar. He had a nice, raspy voice like Bob Dylan, and he strummed well. It was the best part of the meeting.

Afterward, Franklin asked Luca if he wanted to take a walk around the campus.

"I like to walk before bed," Franklin said. "It's nice to see the stars at night. Reminds me of home."

It was chilly, but Luca wore a large puffy coat and a beanie hat. They walked a few times around the main building and Luca looked up at the stars twinkling overhead. A cloudless night brought out a host of sparkling luminescence. Luca couldn't remember having seen that many stars at one time. The shadowy backdrop to the hills and the quietness made it feel like everything would be okay.

"I'm going to head in. You coming?"

"I'm going to do one more lap," Luca said.

The air was crisp, and Luca was getting cold, but he could think out there. It had been a long time since he spoke with God, truly spoke with God; alcohol had replaced God, his new idol. How had that happened? Luca remembered one time when he had first bought into the restaurant and was celebrating with David and his mom, taking them out to a nice steak dinner in Seattle. He had ordered a martini to start things off, a bottle of white wine with the fried calamari, a bottle of red with the stuffed ravioli, and another bottle of red with the steaks. He had ordered a port wine with the chocolate lava cakes and an amaro digestive at the end. David and Francesca had some of each wine, but they weren't big drinkers. Luca finished everything that evening.

"You're becoming an alcoholic," Francesca had said.

Luca scoffed at his mother. "I'm dining like one should dine."

Luca couldn't imagine leaving any alcohol behind, especially the wine—those grapes had died for a cause, and it was only right to consume them as they were meant to be consumed. What was the big deal? He was dining like a king. But that first night at the ranch, Luca realized that that was the first full day that he could remember in the longest time that he didn't have any alcohol. And he knew he was a contradiction, just like the other guys at the ranch. At one moment, his brain convinced him that everything was fine and normal and at the next, he saw the situation as it actually was. Looking up at the stars made Luca feel small, knowing that each one of those shining, glistening spheres was a sun and that probably planets were circling those suns; Luca thought just how small and insignificant he was to the grand scheme of things and yet, there was this god who apparently loved him. And he realized that he did perceive that love when he stopped to feel it, when he asked to make a connection. God never left but patiently waited in the shadows.

Luca went inside and into his room. Franklin was there reading in bed. "What're you reading?" Luca asked.

"Some of the stuff for class tomorrow, but I don't know. It's not really speaking to me. I'm not sure how I feel about this whole place," he said. "I don't know. Anyway, what do you think? How was your first day?"

"It's good so far. Thanks for showing me around."

"No problem. Tomorrow the real work starts. You'll meet our group leader, April. She's a hard ass, but she truly cares I think."

Luca took a shower and wondered what his mom would think if she could see him at the ranch. She wouldn't say 'I told you so'; she'd probably just be happy that he had taken steps to ameliorate the problem. He wondered where she was at that exact moment, what she was doing. It's strange to believe in the soul and its eternal existence. Imagine, to truly imagine that at that moment, his mom was somewhere else, out there, doing something, being something, but not within the realm of his life. Sometimes it was too hard to imagine the possibility. And the foreverness. Luca sometimes wondered if an eternal sleep was the better option. He'd never know it if he were just gone. But that was scary too. To not exist, to not be. Luca didn't know what was scarier, an eternal hell, wherein at least you'd know you existed or an eternal sleep because you didn't exist to know anything at all.

Luca got out of the shower, dried off, put on pajamas and took up a book in bed to focus on other things, fictional things: *Anna Karenina*, a tale of tragic love.

Chapter 5

Luca awoke, a jolt into darkness, enveloped by the ceaseless bellows blasting out of the black hole from the other side. Franklin sounded like a warthog courting a sow and Luca thought seriously about suffocating him with a pillow. The room was blisteringly hot with the heater on high and Luca had had terrible dreams. He checked the time, too early. He had barely a few hours of restless sleep. But he didn't want to venture back to those demon dreams so he got up anyway, took a shower to shake off the sleepiness and then tried to read for a spell. He read the same line over and over and over again to Franklin's oppressive barking. He tossed the book aside and went to walk the hallways and to see about getting coffee.

It was quiet outside the room, but he heard soft snoring and occasional music when he passed other patients' doors. The hallways had been painted a burnt orange like the inside of an old hotel where murder mystery stories were thought up. The carpet a deep russet brown, the ceilings made of perforated tile blackened by cigarette smoke, the cafeteria, large and expansive, was empty of persons so Luca poured a black coffee and sat down at a table to read in peace. He took a sip, surprised at what he found. "Hmm, not bad for drip."

Just as he finished one meager paragraph, Chris sauntered in and sat down at the table, tossing a pack of cigarettes in front of him.

"Can never fucking sleep here man, I don't know if I've slept this entire month, fiending for a hit man, but I'm done with that, got these cigarillos though."

Chris said everything so fast that Luca had trouble catching up and deciding what to respond to. "Not sure if we're supposed to ask, but what is it that you like?"

"Drugs? Fuck, all of em, but I'm here for meth and fentanyl." Chris rubbed his bald head and looked around suspiciously as if he thought there were eyes and ears listening in on his every word. "Yeah, when I get out of here, I'm going to lock in a job, get a house maybe, get a honey, not in that order though. Need that honey first."

"Probably need that job first," Luca said.

"Yeah, yeah, that's true. Wouldn't mind working here if they'd let me, counselor or something. You got to be sober for six months before they let you work here. Shit I'm done with that stuff man, meth sucks. Nah, I'm kidding, I love meth, love it, but I'm done man, that shit wrecks your life. Oh but it's so so so good."

"Anything that good will wreck your life," Luca said.

"Ain't that the truth brother. That's why we're all here, we like the good life."

"Yeah, unfortunately, all good things come to an end, usually a drastic end with the stuff we like," Luca said.

"You got it dude. We gots to learn to live normal lives, boring fucking normal lives, living in our own heads for once. Shit man, that last place I want to live is in my own head. It's a fucking nuthouse in there."

Luca headed back to the room and found Franklin getting dressed.

"You're up early," Franklin said jovially.

"Yup," Luca said, trying to feign early morning glory. Nothing was more aggravating than a person who snored and woke up restful except perhaps a person who ate loudly and was always eating—a person who could pull both of those things off was truly a marvel.

"You get some coffee?"

"Yeah, just talked with Chris for a bit. Interesting guy."

"Oh yeah, good dude, but crazy."

"He's a walking contradiction," Luca said.

"Aren't we all."

"Yup, if there's one thing I learn here," Luca said. "It's probably that everything I know deep down is probably the truth."

With Franklin dressed, Luca found himself once again in the cafeteria. A few other early risers were now there reading the morning newspapers and chatting it up—the news from the outside world suddenly seemed quite interesting and since it was coming from newspapers and not social media, it also seemed more real. Luca had another coffee while waiting for the breakfast trays to fill the line: scrambled eggs, bacon, toast with raspberry jelly, scones, sliced ham, hash browns, and fruit. There was coffee, orange juice, cranberry juice, all sorts of teas. Luca watched as other guys in line loaded up their plates as if they got only one shot at a buffet. Coming off drugs, he imagined this place was a godsend; he figured more than a few pounds were put on at the ranch. Luca surprised himself at how much he ate. One day without alcohol and his body went into hyper-reserve mode—it needed those calories it had been missing.

"Wow, that was surprising," Luca said, leaning back in his chair and sticking his belly out.

"Happens to everyone," Franklin said. "I've put on at least five pounds."

"How long have you been here?"

"Just over a week now."

"You seem like you know the place inside and out," Luca said.

"You'll see. After one week, you'll feel like a junior in high school. Almost top of the pack. But not a senior so you still have some time before you enter the real world. Time flows differently here and you get experience fast. You ready for the first class?"

"I might pop, but got to go sometime I guess," Luca said.

The group was all there as Franklin and Luca walked in and took two seats. There was no sign of April; Luca found himself biting his lower lip again in anticipation to meeting this daunting woman. After a few moments, a short, big woman with squat, dwarf-like legs came in wearing a light blue sun dress exposing her arms like two large pink hams ready to be cooked. She looked around with clear blue eyes and a confident yet abstract smile. She perfunctorily said hello and went straight to her desk to gather up some papers. Luca instantly knew that she knew that this was her domain; he liked her immediately.

"Oh, you must be Luca," she said, looking him square in the eyes and then down at a file in front of her. "Luck-easy."

"Yes ma'am," Luca said.

"Did I say that right, your last name?"

"It's Lucchesi, but close enough."

"No, we respect names here and it's respectful to say

a person's name properly. Lucchesi. Thank you. It's a nice name. I'm April and I'm your counselor here. You've met the guys?"

"Yes ma'am."

"Good, let me sit." April said, taking a seat within the circle of men. "Everyone here has a story and has heard my story, but you haven't so let me tell you.

"Forty-two years ago, I was a patient here just like you are now. I was a lost cause, bad, real bad. I was drinking so much and smoking so much dope, it was amazing I was still alive. I was a skinny-miny too, not like now, but I could drink with the best of them. I thought I knew what I was doing and I wasn't going to let anyone tell me otherwise. It got bad; it got worse. I had to get my stomach pumped, almost died. I was high all the time and was driving and doing stupid things, shacking up with all sorts of bad people. I was poor, stealing from people, in and out of jail and was just living a hellish life. Started at twelve years old. It got to a point I wanted to end it all and I tried. I took a bunch of pills and drank a bunch of alcohol and went to sleep thinking that was it for me.

"The one thing my lousy boyfriend did good for me was wake me up and take me to the hospital. I can forgive him for everything else because of that. I went through hell in the hospital, but it was there I decided to make some changes in my life. I had to or it was death. I had heard about Sundown Ranch and a few of the people I was running with had been here. I thought I had nothing to lose except my life so why not give it a shot. I came here and it was real hell. I had been drinking and smoking for so long and so hard, I almost quit this place because I wanted the drugs and the alcohol so badly. I almost wanted them more than I wanted to live.

"But I didn't, and I did my month. I had never felt better than that time. I knew I needed to be around people that thought that way so I got lucky and got a job here. I've been here ever since, got married, have three beautiful kids, got a ranch of my own, horses, pigs, sheep, a wonderful husband. I'm living life, man. I love my life. I wouldn't trade my life for anyone's.

"That's my story and I'm sticking to it."

"Wow, that's amazing," Luca said.

"Yup, that's me. Lots of stories like that around here. And we'll find out your story too. I'm glad you're here."

\*\*\*\*

At lunch, Luca and the guys sat around the round table discussing the program.

"April seems nice," Luca said.

"Oh, she's nice and a hard ass," Chris said. "You do the work, she's your best friend, you don't, she'll kick your ass. People need an ass-kicking around here though. I know I do."

"Why would you come here and not do the work?" Luca asked.

"Some people have to, court ordered. Some people just want a break from the real world," Chris said.

"Some people just want the food," Mike, the ex-cop added.

"It's an expensive break from life," Luca said.

"Not everyone pays, most don't. Most are state funded," Chris said, rubbing his head. "I am."

"Damn, I'm paying the full amount," Luca said. "I'm not sure even insurance covers this."

"Me too," Franklin said.

"Me too," Edward, the archeologist added. "And I'm only here because my wife wants me to be here."

"You don't think you have a problem?" Franklin asked.

"I don't know, not really. It's not like I'm drinking all the time. I'm just bored."

"Me too. I don't think I have a problem, just go overboard sometimes," Mike said. "But I have to rein it in because my job depends on it. I'm a guard at the federal prison."

"I bet you've seen some interesting things," Luca said.

"More than I ever wanted to. That's why I drink."

**\*\*\*\***

Just before dinner, some of the guys went to go play basketball with the younger crowd, but Luca elected to jog the campus. It was a crisp, gray day with light clouds overhead and the hills seemed to absorb the grayness, dulled by wintry sickness. The estate had a fenced perimeter lined with aspens and oaks, but Luca kept to the main path around the central building. There were women out on their break too, mostly huddled in groups smoking cigarettes, but a few were playing volleyball and frisbee. Luca kept his head down and jogged slowly, trying to keep his body in control and his thoughts on what he was doing there. He only looked up when he felt a presence coming his way. A woman was jogging in the opposite direction as him and just as she passed by, she smiled and instinctually, he smiled back. In the split moment that he made eye contact with her, brain waves sent messages that he was attracted to her; she was about the same age as himself and she seemed rather normal, perhaps there for DUI as well.

Luca kept jogging but thought about the inevitability of encounters he always seemed to have. He found that no matter where he went, he would find some woman attractive, and that woman would somehow enter his world. Luca knew without a doubt, that that woman jogging would resurface again in his peripherals, and he would let it happen, almost as if voicing a call into the wild. It happened at the gym, at the store, at a bar, and now even at a rehabilitation facility.

After dinner, at the nightly AA meeting, the same men who had spoken the previous night shared again their terrible life stories while the others zonked out and waited until the meeting had finished to go about doing whatever it was that they did later in the evening, but that night, Luca wanted to see which movie was going to be shown and who would show up for it.

The movie was American Sniper. Luca casually looked around the auditorium, but there was no sign of his mystery woman. The women had to sit on the left side of the theater, the men on the right, and periodically staff would come in and check to make sure there wasn't any fraternization. Luca thought about leaving to go read, but he hadn't seen the movie yet and became engrossed quickly. Anytime an enemy was killed onscreen, there were teenage-like cheers from the peanut gallery, from the men and women. Luca realized that half the persons there were probably just over eighteen. So young and already destroyed lives; or, getting life back on track. One had to think that the program truly worked.

Just as the movie was ending, the back door to the auditorium opened and in walked two women whispering to each other—the mystery woman had finally arrived. They quickly scanned the theatre and

Luca, hiding in the back, was glossed over. But then, she turned around as if she felt his presence, powerful and wild, and when their eyes locked, even in the darkness of the theatre, Luca knew the connection was mutual. She quickly smiled at him and then turned away before he could even react. His thoughts began to race. What could he possibly do? How could they ever possibly be alone together? There was no way they could sit down and have a normal conversation. No, it was impossible. But it was nice to have an admirer and to play a little game of teenage love in that trapped space—if that was all it ever was.

After the movie, Luca went for a walk outside so that he could be amongst the stars. He thought of her and made-up stories in his mind to who she was. Perhaps she had been a server at an Italian restaurant, and she drove home one night stupidly just like he had. She's been a server for many years, loves wine, loves cooking and reading and drinking wine late at night. She loves card games and tends to be quite competitive; she hates to lose and doesn't lose prettily. She's single because she got out of a bad relationship and just needs time to find herself. She always wanted to be a painter, and she paints in her spare time, but she won't let anyone see her paintings because she thinks they're terrible and she's embarrassed because she likes to paint landscapes. She's educated, but the restaurant world enticed her, and she could never escape from it, just like himself. And, Luca thought, since timing is everything, once she leaves Sundown Ranch, she'll want to become a better person and move on from a life of addiction—also just like himself. But, Luca thought, wouldn't a better person just let her be and let her heal and grow and do what she needs to do here instead of trying to play this game of teenage cat and mouse?

Something flickered out of the corner of his eye toward an oak tree lingering in the shadows. Gooseflesh spread over his arms at the thought that perhaps a coyote was stalking him, or a cougar. Then, he saw a little movement closer to the ground and near the fence. A black and white creature scampered between the fence line and the trees. A skunk. Luca laughed to himself and watched the little guy run along until it was out of sight.

"Thank you, God," Luca said. "Never seen one of those before. Only smelled them."

\*\*\*\*

Lillian sat at the desk in her office looking over notes on some new patients—she had taken on three new patients that week alone. She looked at her phone, nine-thirty and all was quiet and dark; she wondered what Luca was doing at that moment. No cell phones were allowed at Sundown Ranch, but after a week being there, patients could call via the landline phones. She wondered if Luca would call her. She wondered if she wanted Luca to call her. She went back to her notes; she didn't want to think about Luca.

Her newest patient confounded her: twenty-eight-year-old male, living at home with his mother, suffering from delusions that had become increasingly stranger until his mother thought it time to send him to a psychologist. Lillian had met him for the first time that day and was going over their conversation in her head.

"Nick, I'm Dr. Waters. Do you like to go by Nick?"

"Dr. Nick is fine. I'm a bit of a doctor too. I studied psychology in college so I know all your tricks. But it's okay. I want to be here. It's nice to get out of the house sometimes. My mother, goddamn her, always pushing and pulling. Nick, do this; Nick, do that. Why can't she just let me be? I have important work to do too you know, not just dishes and vacuuming and mowing the lawn for allowance."

"What sort of work do you do Nick?"

"Dr. Nick. You and I are on the same level so let's just play nice, okay? Anyway, my work is vastly important and I'm not sure I can explain it to you. It's complicated and time consuming. Sometimes, it feels like too much of a burden."

"Nick, Dr. Nick, pardon me, I would love to learn about it if you'll let me in on the secret."

"Okay, I will because, anyway, I want to tell people. I'm the first to discover it I believe. Anyway, I've saved the most characters than anyone as far as I know. So, you're familiar with video games, right?"

"I know video games exist, yes."

"And lore and legends, right?"

"Yes, and yes."

"Well, what you might not know and most people don't is that when a character is invented in the mind and then put on paper or on a computer or anywhere else tangible, that character materializes in another dimension as an actual, living being. This dimension is called the NetherSphere. Those characters exist through their use here. But what happens when characters are forgotten about, lost to cultural indifference, no longer exciting to the minds of the people? Those characters are sent to the Veldt, a sort of character hell. My work is to find and free the characters from the Veldt and bring them back to the NetherSphere. It's exhausting work. I'm sort of a doctor of anthropology and archeology too."

"I see. And…how do you find the characters that have been forgotten?"

"A lot of video games and research of past civilizations. And I have to talk to people online asking them if they've thought up any characters and to demand their drawings and anything connected to them."

"Okay, I see. So, just trying to understand. If I were to think of a new character right now, would that character exist in this dimension you mentioned?"

"It depends. Just thinking of the character, no. But if you draw it out, give it meaning, then yes. Please don't do it because if you don't tell anyone and forget that you even created that character, he would exist and be sent straight to the Veldt, and no one could ever save him because no one knows about him except you."

"I see."

****

Lillian drove home and could barely keep her eyes on the road she was so tired. She opened the front door and plopped down on the couch, Luca's crummy creamy couch that she still had. It was comfortable at least; it smelled like him. She thought she would fall straight to sleep, but found she couldn't stop thinking about Nick. She got up, went to the refrigerator and took out a bottle of white wine. She hesitated, thinking about drinking at that time of night all alone.

"I'm not the one with the problem," she said to herself. She took down a glass and poured and kept pouring until the bottle was empty. "Should've just drank from the bottle."

Chapter 6

Before classes began that next day, April had wanted a one-on-one meeting with Luca. As she used the restroom, Luca looked across her desk and saw a photograph of her and her husband, their girls, their horses, and a ranch home overlooking a cliff in the backdrop—all smiling and healthy and happy. On the wall behind the desk, he saw letters that former patients had sent her tagged to a bulletin board, a few local restaurant business cards, a calendar with seasonal photos of US landscapes, a certification of completion of an Associate's Degree at Yakima Valley Community College and then a bachelor's and master's degree at Washington State University. Born a bad seed that had grown into an accomplished flower and, she said she was happy, but Luca always wondered if people could be truly happy—he had very rarely seen true happiness, if ever.

April waddled in and sat down at her desk eyeing Luca intently, discerning how he had adjusted to the new way of things. She peeked at some notes and then leaned back in her chair crossing her arms over a colorful, silky, flowery dress. "I'm so happy you're here," she began. "Do you know why you're here?"

"I did a stupid thing," Luca began, but April quickly cut him off.

"I'll stop you right there. Let me help. You're here

because you're weak. You're an alcoholic and you're powerless against it. You're intelligent. I see it in your eyes and I noticed it during our first class. But you're weak and you have a very powerful demon against you. That 'stupid thing,' wasn't just one time. You got caught finally, but that was bound to happen. I'm happy you've come to us before the worst happened. What do you think of that? Heavy, huh?"

"Very," Luca said.

"People get what they want out of here. What you put in is what you get out of the program. This place is filled with druggies and alcoholics. Many don't make it. That's a fact. People quit the program and leave and sometimes they come back and sometimes they die. It's what happens. Alcohol, drugs, they are takers, man. They take, take, take until there's nothing to take anymore. And they seem so good. I haven't had a drug or a drop of alcohol in forty-two years. I love my life. My life is the best. I wouldn't trade it for anything. I still have to be careful. The drugs, the alcohol, it never lets up. It may hide in the shadows, but that demon is patient. One day, you think you're all good and you can have a drink and be just fine. Then bam," April slammed her fist on the desk, "You're done. You're drinking just like you were drinking before. Worse." April suddenly laughed. "But now I mostly need to worry about food. I like to eat that's for sure. Every day big breakfast, small lunch here, and then a big dinner with my family."

"Well, you seem incredibly happy," Luca said.

"I am. And you can be too," April said. "You will be. Follow the plan and do the work and you'll be living your best life. Okay, we're going to start you off with part one. There's some reading and some writing involved. You finish the program in five parts. It's not going to be easy. We're going to ask you to dig deep inside yourself and write about some dark stuff. Do the work or die. It's that simple. Okay, class is about to begin. Here's your homework."

April handed a packet to Luca explaining what it was he had to do. The guys began to clamber in doggedly as if they had just played a rugby match and lost. That day, Chris was presenting his Part 5 and soon after he would be leaving. It was strange to Luca how easily it was to meet, interact and become fast friends, or at least well acquainted with a person in such a short matter of time at the ranch. The one common trait of those there seemed to meld everyone together as brothers despite their complete and utter differences. He felt that he knew Chris well and not that they would be friends in the outside world, but Luca knew he wanted Chris to go out and make that money, get that honey, live that life. Everyone seemed to be pulling for everyone else against their common enemy—addiction.

****

That evening, Luca sat reading at the round table when Chris plopped down across from him looking dejected. He rubbed his bald head, muttering some things Luca couldn't hear. "Fuck." Luca heard that.

"You okay?" Luca asked.

"No man. No. Just found out a buddy of mine got kicked out."

"From here? Damn, man, sorry. What happened?"

"Fucking idiot was doing whippets in his car."

Luca had heard about whippets, but didn't really understand them—something with nitrous. "And just like that he's gone?"

"Yup, they don't let you say goodbye to anyone. Pack your stuff and you're out. If you don't have a car, you walk. And it's life or death out there, man."

The ranch was a fantasy world with very real applications. It was the border wall between life and death, a wall of fog frail and obscure, an in-between safe house that hid life's realities, where the nourishment of the soul could be consumed, learned and applied to real life, which lay just beyond a fence line. But there were rules, rules that if not followed could lead to the detriment of an actual reality. Cozy and warm with books and games, classes and fellowship, it was college all over again, but the college of life.

Luca walked the halls like all the others, but he could see in their faces if they were there to win or there to lose. He heard it during AA, during dinner, classes, all over the estate. He could almost pick out those who would drub the drugs or drub themselves. And what about himself? He had no idea how his own drubbing would take place, but if it hadn't come already, it would come soon. He felt it. Somehow, he was prescient of that.

After AA and taking a customary stroll around the ranch in the moonlight, Luca showered and hunkered down in bed to do some reading. He had now been without alcohol for almost a week and he felt good, his body felt good, and his mind was clearing up. He found he could read for longer stretches of time, focus better and understand what he was reading without constantly re-reading. He was about one hundred pages into *Anna Karenina* when Oblonsky and some friends were at a function drinking champagne. Luca loved champagne; everything about it. It was a gentleman's drink, classy, sophisticated, and wasn't overly filling. It was translucent, bubbly, and beautiful. It went well with oysters, soft cheeses, and seafood. It was better in a riesling glass, but it was elegant in a flute. It sang sophistication. It was heady. Feelings of warmth and happiness flow through the body and into the crowd. Luca liked it when it cut the insides of his cheeks like razor blades; the more acidic the better. Luca felt a thirst throbbing in his throat.

He stopped reading; he had read a full page without comprehension. Thoughts of champagne never waned as his eyes skimmed the words and his brain coveted crystal clear champagne—champagne. He had never felt addicted to alcohol, never felt that he absolutely had to have a drink, but alcohol was nearly always at his disposal so it never had needed to entice. For the first time in years, with no recourse but to stay the course of the ranch, Luca needed a drop, a thimble-full for communion to ask for forgiveness. He needed champagne. He whet his lips just thinking about bubbly liquid gold, the sensations to the mind and body, the feel of sophistication holding the glass at the stem, clinking it with another human body, soul, perusing a room with a superior air—drinking champagne as a king. Luca set the book down and got out of bed. He had to get his mind thinking of something else. His heart was beating fast, his hands shaking. He went to the cafeteria and poured some decaf coffee.

Those first few sips of anything always seemed so harmonious with living life to the fullest. It was instantaneous. A room brightened, a person sparkled, air felt jovial, beauty blossomed bounteously. But he never stopped. He always wanted more and more and more. Too much of a good thing is, grand. And the more and more and more he continued, the more he was missing from life—blackout. There was no off-switch. He would wake up and not remember what it was that he had done the previous night, especially near the later hours. Alcohol eventually cut off his mind from making memories. Those black, blank spaces of time were lost time, forever. For twenty something years, he had huge gaps of lost time that were forever gone. Some weren't important, but whole conversations, meeting new people, driving places, situations Luca knew not what they entailed simply because he kept pouring. And for what? Was it fun? And there was always a horrible sensation of questioning what it was that he did or said. He had had to apologize many times not knowing what it was that he said or did, not believing it, but since he didn't have the memory, he had to apologize anyway. Luca had lost some good friends; he'd lost some good relationships.

And now he had lost Lillian. He went to bed trying to remember everything about the night he met Lillian, to try and fill in the gaps.

****

Occhi Belli had hardly been open a few months when Lillian had gone on a date with Sarah, her best friend. Luca was still serving back then, trying to make a name for the restaurant. They had been celebrating themselves, Lillian for getting an office and her own practice, Sarah for getting a long-needed divorce, which she was incredibly thrilled about. Luca had been happy to be waiting on two gorgeous women who came in ready to celebrate.

"We just *must* begin with champagne," Luca said.

"Begin, during and end," Sarah exclaimed. "It's the

end of an era for me and the beginning of one for Lillian here who is also single."

"I can't take you anywhere," Lillian said. "Anyway, you're the single ready to mingle one now."

"Oh, like you've gotten laid lately," Sarah scoffed.

"Ah…I'll get the wine," Luca said.

"Be quick. Momma's getting thirsty," Sarah said.

Luca didn't know who momma was, but he quickly brought the bottle and three glasses. "First bottle is on me."

"Can you do that?" Lillian asked, peering around the restaurant as if some 'owner' would come and ruin the parade. "I mean, won't you get in trouble?"

"Well, I own the place so I doubt it, but *we* could get into trouble," Luca said.

"I'm happily getting divorced, Lillian's opening a psych ward—"

"It's not a psych ward."

"And cute server boy here owns a restaurant. I'd say we have a trifecta of celebrations."

It had been a slow night and Luca closed the restaurant early—Lillian and Sarah were still there and Luca was pouring the fourth bottle of champagne.

"And then I found him in bed," Sarah said, indignantly. "At our house."

"With the woman?" Luca asked.

"No," Sarah screamed out. "With the man."

"What?"

"It was the man he was eyeing the whole night. I guess I should've known. It still hurt though. But good riddance. That is all over with now. And I still got a hefty payout."

"Wow, what a story," Luca said, drinking half his

glass.

"You drink fast," Lillian said.

"Must be the company I'm with," Luca said.

"Ouch, are we such a bore?" Sarah asked.

"Oh, not even close. You guys are great. I'm having the best time."

Luca closed up the restaurant and locked the door. Lillian and Sarah waited for their ride.

"The restaurant closes early," Sarah said. "It's only ten."

"This neighborhood shuts down early," Luca said.

"We're going to Lillian's. You coming?"

"Sarah," Lillian objected, grabbing hold of Sarah's arm.

"Ah it's okay. I'm not going to invite myself over," Luca said.

"No, I mean, you can come over," Lillian said.

"No no, I won't take pity," Luca laughed.

"She wants you to come over," Sarah said.

"You sure?"

"Yes," Lillian said. "But no funny business."

They drank well into the night until all three made it into Lillian's bed to watch The Princess Bride while falling asleep. Luca was in the middle with Sarah snoring on his left and Lillian breathing in his ear on his right. He could hardly keep his eyes open, but felt like he just had the best time.

****

Luca lay in bed at Sundown Ranch, Franklin snoring away from the other side of the room. That memory was a good one, back when Sarah still liked him and Lillian only thought his drinking was part of the restaurant persona. That was ten years ago. For the last ten years of his life, Luca realized they had all been spent inside a restaurant, a bar, or some other place that involved drinking and eating. A quarter of his life devoted to drinking. And before that too, eight years before that. Almost half his life devoted to drinking alcohol, to find pleasure, to escape reality.

****

David sautéed two chicken breasts in white wine and lemon and capers and prepared a house salad with olive oil and balsamic vinegar and sliced cherry tomatoes and red onion, added some caraway seeds. That had been Francesca's favorite meal, simple and healthy. He sipped on some white wine as he moved the chicken around nonchalantly in the pan with a wooden spoon. Ludovico Einaudi's soft sounds sonorously sifted in from the dining room—he had been Francesca's favorite musician. The night she had met him at the Seattle Repertory Theatre after a concert was one of the highlights of her life.

David simmered down the wine, whisking in a bit of flour to thicken the sauce, and then sat alone at the dining room table eating slowly, methodically. He stared at a painting hung on the wall of the city of Florence that Francesca had bought at the top of the Palazzo Michelangelo and given to him later that night in their hotel.

"It's beautiful," David had said.

"I sat there and watched him paint it. Water colors. So you know it's an original."

"I love it."

"I love you," Francesca said.

The chicken tasted bland. He must have forgotten something. Francesca knew how to prepare it. David

93

pushed his plate away and poured more wine into his glass, sat and stared at the painting and tried to remember everything about that day. It had been the first time they had traveled abroad together. That was such a wonderful trip, David thought, sipping his wine. Gosh that seemed like yesterday. The time had gone too quickly.

David got up, scraped the rest of the chicken into the trash and put his plate in the sink with all the others. He turned off the lights in the kitchen, the dining room and went into the living room and sat down in his customary chair by the fireplace, the chair he'd read in while Francesca would watch Shakespearian movies on the laptop. She loved Kenneth Branagh and Laurence Olivier. David preferred to read in silence, but having Shakespeare in his ear never distracted him.

Francesca's laptop still rested on a small table in front of the couch. David stoked up a fire and poured himself a scotch with two little ice cubes. He was re-reading the *Lord of the Rings* for the third time, the last time he said to himself. The Council of Elrond—for some reason, he couldn't get past it. Three nights now, he read the words and continued reading until he realized that he had no idea what it was that he had just read. His mind was elsewhere, in the fire perhaps. He stared into it, the flames crackling over the wood. Fires always brought out old memories, nice memories, dark memories. He sipped his scotch and looked into the fire and couldn't help but remember Mary Anne Morehouse, the one splotch on his relationship with Francesca.

The fire burned David's eyes as salty tears strove to make their way to the floor. "I'm sorry, my love, I was so stupid back then. I let myself get carried away. Please forgive me." David finished his scotch and poured himself another. He set the book down and let the fire re-open all the old wounds.

\*\*\*\*

Since Chris was leaving that next day into the wide known world re-mastered, the group gathered at the usual round table at dinner. Chris heaped upon his plate chicken tenders, sausage links, mashed potatoes, kernelled corn, two types of pie, cherry and pumpkin, all the while drinking black coffee and talking of his plans as usual.

"You even took broccoli," Franklin said.

"Yeah, won't eat it though, just took it because it was there. My last supper. Won't have good eatin' for awhile," Chris said. "I think I'll go back for seconds."

"And end the night with the biggest dump you've ever had," Mike said.

The guys all snickered. "Man, I've been regular since coming here," Chris said. "Three square meals a day and no drugs or alcohol. I'm a Swiss watch."

"And all that coffee," Luca added. He had amped up his own coffee intake since being at the ranch and that was something coming from the restaurant. He estimated he was drinking about eight cups a day. "What kind of work do you want when you're out?"

"After six months sober, I'll try to get in here. They like me so it's a shoe in I think, but damn man, got to wait six months, I don't know. For now, get in a car garage or something like that like old Billy Bob here."

"You found a place to live?" Billy Bob, the mechanic, said.

"They got me set up in an Oxford house here in Yakima. No women though. That might be a problem."

"Focus on the job and getting sober first you know

what I mean?" Franklin said.

"Yeah, yeah, got to do the work on the outside, I'm done with all that shit." Chris rubbed his head. "Got to stay away from those people."

"Why don't you try a different city, really start afresh?" Luca asked.

"Nah, I like it here, I know Yakima, know the culture."

"Yeah, that's the problem," Franklin said. "You're too familiar."

****

Chris's final goodbye speech at the AA meeting was a raucous affair with whooping and hollering, the boys really giving him the treatment. There were usually always a few guys who skipped AA, but that night, everyone was there. The auditorium was glowing with the soft yellow light of the evening and the guitar man waited patiently on the stage for everyone to take their seats.

Luca sat with his usual troupe. Chris was chatting it up with a bunch of guys, feeling the warmth of the brotherly love he found at Sundown Ranch. Luca watched him weave seamlessly in and out of the groups of men, talking with the young and the old alike. Luca always admired guys like that, guys who looked and presented themselves in such a way that made other people feel comfortable, at ease, and easily found themselves making friends with everyone. Luca could never pull that off; he thought too much, hung around the walls. He only blossomed when in his own idyllic element. That's why he loved the restaurant. It was his home base and he was the master of that domain—he felt like that at least. Take him outside of that element, and

Luca lost his way—he could only perform after ingesting enough alcohol, the tragic foil.

Chris took the stage to whistles and applause. "I'm a little embarrassed. Most recognition I've ever got," he began, rubbing his head. "Some of you don't know me. I'm Chris. Most know my story. Came here half dead, in a real bad way. I've been a user a long time, it just seemed like that was my life.

"Coming here, I know now it doesn't have to be like that, I can start fresh. And I'm old. So you young guys out there, you gots your whole life ahead of you, do the work now, seriously, do the work now, don't be like me. I'm just happy I got here when I did. I can still use my legs, my arms, my body works, sort of. My brain doesn't. But I have to live with that. Do the work guys. I want to thank everyone here at Sundown Ranch. This place is awesome.

"I want to thank my counselor, April, she's amazing, all the counselors are. Ever you guys need an ear, use the counselors guys, they have your back.

"What's next for me I don't know, but it's going to be better than my old life I know that, try to work here if I can. I'm excited for it, I'm excited for all of you too. Do the work, do the work.

"Okay, won't take up everyone's evening up here. I'm out."

The auditorium stood up and cheered, lauding over the words Chris spoke, the truth of it—standing ovation, approbations to the man who had changed, the man who lived. Here was a man of the people who was about to start life anew. It was inspiring if not a sham, Luca thought, but quickly tried to drub that pessimism away, but he couldn't assuage that aching thought that everyone here was doomed, even himself. Redemption wasn't for people like them. April's story was myth, legend, but she stood there in front of them, a living legend. How? It was all a paradox.

That night Luca took a long walk around the ranch; instead of the usual path, he went along the fence line bordered by the trees. He thought about what Chris had said in his goodbye address. Doing the work and living better, having a goal to work and live toward. Alcohol was so ingrained in Luca's life, he couldn't see through the nebulous, tenebrous doldrums without it. He wondered who he would be without not only alcohol, but the stages where alcohol played such significant roles in his life. He couldn't imagine pure avoidance of his bars and restaurants, his wineries and tastings, his vacations without indulging with the spirit of the culture. For eighteen years he had been involved in the restaurant business; he was the restaurant and the restaurant was him. It takes over the soul. Was it even possible to get the soul back?

An owl cooed overhead and then silently flew off into another tree. Luca watched the owl perched high in the night sky staring down at him as if it were seeing through his soul and discerning if he was benevolent or malevolent. Luca hoped that the wise old owl would tell him. He didn't know how he felt about himself. He always thought he was a good person, but perhaps that was still up in the air.

His thoughts trailed off to Lillian. He had hurt her; he had hurt her badly. He had chosen alcohol over a life with her. The woman he was supposed to love more than anyone. A liquid substance over a life with someone. He had taken her for granted. And now it was too late. A scorned woman is forever encapsulated within the memory of that scorn. No, the best Luca could hope for is her friendship, but maybe that was impossible to have. He could not blame her for leaving; it was inevitable.

The owl flew off to find a new tree and Luca looked up into the bright lights above him. Those magnificent stars. And those were only the visible stars he could see. Imagine, just imagine a whole range of stars in the universe and all the planets orbiting those stars. It was too grand to think about. Luca and Luca's life was too minuscule to comprehend. He was just a small speck of an electron compared to the complete bodies he was attached to. His life was meaningless save to him and perhaps a few of those bodies he came in contact with. Those connections. The universe was grand; his life was infinitesimal.

And yet, he thought, he was the Lord of his Life and only he was the Lord of his Life. Being insignificant to the grand scheme of the cosmos and yet lordly to the grand scheme of his own life, he knew he had to be better, to become something better than simply a man who wasted away in the poison of his own hubris—to control his passion for hedonism, to elicit escapism and reject it. That was the beginning, his first steps to the new life that Chris was talking about earlier. Understanding what drove Luca to do the things he did. It was a passion for hedonistic pleasure and ultimately sleep, to not have to think or do anything. He simply had to answer the question: why was he escaping from real life?

Luca walked back to his room under the heavenly blanket of stars. What a base thing to drive a person, he thought: hedonistic pleasure. As if there were no greater things in this world to strive toward. It made Luca sick to think he was a pawn in his own life.

He took a shower wanting to wash away the evils of all the things he had ever done, but absolution doesn't come purely from water. He knew in his heart it was time to make changes. His mind for once felt clear of something—the clouds lifted, the way forward shown.

Chapter 7

Chris left early the next morning, which proved to be a bright sunny crisp day. A friend of his picked him up and together they rode off into the hills, presumably laughing and telling stories. And that was it. Chris was forever gone out of Luca's life. People come and go, he thought. Sometimes, little impacts affect the most. Chris's life helped Luca think about his own.

Losing someone at the ranch was only momentary lugubrious. Ranch life moved on quickly: new lessons, new people constantly coming in, new stories were heard. The group seemingly forgot Chris shortly after he left. That was the way of things. Chris had ascended. His name was brought up a couple of times that whole next week, but soon it died down to naught. Billy Bob was next on the list to exit so the group was beginning to focus on his departure. The fateful eight, one by one, were graduating.

Luca went for a run before dinner and was happy and surprised to find his mystery woman running the track as well. He smiled at her as they passed each other and she smiled back. It gave him something to think about, even if nothing would ever come of it. A little teenage crush to keep the time flying.

After dinner and before the AA meeting, Luca sat in the cafeteria reading. It was nearly empty save for a couple of guys playing Go Fish. That's when she walked in. She went to the coffee machine, poured herself a cup of decaf, added some whole milk, some fake sugar, and then began walking straight toward Luca. Just as she came upon him, she dropped a small piece of paper near the table and stalked off as if she was confused why she was in the cafeteria. Luca looked around, nobody seemed to notice anything. He set his book down, picked up the paper, and read it.

*—Michelle. Room 116. No roommate. Come tomorrow night, late. Leaving next day.—*

The flurries of temptation flew furiously around his head like sprites, vying to concede to his infatuation. Paradoxical after all that he had learned. It was stupid; it was too dangerous. Oh but his hands began to sweat, his heart began to beat thinking about going there. Tomorrow night. His ever-tormenting hedonism leading him astray. He had a whole day to think about how he could make it possible. All the rooms had doors leading to the outside so he could avoid the hallways. He could slip in and out quickly and no one would know the wiser. It was possible.

The siren's song beckoned him. He would have to go. He would have to know.

****

Luca woke up the next morning having hardly slept. He read the note in his mind, the possible diction, the succinct grammar, the directness. He tried to imagine what it would be like with someone who he had never said one word to—no alcohol to lubricate the senses. They would also have to be quick for fear of getting caught. Luca, the wallflower, couldn't imagine how it would go down—it wasn't a story he drew up in college—he would have to timorously tap on the door clandestinely hiding within the doorframe. She would open the door, whisper 'come in', something like this. He would tell her his name; or maybe he wouldn't tell her his name. There would be a moment where they would look at each other shyly, but they both knew why they were there so perhaps he should just kiss her straight away. Then, naturally things would slide in the direction they were meant to go. Then what afterward? He kisses her goodbye, leaves his phone number and maybe she calls him weeks later.

Could he go through with it? Yes, he had to—his life was built around these sorts of clandestine missions, another story for the masses at the bar. The possibilities of the unknown were what excited Luca the most. He felt like James Bond. But having no protection seemed stupid. What did he know about her? And she knew nothing about him and yet slipped him that note. Luca's brain oscillated between the going and not-going. It wasn't smart. But it was exciting. They were running on pure adrenaline and attraction. He had all day to ponder the possibilities in his mind.

The day sonorously crept by and Luca felt a torpor toward his reading. He just wanted the night to come. But he hadn't decided yet. They didn't have to do anything together. They could just meet and exchange numbers and promise to call each other once both were free. But that seemed a bit too risky for the reward. Breakfast came and went and finally Luca found himself in the first class of the day.

April came in looking tired, angry. She fidgeted with something at her desk and tossed an envelope down in disgust. She looked at the guys with bloodshot eyes filled with a fury Luca had not seen before. The boys were terrified, silent. "What're you guys doing here, huh? Why're you all here?"

Nobody said a word. Finally, through the thick, silent air, Franklin perked up and said, "Trying to get better."

"Yeah, okay," April said. "Look I don't know how to tell you guys and I don't want rumors to be flying around so I'll just tell you." She paused, shaking her head. "Chris OD'd last night."

"What?" Luca said, popping up in his chair.

"What do you mean?" Franklin said.

"Yeah, he died. He's dead. Him and another guy. Fentanyl."

"No way," Luca said. "Just no way."

"Yes, way. The enemy is so strong guys. Out there, it's real. I've seen it many times. I'm so pissed off. I'm pissed."

\*\*\*\*

Luca walked in a somber dream the rest of the day, like trying to wade through pressurized water wearing iron boots. But the news spread through the ranch quickly and it felt like everyone held their flag at half mast, but it wasn't enough. The reality wasn't enough for the younger guys and that sickened Luca. A man was dead because of his addiction, his disease. He had been alive just the day before with dreams and aspirations. Luca walked the hallways and anger bubbled up within him knowing that these guys would continue joking about the drugs they would be taking once they were out and free again. As if it were all a joke. The jocose life was the joke.

The counselors were agitated, enervated as if Chris had sucked their vitality with a straw, spitting it out into the wind and dissipating into nothingness. They held their classes lugubriously with faces long, without mirth, their eyes were gray and misty. Luca couldn't understand how it happened. Impossible to think that Chris, who was just here a short time ago, a moment ago, was now gone into that nether void. If Luca had never heard anything about Chris ever again after he left and life went on until Luca's dying day, he would still feel that not knowing was better than knowing. He could go about his life and know that people were still possibly out there living, but hearing about Chris's death made it real, concrete.

Luca thought of his mother. What would she say if she could see him at that time of his life? And maybe she could. Maybe she was watching from some heavenly sphere. If he knew that she was watching him, would he perhaps make different choices? Luca cringed at some of the things he had done that perhaps his mother knew about now. No, he had to make changes. He was there at Sundown Ranch because of the choices he had made up to that point. Maybe it was time to fully realize that something must be done, to change a potentially ugly future life's outcome. Chris had had such high ambition for change. He wanted a good path. Work, a relationship, something meaningful. How did he get caught back up so quickly into that vile world? That's the problem. The wall of fog only extends so far; and it is thin. That world must be fully excommunicated. Those same demons will always be out there lurking and tempting. And what about you, Luca, he thought. What world is out there waiting to tempt you?

Luca took out the piece of paper with Michelle's note on it. He ripped it up into tiny little pieces and tossed them into the trash can, covering them with other trash so nobody would ever find them. He wasn't going. That was the life he left behind, had to leave behind. That life only led to trouble, damnable trouble. If he was going to make a change for the better, he would have to start at that moment.

Luca took out a piece of paper and wrote down:

—*Luca, Can't come because of Chris's death. Sorry. Wanted to. 667-2020.'*—

He'd get the note to her somehow.

\*\*\*\*

Chris's death had sobered up the ranch for a few days, but then things began to get back to normal, no more than with the younger kids who weren't touched by death. Talk of girls, which drugs were best for getting high, which jobs people did or didn't want, the usual stuff beginning to creep its way back into the fold. Michelle had left the ranch much to Luca's relief. There was now nothing and nobody to tempt him.

Luca was reading *Anna Karenina* quickly—if he could get back to a life of study, perhaps he would find what he was looking for and step upon the road to redemption. Luca spent less and less time with the group as they began to dwindle away one by one. When it was time for Franklin to leave, Luca finally felt like the senior in high school and that he would soon be alone and then leaving himself. Everyone at the ranch liked Franklin. He had a grizzled nicety about him that made him easy to talk to. He could connect with a range of people. Luca was thankful that he had gotten Franklin as his roommate.

The night before Franklin was scheduled to leave, he gave a heartwarming goodbye address at the AA meeting and afterward, he invited Luca on a last walk around the ranch. They had now been walking together for almost three weeks and Luca enjoyed their conversations. They had talked much about books and teaching, students and parents. Luca had thought at one time he wanted to be a teacher, but quickly gave that up thinking about school administrators and the lack of power teachers possessed. Franklin agreed with him, but Franklin persevered.

That night was moonless and chilly. They dressed warmly and were walking at a good pace. Franklin seemed a bit frazzled though, shaking his head as if he were conversing with another person in there.

"You okay?" Luca asked.

"I don't know. This whole experience has been weird. I don't know what to expect when I go home."

"Your kids miss you; your wife misses you. You're going to be just fine," Luca said, hoping to sound reassuring.

"The problem is that I'm not sure I have a major problem. I know what the literature says and what April has been talking about. And it's true. I was drinking way too much. I don't know. I feel like I was drinking because I was bored. You know? Living in Republic is not exciting. I mean, I like it. I go fishing. I coach basketball. I find things to do. Stuff around the house and yard. My wife and I talked about getting a cow. I like the teaching, but the kids can be a pain in the ass. Drinking is all I really have out there. I mean, something just for me. I go fishing alone and bring a few six packs. Big deal."

Luca was silent, didn't know what to say, didn't even know how he felt. He could tell Franklin that alcohol was the great destructor in life, but how could he give admonitions when he wasn't so sure he believed them either? He had his own reservations with giving up alcohol completely, but perhaps that was his alcoholic brain trying to convince him that he just needed to change certain things.

That's what they'd been learning at the ranch, the conniving alcoholic brain, the schizophrenia of the alcoholic brain and its manipulation of the rational side. Rationally speaking, the brain knows that alcohol and drugs are damaging to itself and leads to unwanted outcomes. Yet, the siren's call is singsong and alluring, amenable to the rational brain, allowing the soporific effects to essentially put it to sleep, which allows the alcoholic jester to dance as it wishes, the Dance of More and Forgetfulness. This singsong melody alluringly whispers lies: 'it'll be different this time', 'only have a little', 'only have wine', 'only drink with friends', 'only drink with company', 'only drink on the weekends', 'only drink if you've exercised', 'drink one drink, run a mile.' The rational brain cannot compete as long as the alcoholic brain is allowed to have a voice.

Luca knew he gave his alcoholic brain a voice. He knew he was paradoxical and that he wanted a dualistic fantasy world that allowed him to drink as he wished and yet have different outcomes than those that happened. A tale of two brains vying for control. But the outcomes weren't different, ever.

"I don't know what to say Franklin," Luca said. "I'm not really any help here. My brain isn't in a reasonable place right now. I feel like a walking paradox."

"Yes, exactly. Me too. I know drinking is bad for me and it's what got me here, but I also know that having a beer or two after work every now and then isn't a big crime. Even my wife doesn't think there's too much of a problem. She just wanted me to get some help. And I got it."

"And your kids?"

"They just want me to be present. Not be checked out. A few beers isn't going to do that."

"Yeah, but that's the problem. When do we ever stop at a few beers? I know I've said that countless times. I can only think of a handful of times wherein I've actually stopped drinking. Usually a few beers, a few drinks, whatever ends up with me pissing Lillian off, or driving drunk or saying something stupid to some person. But that's just me. I think about Chris and what happened. He seemed like he was beating his addiction. But that's because we're at the ranch. He went outside and then, bam, just like that, gone."

"But Chris was into hardcore drugs. That's different. I don't know. Maybe I'm just searching for excuses."

It was getting cold and the chill was beginning to break into their skin so they decided to head inside. Luca went to the cafeteria and made himself an herbal tea and sat and read for a while. He finished *Anna Karenina* just as Franklin came into the cafeteria and sat down with Luca.

"I thought about what we talked about. Yeah, I think I'm going to try this not drinking thing and see how I feel. What's the worst thing that quitting can do to me?"

"You've come a long way my friend."

****

The next morning, Franklin left just after breakfast. His wife picked him up and Luca was disappointed that he wasn't able to meet her as he had heard how wonderful she was, but he was able to wish Franklin well and hopefully they would stay in touch. Franklin got behind the wheel of the blue pickup truck and was off. The original group was all gone now and it was just Luca and the newbies. In one week, he would be leaving as well.

As Luca's departure day drew near, he tried to keep it under wraps—he didn't want the hoopla of leaving in a cavalcade of triumph. When he did give his final speech on the eve of his departure, many of the guys there were surprised he had been there a month as they didn't even know his name. He thought it best that way. He didn't want to pretend to be interested in their lives anymore. He was ready to get back to his life, to move forward onto this new path.

The ranch had been a departure from real life. A blip in time, but a full month of recovery and awareness. Luca left with the hopes of never having to return to such a place despite its benevolence. And Luca knew it was time to go. Gabriele, from the restaurant, was to be there in less than an hour.

Luca packed up his things amidst a bout of melancholia. He did want to begin life anew, but the ranch was such a comfortable place. He felt he could stay there longer, maybe even needed to. But there were things to do and there were things to figure out and some things could only be figured out in the real world. Luca didn't know how his life was going to look. The restaurant loomed over him and he was filled with trepidation he had never felt before as if he were a newborn babe cognizant of that fact.

Gabriele arrived on time and hungry. They drove to a burger joint nearby and Luca told him all about the program. Then, they were off racing down the interstate.

Luca's myriad thoughts conflicted with each other. He couldn't think of his mother; he thought of his future. For ten years he invested his energies, his body and soul, hell his entire thirties into Occhi Belli. He met and married an amazing woman, messed that up through drinking. He made money; he bought a house with Lillian. He drank a lot of that money away. He made a lot of friends; he made some enemies.

It seemed like one big party that decade, and that party seemed to be coming to an end. He went toward the sun sinking into the dark mountains with thoughts so peculiar to him he wondered if this was his mother infiltrating his mind. What if he sold the restaurant and got out of the business entirely? What would he do? What were his skills? He had been an English major and had spent the last eighteen years in the restaurant business. He had no skills. He had managed a successful restaurant for ten years; that must count for something in the working world.

As darkness deepened his brooding thoughts, he became acutely aware of the night and the shadows that permeated the forest. He could have sworn he saw moving shapes within the trees. The apparitions were there again. Something was hunting him, wanting to devour him. Luca felt his spirit had been weakened, his soul open for evil to enter, his heart dead, and his mind turned to mush. He needed a shower, a fire, a book, and a scotch while wrapped up in a blanket. He needed Lillian's smile to shut out the dark thoughts in his mind. He needed the church, sanctity and absolution. He needed to confess to God his unworthiness, his sins against man, against woman, against animals and children, and against the world.

Had he helped anyone? Had the restaurant helped anyone? Who or what was he but an entertainer? Was that a justifiable position to take in a world such as this? Yes, a broken world needed people to give just a little bit back in the form of art and beauty and laughter. How arrogant to think that he was that thing that brought happiness to anyone. Yet, he knew he did at times. But was he a fake, a fraud, a *pagliaccio*?

An hour more of driving; he wanted that scotch, fiending, like Chris must have been. He even wanted to see Lana. He wanted a filet mignon and mashed potatoes and a glass of nebbiolo. Want, want, want Luca, why not give, give, give. He took from people the things that were there to take and sometimes the things that weren't there to take. And he hid behind that façade of a smiling, gregarious persona: Luca Lucchesi, restaurant entrepreneur and golden boy of north Seattle, DUI recipient, divorcee, a pariah of Woman and a lonely alcoholic *bastardo*.

\*\*\*\*

Lillian knew Luca would be coming home that night. She paced around the house tidying up, doing the dishes, putting her work in order. She put on a black bra, black panties, black jeans and a black blouse. She looked at herself in the mirror. Too L.A. She took off the black jeans and put on dark blue jeans, a black belt, black high heels. She took off the black blouse and put on a red blouse. Too Valentine-y. She took off the red blouse and put on a light blue snug sweater. She grabbed her work bag before taking the train downtown.

When she walked into the bar, she instinctually looked to see who was working. He had his back to her, but she knew it was him. She found an empty seat next to the wall and took her laptop from her bag and set it in front of her. She felt his approach and she tried to nonchalantly continue looking at her laptop until he was practically upon her. She looked up and smiled what she hoped was simply a gregarious smile that didn't mean anything.

"Well hey," he said, putting his hands out in front of him as a welcoming symbol. "You didn't call but seeing you in person is even better. Vodka martini, olives?"

"Well, hi, and yes, I'd love one."

"You got it. You're meeting your friend?"

"No, not tonight. Working. I needed to be in a different space."

"Oh, what is it that you do if I may ask?"

"Psychologist."

"Oooh, fascinating."

"It sometimes can be. I'm Lillian by the way. I don't think I actually introduced myself last time."

"Yeah, I sort of thrust my number upon you without catching your name. I'm normally not this terrible. I'm Antonio."

"I do remember that," Lillian said.

"And I still haven't made your martini. I'll be right back."

Antonio flitted away and Lillian found herself watching his every move. He took a shaker, filled it with ice, took down a bottle of vodka with a polar bear on it and poured heavy and shook vigorously. He speared three small olives with a plastic sword, took out a chilled glass, and poured the martini to the brim. He set the lake of ice crystals in front of Lillian and shrugged his shoulders.

"Best one I've made tonight I think."

"How'd you know I don't use vermouth?"

"Your friend mentioned it last time."

"And you remembered? I'm impressed. But not that I had gin last time. This is vodka."

"Oh, man, that's right," Antonio said.

"No, I'm just playing. I want this. What was that vodka?"

"It's from the region of Champagne. Distilled seven times and just as good or better than most vodkas and yet half the price. Not that I think you can't afford high-end vodka, but…"

"No, I appreciate it. That's very thoughtful of you."

"You hungry?"

"No, just the martini for now."

"Good. I'll let you work. Let me know if you…need anything else."

When he walked to the other side of the bar, Lillian let out a deep breath. Her chest was pounding and she all but thought everyone in the bar was about to do a rumba to the beat of her heart. She didn't know if Antonio thought that was her flirting, but she hadn't talked to another man like that in nine years. At least that's the way it seemed to her. But maybe not. What had she said? She said she was a psychologist, that she was there to work, she had introduced herself, insulted his memory of the gin. She asked a question—what was that vodka? Was that flirting? Actually, she didn't really say anything at all remotely flirtatious. She said thank you, that's nice of you, not hungry. Oh god…she was terrible at this. Boring old Lillian. He probably talked to all his customers like that and maybe her drink order was so boring that it didn't matter if it had been gin or vodka. He did mention her not calling though and that it was good to see her. Well, he had to say that so it wouldn't be awkward.

Lillian's laptop had gone to sleep and she started it back up. She took a big pull of the martini—he did make an excellent martini—and then she began furiously writing notes on her new patients.

After an hour, she closed her laptop and put it away into her bag. She finished the martini and ate the remaining olives. Antonio approached, pointing to the glass. "What did you think?"

"It was amazing."

"I've never seen a person take that long to have a martini that was amazing."

"No, I—"

"I'm giving you a hard time. You, want another?"

"No, I need to be getting home I think."

"Well, that drink is on me. It was nice to see you."

"Oh, you don't have to do that…but, thank you. Maybe, I can repay you and take you out and buy you a drink sometime?" Lillian couldn't believe that she just said that. Time seemed to stop and the waiting for his response seemed to last an eternity.

"Yes, yes, that would be great. Anytime. You have my number."

"Okay, okay then I'll just text you and see when you're free."

"I'll look forward to it."

"Okay, me too. Well, bye now."

"Text soon."

Lillian left with the jubilation of having done something that seemed impossible or at least forgotten within her. She felt that perhaps she could move on, she could be her own woman again. She took a car home and decided that night she would not continue working and do something else for herself—she didn't know what it was going to be, but she would find something.

\*\*\*\*

Luca awoke that first morning after returning home in a stupor from all the wine and scotch and partying he did at the restaurant the night before—his glorious return. He shook the sleep from his eyes. He showered, dressed, made some eggs and sausage, had some coffee and took a good look at his surroundings. He was forty years old living in a studio apartment with barely any furniture in it, barely any life in it. He wore an old maroon bathrobe over his clothes and wondered just what the hell he was doing. He had fallen the first night.

But there was a brief moment that night before that he felt like he had lived.

Chapter 8

Grief begins as a seed hardened and knotted away deep inside the psyche until corybantic shock explodes out like a supernova, pulsing frantically before dying away; then throbbing softly inside its carapace, through memories and emotions, above all love, grief begins to manifest itself. To become whole again, it must be allowed to; the stagnation of feelings stymies the healing process and only a shell protecting emptiness, then, is allowed to exist. It had been three months since Luca had left Sundown Ranch and forgetting everything, he had killed his emotions and memories with drink. Without Lillian in his life, without his mother there in his world, he had a license to kill, himself.

Luca left Occhi Belli mid-day cheerily, walking down the street basking in the sun that had come out after a week of rain. Chickadees were gossiping away up in the cherry blossoms that had just begun to bloom that morning—the streets would soon be littered with white and red and pink petals. A soft breeze blew clean flowery fragrant air and Luca heard the buzzing of bees roving in and out of his periphery. He began to whistle "I'm Henry VIII, I am" as he made his way down to an Irish pub for spicy wings, a cup of soup, beer and Jameson, his usual lunch.

It felt good walking under the sun. It had been a stressful week with Valentine's Day and the Valentine's

Wine Dinner. The restaurant was booming and Luca's wallet was booming right along with it, but felt he was dooming himself with the drinking. It had been party after party and springtime was coming so soon the patio would be open to the buzz of summer excitement—no rest for the weary. He could handle it; he felt good. He tried to jog every day to burn off what he drank, a mile for each drink, to even things out.

The pub looked menacing enough on the outside with thick, dark opaque windows and gray slats when closed to ward off the high school students lingering nearby—an immutable, amnesiac, pandering place for inveterate persons to disappear into. The air was heavy and dark, only the back bar lit up to highlight the endless pleasures to quaff down. The russet walls were adorned with the signed jerseys of accomplished men, heroes and villains, a constant reminder that as the beer, the scotch, the vodka sodas dwindled down from the glass to the gullet, that to genuflect to the drink would ameliorate the hubris of thinking just anyone can be a winner.

Luca swung open the door and marched inside. Dark shadowy faces with hoods or sunglasses drank thick, dark liquid and whiskey at the bar top. The Irish bartender, a beautiful elven woman named Aoife O'Flannery, a Serinda Swan shorter sister of sorts who hid her sensual body behind baggy black trousers and baggy black heavy metal T-shirts and sports bras, hustled up and down the bar pouring drinks or cleaning spoiled surfaces. Her luscious, undulated hair was tied up with a rubber band and she looked like a rooster bobbing back and forth along the bar. She glanced up at Luca as he approached and she only gave him a perfunctory hello as she began pouring shots for those already seated and waiting at the bar. Her mood seemed forbidding so Luca ordered his usual beer and shot and took it outside onto the patio to bask in that day's sun.

He sat under an awning and watched the football game on a large screen television next to a blackboard with all the drink specials—Everton versus Crystal Palace. Whenever Luca saw Crystal Palace play, he imagined a palatial kingdom out on a cliffside overlooking vast stretches of raging green waters in Cornwall, not a club in the heart of London. Luca's team was Fiorentina, La Viola and his one wish before he died would be to go to a match in Florence, preferably winning against Juventus. Luca sipped his whiskey slowly, but drank his beer quickly. Not a bad life. Freedom and time. Money and excitement. Nothing tasted better than that first sip that whet the lips and excited the mind. Luca had no idea he would grow up to be such a roué—his parents having come from war-torn Italy hadn't ever envisioned that sort of life, but perhaps it was inevitable for first generation boys in a land such as America. He finished the beer and the shot just as Aoife burst through the back door in a rush.

"Sorry, it's been a hell of a morning. Dealing with my brother stuff and parents and my brother's kids. You know the story. Another round?"

"I will. I'll come inside, though, because I'm going to get the wings and soup too."

Aoife had a morass of her own that Luca could understand. Her parents, who lived on an island in the far distant land of Ireland had health problems and it was nearly impossible for Aoife to attend to them and her brother, who had married an American, now had a little girl to raise on his own as his American wife had suffered traumatically severe postpartum depression and had succumbed to a pill addiction.

Luca took his round at the bar and watched the game from an uncomfortable stool without a back, a stool that promoted brevity. Street walkers came in for quick shots and went on their merry way—it was a bereft way to the road to inebriation. Steaming wings came and he let them cool to the touch. He finished his round and ordered another. Crystal Palace lost to Everton and the bar started to fill up for the next match.

Luca was feeling good and wanted to chat so he bought a round for everyone at the bar top.

"You want one, Aoife? Just one?"

"No, I'm good," she said. "But thanks. That's nice of you to get everyone a round."

The company cheered and more whiskey shots were taken. The quintessential Irish rock band Mumford & Sons blared out from the jukebox and everyone was feeling good. By four in the afternoon, just as Occhi Belli was opening, Luca decided it was time to head to the restaurant. He said *ciao* to his new friends and staggered up the street. The day had turned gray and a brisk wind had picked up. It looked to rain as Luca felt the capricious nature of drink, his thoughts beginning to brood as the looming ochre building began to grow larger and larger with each slow, sideways step.

Occhi Belli was quiet, but it was always quiet at four in the afternoon. When Luca walked in, he immediately noticed that the setup wasn't complete. The open sign wasn't turned on, the lights weren't on, the bread station wasn't set up, and Gabriele was nowhere in sight. Then he heard the bathroom door open and close in the back of the restaurant; Gabriele came out with his shirt untucked and his facial hair unkept.

The drink bomb exploded. "What the fuck man? This place looks like shit," Luca yelled. Gabriele ignored him, having seen this before, turned the open sign on, and then went behind the bar. "Are you clocked in right now and not doing shit?"

"How much you drink today?" Gabriele said, his voice even.

"It doesn't fucking matter," Luca yelled. "Get this place ready to open. We should be open already."

"Okay, boss. You're right, boss. Sorry, boss."

"Patronizing asshole."

"You want me to leave, boss? You want to fire me, boss?"

"Fuck off," Luca said. "I'm outta here."

Luca stalked out of the restaurant, into the rain and headed back the way he came. He needed food and drink and what better place to go than the friendly neighborhood competition, Gino's Il Polpo Danzante, The Dancing Octopus. Gino was unscrupulous with his serving of octopus—grilled and served with salad, marinated into a sort of ceviche, sautéed into seafood soup, seared and served with potatoes, grilled with sausage, the list went on. Luca refused to serve octopus as it went against his principles—he even oscillated with pork, but he had a restaurant to keep open; so, pork was served.

Luca's envy of Gino's place was well-known within the neighborhood. Gino had been in business for thirty-five years and counting and had a nicer setup than Luca. Il Polpo Danzante opened with a foyer and a bar with bench seating along the walls, underneath a giant bronze metal octopus with coal-black eyes clinging to a corner, peering down upon those who came in. Stools lined the bar counter and one would walk into the fray and feel the energy of the place immediately. Except for the bored host who seated those after going through a stone archway—the whole interior of the restaurant was compacted with stone—the restaurant felt right. It opened into a dining room with succinct tables covered with white tablecloths, had arched windows with ruddy pink curtains, and the famous murals painted by Gino of gorgeous seaside scenes of fabled Puglia. And the best part, Luca ruminated, was how the restaurant veered off around a corner into a semi-circle of private seating and the maw of the kitchen opened up. Luca dreamed of a sectional floor plan that separated his guests rather than his own longhouse.

Luca was shown to a window seat and promptly ordered a bottle of barbera and a roasted beet salad. Table bread was brought and Luca scarfed it down with a glass of wine. The beet salad came and Luca finished it in a few bites. He ordered next a mushroom pasta with truffle oil and artichokes. More wine quaffed down. He then ordered beef medallions.

Gino came out of the kitchen wearing red jeans and a white long-sleeved shirt with aquamarine cufflinks with an octopus insignia engraved within them. Gino was not a tall man, but his rocklike exterior was about to pop out of his shirt, his biceps bulging like taut, rounded pillows. He adjusted his glasses as he approached the table. Luca looked up and wiped his mouth of the pasta sauce and stood to shake Gino's hand.

"*Ah che schifo,*" Gino said, taking Luca's hand in his. "*Come stai bello?*"

"*Bene, bene, molto bene. Come va?*"

"*Eh, cosi cosi. Cosa fai? Ceni?*"

"*Si, vuoi un bicchiere di vino con me?*"

"*Beh*," Gino said, shrugging his shoulders. "I'll have some wine. What're you getting? The medallions? Okay, I'll get them too."

Luca ordered a bottle of Brunello and Gino sat down and naturally, conversation geared toward restaurant life.

"I'm ready to retire," Gino said. "You want to buy this place?"

Luca scoffed at that. "I'm ready to retire too."

"Beh, you're young," Gino said. "Wait till you've done what I've done. Then talk to me about retirement."

"I would retire right now if I could and move to the south of Italy where it's cheaper, the food is amazing, and the wine flows like the salmon of Capistrano."

"South of Italy. It's terrible," Gino said. "The Africans coming over in boats, working illegally in the vineyards and then the bastards cutting them loose afterward. But where they go? They don't go home. *Che cazzo*, they stay there and live off the government or sell drugs. Thousands, millions of them. It's terrible. Sicily's a shit hole. My Puglia is being taken over next."

"It can't be that bad, right?" Luca's face went from tepid to glowingly flushed from the wine as if it were radiating its own heat. He felt full of pasta and was about to implode. But the medallions came and he kept eating and he kept drinking and he kept talking with Gino—Gino finished off the Brunello and had another bottle brought to the table.

"Bad? *Che cazzo*. It's a mess. It's like the border problem here. People coming over, taking tax money, setting up gangs, bringing whole families over. Take it from the Italians, it's no good. You should know."

"Yeah, but those people are fleeing for a reason," Luca countered.

"I don't give a shit," Gino said. "Parasites is what they are. Let me tell you, all they do is take and they want to send everything back to the mother country. You think they want to become American, like really American and build things and do good here? Never going to happen."

"They contribute. Everyone has to contribute."

"*Che cazzo*. You're living under a rock man. It's all going to be *un pezzo di merda*. Terrible waste too. This country is good. Liberals are destroying it. Don't be a liberal man. Wake up. You own a business. You should know."

Luca looked around the restaurant at the faces staring at the two of them. He felt their embarrassment and ate his medallions without saying a word. Gino got up and stormed off into the kitchen and Luca asked for the bill that had all three bottles of wine and both plates of medallions on there—he paid it quickly fearing the wrath of Gino's biceps, and left.

Back out in the streets, the air smelled of smoke and ash—something was burning nearby—a haze blinded Luca for a moment as he passed two men huddled in the corner of a building, their backs to him. They wore dark clothes and shaggy beards. He knew what they were doing. He kept moving. The wine and pasta and beef and salad and bread all sloshed inside his stomach into a gruel, but Luca had to keep moving. It must have been early still. Cloud cover shielded the moon and stars and there was nothing to see above. He kept moving.

He was tired and inebriated, but he didn't want to go home. If he was a roue, a true roue did not abandon the nascent night. He came to the train station and took the escalator down until his ears plugged up and he felt the cold against his skin as if inside of a cave. A draft blasted into his face and the train arrived a moment later. He stumbled on and plopped down on a seat. He felt the ostentatious stares of other passengers, but he didn't care. People scowled, but whether it was because of him he knew not. Then he saw that somebody had passed out on the floor. A man wearing a ripped Seahawks coat from the '80s, stained blue jeans and only one shoe lay in a corner seemingly dead. Terrible what is allowed on these trains, Luca thought.

The train passed the university, Capitol Hill, and made its way downtown. Luca got off in Pioneer Square and headed toward the water. There was a bar there he used to frequent, another Irish pub, Pied Piper. He had gone out with some college friends about fifteen years ago to the Pied Piper and they had gotten so drunk that when they left, they were singing and they were spread out and didn't even notice the group of guys that came up to them swiftly and silently demanding their wallets with brass knuckles and shanks. Luca didn't even see the guy that punched him first, the alleyway being a long dark abyss. He'd felt a second punch that split his lip open, though, and that sobered him up for a second to run toward an ambulance that was parked nearby and screamed for help. That saved their wallets, but the ambulance had taken Luca to the hospital and that had cost five hundred dollars that insurance had refused to cover.

The immutable Pied Piper still had the same ocher walls and russet floors and doors, but the surrounding area had become something else entirely: that same alleyway now had a six story apartment building next to it and the old, decrepit parking garage that had been an eyesore had been turned into a ferry terminal hub with cafes, restaurants, shops, and studio apartments. Even downtown was changing.

Luca sauntered in and took a seat at the bar. The place was full of characters, mostly regulars and hotel skips as Luca called them—people who went from hotel to hotel downtown to find the ones that were lenient toward prostitution. He ordered a beer and a whiskey from the leggy bartender who could have been walking on stilts.

"You have a card, love," the bartender said.

Luca hated depositing his card into the capable thieving hands of a bartender when he had already been drinking, but as this wasn't one of his usual haunts and he was an unknown entity there, it was unavoidable. He handed over his card hoping to remember to collect it before leaving. He had walked out from bars before, forgetting to pay, and that always proved costly and time consuming. He drank for a bit hoping to engage the giraffe behind the bar, but she was busily leaping from one end to the other. He turned around and listened to the band that was playing there instead. It was too loud to think, though, so he took his card back, paid the bill and left.

He needed to relax, he needed to lay down, he could hardly see through the blurriness that was seemingly surrounding him. He vaguely remembered that there was a massage place nearby. After wandering around side streets for almost half an hour, he found the hole in the wall in a back alley in the south end of Pioneer Square. Luca knew he shouldn't even be in that neighborhood when the sun went down, but he opened the door to darkness. A tiny Asian woman in a skimpy red dress coalesced out of nowhere. Her straight black hair fell down her back and her eyelashes were almost as long as her arms. Luca had no idea how old she was.

"Massage?"

"Yes, please."

"Sixty dollar. Cash."

"I don't have cash. Card okay?"

"Cash machine here," the woman said, indicating an ATM against the wall that Luca hadn't noticed before. He put his debit card in, tried to remember the pin number. He punched in a few different numbers, but none worked. Finally, after the fourth try, he was able to request money. He took out one hundred dollars and gave it to the woman. "No change," he said.

They went through a doorway of colored beads and into a room lit by a prismatic lava lamp. The masseuse instructed Luca to take off his clothes and lie face down onto the massage table while she went presumably to lock the front door as she seemed to be the only person there. She came back in the room a moment later.

"You want hard or soft massage?"

"Hard please. My lower back is what's killing me."

She squeezed and rubbed oil on Luca's shoulders, arms, back, buttocks, legs, calves. She softly massaged it into his muscles. He felt drowsy and it was impossible to keep his eyes open, but he tried to focus as the room began to spin. Just as she was about to climb onto the bed and dig into his legs with her knees, Luca felt a surge in his stomach and a tightening of his intestines. He bounced up quickly and went straight for the trash can. He puked inside and chunks of food sploshed to the sides of the can, onto Luca's face and onto the floor. He puked again and the smell of wine and a mishmash of food permeated the room, threatening to force Luca to puke again.

"I'm so sorry," Luca cried, trying to get dressed as quickly as possible.

"Go, go," the woman yelled.

Luca scrambled to put his clothes on as he hurriedly left the parlor. He flew into the streets and got away from there as quickly as possible. His mouth tasted of regurgitated meat and smelled of sour grape juice. He looked around for a bar or someplace he could go to get the taste washed away.

He didn't see anything that he liked so he trekked back to the Pied Piper to order another round but his eyes, bloody and veiny, betrayed him and he was denied. He trudged away disgruntled and embarrassed and headed for the waterfront. He belligerently stumbled toward the Puget Sound, one foot first, then another, one foot next and then one more. He tried counting how many steps he was taking, but lost count and his mind drifted to thoughts of bed.

He came to a railing and looked into the sea. A lamppost was brightening up the emerald green water, the slimy rocks under the docks and the starfish clinging desperately to anything as the waves rushed over them. Luca clung to the railing, swaying side to side focusing on the starfish. His eyes had lost all their vim and he vigorously blinked to waken himself. He began walking up the waterfront again toward Pike's Place.

He wanted to cocoon himself into a warm blanket, but there was nothing like that there so he kept moving. Two men wearing plastic garbage bags were huddled together outside a closed shop. They looked up at Luca as he was passing and he saw that they had a metal frying pan lit up with a white powdery substance and Luca incomprehensibly stared at them.

"What's your problem man?" one of them said.

"Get out of here, this ours," the other said.

Drugs, Luca hated drugs, a waste of life, a pandemic killer of the body and minds in America. Feeling angry and emboldened, Luca rushed toward them and kicked the pan out of the way. It scrambled toward the water and Luca rushed after it, continuing to kick it until it went over the edge of the dock. The two guys tried to get up, but one fell over and the other fell over top of him. Luca began running awkwardly up the street as they were yelling after him. He ran and ran and ran until he was well out of sight and well out of breath. He meandered out onto a pier and hid behind a large wooden dock post.

After about fifteen minutes of waiting there, there was no sign of the two men. Luca inconspicuously peed into the sea and onto his hands looking over his shoulder and then sat down on a bench, wiping his hands on his jeans. It had begun to rain, and the sky was a hazy grayish black, the air chilly, and only lamp light lit up the pier. He smelled the saltiness of the sea as he sat swaying uncontrollably, shivering from the cold.

****

As Lillian's last patient was leaving, she gathered up her papers and notes and put them in her briefcase. She put on her jacket and was out the door almost before her patient left the parking lot. She got in her car and speedily drove to her favorite cafe; she needed to get away from the office as quickly as possible. She ordered an espresso and a brioche and sat down at one of the tables expecting to do a fair amount of work—at least she was out of the confines of that morgue—the office had begun to become stifling, her own walls enclosing her within, threatening to suffocate her.

But within seconds, she glanced up and saw Antonio sitting across from her, finishing an espresso. He apparently looked up at that exact moment and after a slight hesitation, he smiled and got up to say hello.

"Hi, wow, it's been a long time since I saw you," he said. "I didn't know if it was you at first."

"Yeah, I've been meaning to swing by. Work has been busy and—"

At that moment, a lovely young blonde woman, probably in her late twenties, wearing a cute black dress, tights, and a long overcoat came up and took Antonio's arm. "Okay, I'm ready," she said.

"Um, Lillian…this is my, partner, Julia. Julia, this is Lillian who comes to the restaurant sometimes."

"Nice to meet you, Julia," Lillian said as cordially as she could muster.

"Nice to meet you. Anthony meets so many people at the bar. He's so loved. I'm happy we met in a completely different atmosphere. We met at a Seahawks game."

"Getting drinks at a Seahawks game," Antonio corrected. "Anyway, we need to get going. Lillian, good running into you. Hope the workload lightens up."

"Yes, good seeing you and thanks. Have a good night."

The couple paraded off and out the door into the ephemeral joyous night of nascent lovers. Lillian watched them as they got into Antonio's black SUV, the lights coming on like two stars dissolving a cloud, and they drove off into whatever sunrise they would probably be seeing with each other. Well, it wasn't like she really tried; she hadn't been there in three months. Of course he was able to date other people; Lillian just assumed he wouldn't. Where did those three months go? And why did she have to be a younger blonde with a great body in a sexy dress and snarky as hell? "We met at a Seahawks game," Lillian imitated.

She opened her briefcase and began looking through her patients' notes. She now had too many clients to see—she took on two more that last month alone. She was seeing eight patients a day at an hour each and then had to do all the notes and case files frequenting all the bars and cafes in Seattle and the rest at her house.

When she got home that night, she took off her blouse and saw that she had had to tighten her belt loop one more hole away than usual. It looked like a tourniquet squeezing an albino leek. She took off her slacks and scrutinized her body in the mirror. She had lost weight somehow. She felt like she was eating regularly, but she couldn't say for sure. Too much stress.

She took a shower and then dressed in pajamas before going into the kitchen and looking to see what was there. Not much. Frozen chicken and some peas. She needed to do some shopping. There was some fire roasted tomato soup that hadn't expired yet so she heated that up in the microwave and grated some cheddar cheese over it. She dipped crackers in the soup until it was gone and then went back to her work.

After a couple of tired hours and her brain beginning to shut down, she closed everything up in her briefcase. Tomorrow would come early, but at least it was Friday. She texted Sarah.

Lillian—*I need a night out. Your free this weekend?*

Sent.

She laid back and the couch absorbed her; her eyes promptly closed, and she was fast asleep.

\*\*\*\*

Luca squinted his eyes open and they were filled with water. He sat up; he was in a bathtub. His head was pounding and his arms and legs had gooseflesh as the cold water nearly filled the tub. He moved his leg and the water began rushing down the drain—glug glug glug—the water was cold. Luca turned the shower head off. He lay in the tub naked and shivering. He was in his bathroom, but he had no idea how or when he had gotten home.

It had been three months since he had come back from the ranch. Everything had gotten worse. Every day drinking, getting wasted, causing problems at the restaurant, getting in arguments. A downward spiral worse than before. He knew he was going to die; it was only a matter of time. His head was pounding and he couldn't think. He only knew he was going to die. He had to change. If he wanted to live, he had to change.

"God, what am I doing?" he whispered. "I'm killing myself. And for what? This is not life; this is not happiness. I must stop, I must stop, I *must* stop. Is this rock bottom enough for you Luca?"

## Chapter 9

Luca felt weak. He knew he could not control his desire for alcohol and the hedonistic thrills he coveted. It seemed to be ingrained in his DNA to seek out pleasure and debauchery with drink as the necessary lubricant. Why the debauchery, he didn't know. It seemed the baser the better: dingy dive bars, dingy massage parlors, dingy streets. None of it was new and none of it ever filled that void that gnawed away at his interior. What was it about those places that he felt so at home, at least until he ruined those relationships through inebriation? Alcohol brought the lizard out of him, that ancient reptile for love and fulfillment. He had fallen a long way since his days as a poetic romantic.

The dopamine lizard creeped up and dammed the rivers of thought, poured in its sticky poison and waited to gorge on the pleasurable nutrients. Munch, munch, munch, gulp, gulp, gulp—and it could never get enough. Luca kept drinking, kept eating, kept watching the women. He consumed, consumed, consumed. It was a façade, cute like a blue koala, his magical invisible friend he had when he was just a kid dreaming of growing up to be something special.

Luca knew he had to tame or kill blue koala. He had to go hunting, but how? In the meantime, he knew he was weak. He had to escape. He had to physically escape, leave completely or he'd never get well. He had to run, but to where? Where else…to the only place that made sense, to the place wherein he could possibly find redemption, to the motherland—*Italia*.

****

The restaurant greeted Luca icily, forlornly, menacingly, dauntingly. He felt the hollowness, emptiness, discombobulation, consternation. He felt he had fallen out of love and was just realizing it. The smells of garlic and onion, carrots and celery were pungent; the simmering *bolognese* and *cinghiale* were vapid. The knife's edge on the cutting board was grating and the cutting of the beef gag inducing.

Luca paced the restaurant, went into the kitchen to record what it felt like to be a part of that atmosphere. It didn't take much for a restaurant to burst with energy—it only took two people who were passionate about what they did—the chef and the clown, the *pagliaccio* for that's what Luca felt like most of the time.

Salvatore was stirring the pots and slicing the beef when Luca came in. "*Ciao bello! Mama Mia*, you really want to sell?"

"Yeah, I do."

"Why? What happened?"

"For me, it's time. It's been ten years. It's time for me to move on."

"What're you going to do?"

"Not sure yet. I guess I'll have to figure it out," Luca said, shrugging.

"You should move to Italy. I have cousin there in Florence. His name Marco. You live with him. You like wine. You learn how to make wine."

"Yeah? *Che interessante!*"

"Okay, the restaurant. You serious, let's talk

numbers," Salvatore said as he put on his glasses and sat down at the bar with a pen and paper.

\*\*\*\*

The number was agreed upon; the sale was done. Luca handed over his keys to Salvatore and left Occhi Belli melancholic. The emptiness he was feeling surprised him—ten years and he simply walked away and he didn't even feel like looking back. Luca gave Salvatore all the passwords, logins, client list, and showed him how to access all of it and then walked out the door. He was done with the restaurant and his mind was empty. Soon he would have to think about what came next, but for now, he felt like he simply wanted to exist without thought.

He planned to leave for Italy within a week. He would donate his bed, his couch, the cooking ware he took from the house, his lamp all to Goodwill. He would take only his clothes and some books, his laptop, and some personal items. He was forty years old and he felt once again like a young man going out to sea to discover the world and adventure. But first, he had to say goodbye to Lillian.

She was still at work when he showed up at the house so instead, he walked over to the local bar that he'd been going to for years to have a few drinks while waiting. The usual crowd was there, but Luca didn't have the heart or the energy really to tell them about his imminent departure to the land of his forefathers, nor about the divorce, nor the DUI charge, nor anything really about his life. They weren't interested anyway; they were there to talk about themselves.

Luca walked back to the house in the rain and luckily Lillian's car was there. It felt strange to ring the doorbell of what was once his own home, but he was walking on eggshells with Lillian and he didn't want to crack any more than he already had. At that point, he simply wanted to say goodbye.

Lillian opened the door still wearing her work clothes. Luca had always liked her work dress since it was so different than what he wore to the restaurant every day.

"Always beautiful," Luca said.

"Right, anyway, come in."

"I mean that. Just a natural beauty," Luca stressed.

"Well, thanks," she said. She tried to dress as plain as possible and look as plain as possible so that her patients could focus entirely on their problems at hand without having any distractions. It was tough to be an attractive woman in psychology. "You want something to drink? I don't have much: juice, milk, water."

"No, I'm fine. Thank you."

"You're sure you want me to have the house? I can give you some money for it when I have some."

"No, you take it," Luca said. "I put you through hell over the years. You deserve it. I have what I've been saving and anyway, I came to tell you something important."

"What's that?"

"I sold the restaurant."

"You did *what*?"

"And I'm leaving the country. I'm moving to Italy to learn how to make wine. A new start for me."

"Luca…you've been through too much these past few months. You sure this is what you want to do? You think making wine is a good idea?"

"Yes. I just need a change. I needed to get away

from the restaurant. It's hold on me was too much. It's helped me ruin our marriage. I understand that it's not the restaurant's fault and I did it to myself, but it didn't help that I had access to so much alcohol."

"And you think making wine is going to change that?"

"Look, that's the only business I know, this sort of business. I know I need to work on myself and I will. I leave Friday."

****

David dressed in a light gray tweed suit and herringbone cap. He wore a yellow tie and burgundy leather shoes with laces succinctly tied. He put on his spectacles and looked at himself in the mirror. He had had to roll a lint remover all throughout his clothes to pick up dust, had had to iron his shirt, his tie, and had had to polish his leather shoes. He hadn't thought it had been so very long since he had worn these things, but the dusts of stagnation gather quickly. He had shaved just a couple of days ago and stubble had already begun breaking ground again. Things moved too fast for him.

He was meeting an English department friend at the Richland Players Theatre for a showing of *The Curious Savage* by John Patrick. He got to the theatre punctually and scanned the crowd for his friend, but he was nowhere to be seen.

David went to the bar and ordered a gin and tonic. He stirred his drink with a plastic spoon and then turned around, leaning on the bar, hoping to appear casual. It felt strange to be out in the world again as a widower. Everyone was dressed casually, not like the past when going to the theatre was a special event and everyone wore their best duds. He had tried to take Francesca to the theatre often and he could still remember the first play they attended together; she insisted on bringing Luca with her, her little bodyguard back then. The play had been Tennessee Williams' *The Night of the Iguana* and David remembered the excitement of the theatre, the thrill of the storm, the actor who played Lawrence T. Shannon who portrayed the destruction from desire all too well. Francesca had fallen in love with the theater that night and David liked to think with him as well.

He looked down at his drink when he surprisingly heard the rough clinking sound of sucking on just the ice in a glass. He ordered another gin tonic when he heard a voice calling him from across the foyer.

"Dr. Adamson? Is that possibly you?" A lovely young woman wearing her hair in a half updo style and thick red lipstick against an aquiline pale face came rushing up to David, but in the excitement of seeing the young woman, he couldn't place her straight away. He assumed she had been one of his students from the past, the near past he gathered as she appeared quite young, perhaps twenty-six or so. "I can tell by your expression you don't recognize me. It's Diana. I took your 201 Shakespeare course, oh gawd, must have been years ago."

"Diana—Miss Rosewood," David exclaimed. "Of course I remember you. And it couldn't have been too long ago. You look…" David couldn't think of words to describe her.

"Lost for words? That's a first. But I think what you're trying to say is that I still look young. But I'm a good twenty-eight now. You look great. That's a beautiful suit. What're you doing here? Obviously going to watch the production, but are you here with anyone?

Your wife?" Diana immediately noticed the change in David's face upon hearing the word 'wife.' "Are you okay? I'm sorry. Did I strike something?"

"No, it's okay. My wife passed away recently and it's still so new to me."

"I'm so sorry Dr. Adamson."

"Please, David, hearing doctor outside the college only makes me feel old. Anyway, I'm retired and you're no longer my student."

"Fine, David."

"I'm meeting a colleague here to answer your question. In fact, I think I see him now."

An older gentleman wearing dark mahogany corduroy pants and jacket and a white button up shirt approached steadily, walking with a cane. "Well, you little devil," he said to David.

"Diana, this is Professor Wagner of Humanities. Bernard, this is Diana, an ex-student of mine."

Bernard seemed to scrutinize Diana completely and finally said, "Well Diana, I hope you enjoyed as much as possible David's courses. I'm sure he enjoyed having you in his class."

"Ah, yes, of course," Diana said. "Anyway, I should go as my friends are over there waiting for me. Dr. Adamson, David, I hope to see you again. I'm in the middle of reading all of Hemingway's short stories and novels and I have many questions for you if you'd be interested in having coffee."

"I'd love that," David said. "Another reason to leave the house."

"What's your cell number?"

David rattled his number off and Diana went to meet her friends. David turned to Bernard knowing some shrewd remark would come.

"How's your heart?" Bernard asked.

\*\*\*\*

Luca first flew to Charles de Gaulle and found the airport hectic and confounding and not the least bit giving to intuition. Bustling like a Vietnamese intersection, Charles de Gaulle was an amorphous oozing gelatinous watery soup with specks of humans swaying to and fro unbalanced in undulated billows crashing into each other with shrieks of rage and discombobulation. Luca twice got on the wrong bus to go to the wrong terminal after his gate had been changed to exactly where he had begun in the first place. He highly doubted his luggage would make the connecting flight.

Finally, he was on to Rome wherein there would be a certain systematic order—the Romans had developed the first grand road system after all—and a language that made sense, words sounding like they were spelled unlike English and French. But Luca found it was difficult to understand anything being said on the Alitalia connecting flight, hearing what sounded like a cacophony of gibberish with accents a bit high-pitched and nasally spouting out words at such a pace he wondered if there was any breathing allowed in the language. Every so often, he heard a word that he understood, but unfortunately, it would linger in his mind like big block letters—VINO—as countless other words were already being passed through the tunnels of incomprehension, thus losing the meaning of the entire sentence. He realized he should have listened and learned more from his mother growing up.

The touchdown at the Fiumicino Airport was rough

as the plane bounced along the runway, skipping as a floatplane performing a water landing. Luca sat with his eyes closed gritting his teeth, visualizing the plane bursting into flames. The jovial voices and laughter resounding like echoes off the enclosed walls seemed preternatural and surreal; he had been an American for too long and had lost the Italian jubilation of simply being alive, thankful for safe passage, which is not always guaranteed. When the plane came to a stop, Luca opened his eyes to glimpse the new world from the round, opaque windows. The sun was beginning to set and the mere shadows he saw were of flat land with darkened mountainous ridges resembling jagged teeth.

Luca had no time to dawdle in wonderment in what would be his new home. He left the airport, unbelievably *with* his luggage, along with a plethora of Italians to take a short train directly to Rome. The excitement was outstanding as Luca sat amongst the beautiful people of Italy listening to the prattle of what he assumed was unnecessary conversation, but conversation for the sake of conversation to be heard and feel connected. He loved it.

The Italians would speak at length upon a subject; rarely, if ever, had any American he knew ever said more than five words in a row without the clipped staccato of American slang or the gruff single-word responses that is ingrained in American culture. *This,* on the other hand, was mesmerizing as it felt like he was in a school of fish listening to the fish give their opinions of the open sea.

Without comprehension, Luca was sure the Italians were complaining about their jobs, their day, their families, their lovers, their mistresses, their political situations, but all of it with gusto. Only when he heard words describing food did their faces perk up jovially. Yes, the blatant discussion of what was going to be prepared for dinner that night was obvious. And Luca felt the pangs of jealousy creep up through his stomach knowing that his dinner was a long way away somewhere in a neighborhood in Florence where he was heading. He imagined heaps of pasta, plates of starters, and mounds of meat being served in three, four courses: *tiramisu, panna cotta, almond pandoro* for dessert. He would be going through Rome and missing out on the chance to try *carbonara, cacio e pepe, amatriciana*; he vowed to return at some point to spend time in the fabled city.

After arriving in Rome, Luca immediately took the next train to Florence, which was comfortable and fast. He took a cushioned seat next to a window hoping to catch the last of the sun lighting the landscape as the train passed through the provinces, but it was getting dark quickly and Luca had two hours of travel, so he began to re-read *The Fellowship of the Ring.* A group of Italian women took the seats across the aisle and Luca found it difficult to focus on the book's English words as their Italian bombarded into his mind. Luca glanced over and watched as they played with their hair, twirling it within their manicured fingertips, peeking over at Luca as if he were a rare animal intruding on their space. He found the women intriguingly beautiful as a traveler finds things in a foreign country automatically beautiful.

The dark countryside strode by and the train eventually arrived in Florence. Almost immediately after leaving the train station, Luca stumbled upon the most glorious sight he had ever seen: the Cathedral of Saint Mary of the Flower, the Duomo of Florence, a majestic, gothic edifice looming with ostentatious grandeur among the red-tiled roofs of the city. Luca couldn't adequately take it all in, the magnificence of it all. Building began some eight hundred years ago and it being absolutely stunning, it was too much, he had to turn away and keep walking or he felt as if he would be absorbed into that moment forever becoming a part of that building like one of its stones.

Luca checked his map and the address of his studio and began the long walk up Borgo Pinti toward the Four Seasons Hotel. The streets became quieter and quieter as he moved away from the Duomo until he was seemingly the only one meandering up them. He walked past a small *trattoria* filled with Italian families and thought that once he dropped off his bags, he would head back there for something to eat. His small studio apartment was in a neighborhood just past the restaurant and when Luca came to an iron gate, he was buzzed in by a plump man who came out of the apartment office a moment later. He had short, cropped hair cut as if with a bowl and a large head with a round, pudgy face. He squinted his eyes at Luca, "*Si, posso aiutarti?*"

"Ah, hi, I'm Luca…Lucchesi. I believe Marco has me set up here."

"Oh yes, okay, good, come, come. I'm Armend," he said.

"Nice to meet you. Armend, that's an interesting name. Not Italian I take it."

"No, Albanian. Let me help," he said, taking hold of Luca's largest piece of luggage.

The studio was quaint, but everything Luca would need: fully furnished bedroom, bathroom, kitchen, dining room and balcony. Armend mentioned a few rules the place had and then was off to guard the gate. Luca set his bags down in the bedroom to be put away later. He wanted a shower and then a meal. The water was hot and the pressure was good; he almost didn't want to get out, but his stomach, famished, began growling in anticipation. He dried off, got dressed, and headed out to that little restaurant he had seen down the street.

The night was clear with inky black skies above, but the stars were hidden by a faint fog that seemed to engulf the entire city. Only an opaque waning moon shone through. Luca walked his new streets with heightened excitement; he couldn't believe he was really there in that new country, his old country. It seemed surreal as if this dream he dreamed would fade soon enough. But until then, he would enjoy every moment of it.

He opened the door to the restaurant and was greeted perfunctorily by a server and motioned to sit in a space in a corner, which Luca was grateful for so that he could people watch without being so much watched himself. The smells of garlic, onion, and roasted beef coming from the kitchen overloaded his senses and as he perused the menu; he had a desire to have a little bit of everything. He ordered a glass of wine straight away and some bruschetta with tomatoes. Then, ultimately, he decided on the *pappardelle* in a wild boar ragu followed by the veal *saltimbocca*.

"*Una bottiglia di vino rosso con la cena per favore,*" Luca said to the server. "*Che mi scegli?*"

"You want a bottle for just you? *Non e' normale.*"

"Ah, yes, I'll take what I don't drink home with me."

"Okay, okay. Sangiovese then?"

Luca stuffed himself to the point he had to decline dessert. He whittled down his bottle of wine as he watched the Italian families engage with each other. Words seemed to bounce off the walls, a cacophony of sound, hectic and poetic. He had found his people. No one seemed to take notice of him; he was just another Italian eating a good meal and that felt sublime.

Luca flagged down the server to pay the bill and headed out into the night. He stopped at a hole-in-the-wall shop and bought two cheap bottles of wine, took them back to his studio and began unpacking and drinking out of the furnished wine glasses. He took out his books, roughly a dozen, and then after everything was put away, he went out onto the patio with his bottle of wine and looked out at his new city—he could just see the top of the Duomo from his apartment balcony. After polishing off the first bottle, Luca was in ripe condition to go and explore the city. He was tired but was working off adrenaline bolstered by the excitement of his arrival. He filled a plastic bottle full of wine and set out with his map.

Luca walked toward the Duomo and then from there along the Arno toward the Ponte Vecchio, the bridge the Germans refused to bomb during World War II because of its cultural heritage or because the pastrami sandwiches being sold there were just too damn good. Luca walked across the bridge, stopping to gaze off into the river. He crossed and headed north through the neighborhoods. As he sipped his wine among the two- and three-story houses and apartments, Luca kept walking north until he had no idea where he was. He couldn't see the Duomo from there because the buildings were too tall and he finally came to another bridge, one flat and a lot less intricate. He crossed that back to the other side and eventually came to *la fortezza*, a fortress with immense barbicans connecting the fourteenth century walls built around the city. Luca staggered north or west he couldn't tell.

He eventually came to Cascine Park and walked among the barely lit bushes and trees. All was quiet and Luca felt the eeriness of the quietude as if he were being watched. At one point, he thought he heard rustling from within a bush, but he kept staggering onward. He came to a play area with fair rides and booths, but they looked like they hadn't been operated for some time. He had no idea where he was. Finally, he came to a sign that read 'Scandicci' and he knew he was not even close to his studio. He finished his wine and reached for the map out of his back pocket. His hand came back empty; he had lost the map somehow along the way. He turned around, trying to aim toward south and east. He staggered through neighborhoods passing all sorts of restaurants and shops and bars filled with Italians enjoying conversation and drinks. He just wanted to get home then; jet lag was overtaking him.

He put his hand out and steadied himself at the corner of a building, looked up to locate the Duomo, but it was nowhere in sight.

The sky was dark, and the eaves of the buildings loomed over Luca casting their shadows. He wasn't about to sleep on the streets, but he was cold and tired and just wanted to rest. Then he saw some commotion ahead. An ambulance had arrived and men and women in white jackets were bringing a stretcher toward a shop of some sort. Luca sauntered over and saw a body in the middle of the sidewalk draped under a white sheet. A dead man. A crowd of people were gathered around the man and were excitedly talking and gesticulating with their arms what they had seen. Luca tried to get close enough to hear what they were saying, something about the man leaving the bar, driving through an intersection and flying over the handlebars of his motorbike after hitting a curb and crashing through a window. Luca caught none of that in words but only understood it by the pantomime of the people. He saw broken glass all over the sidewalk and a motorbike nearby. The EMTs were loading the body onto the stretcher and into the ambulance. It was a terrible sight. Luca approached one of the EMTs and asked which way the Duomo was.

Finally pointed in the right direction, he began making the journey back to his apartment.

After what must have been an hour, Luca finally recognized a street and began making the arduous journey through the gobbled stone roadway. He shifted left to right with his arms hanging down his sides, his head wagging back and forth—he was so tired he wanted to lean against a building wall and simply fall down the sides. Suddenly, Luca caught one of the road stones with his foot and he fell forward. He put his arms out just in time as his head came down upon the roadway with a dull thud. He lay there for a moment feeling the pain. With his face cut up, he looked at his hands. A huge gash produced blood and stone rubble. He twisted his left wrist and felt sharp pains.

He got up onto one knee and then stood up. His jeans had a hole in them and his knee was bleeding as well. With throbbing pain, he began hobbling down the street until he came to the gate of his apartment complex. He inserted the key, hobbled up to his studio and let himself in. He washed his hand first and then wiped the blood away from his scratched face. He took care of his knee next. He looked at himself in the mirror. Cut up, bleeding, face flushed, bloodshot eyes, chapped lips. "Different place; same story," he whispered.

Luca went into the kitchen, got a glass, and poured some water. He went out onto the balcony. He sat down and tried to focus. He waded through his staggered thoughts, his mind fuzzy, feeling the frenetic frenzy of thoughts overwhelming him when, suddenly, he looked up as if sensing a spirit watching over him. He saw a woman, a small, elderly woman in a window across the way. The woman turned and looked Luca in the eye and the blatant similarity of this woman to his mother he felt he was looking right at her. The woman watched Luca as he gazed back upon her in wonderment wondering who or what she was. His mother. That loving soul, that woman who had born just her one son and who loved him above all things, that woman who gave him everything and only wanted what was best for him at all times even sacrificing what she wanted in life so that he could do the things he wanted to do once his dad, her husband had died. What was Luca doing for his mother now? Had he even thought of her? It was terrible what Luca was doing to her memory—drinking, getting drunk, and wasting away a life.

The woman in the window seemed to vanish and Luca was left alone with his thoughts. He saw the man in the white sheet, face up, covered in a shawl of death. That was him; that was the future Luca. He got down upon his knees and put his hands together and looked upon the moon shining now brightly above his head. "I vow, Lord, I vow that I will change. I will become better. For you, for my mother and for me," he said. "I'm a lost soul, Lord, and I need help. I need to change. I'm so unhappy and I feel I will die. I'm killing myself. My momma sacrificed everything for me and I'm doing nothing but killing myself. I vow to change. But—I need your help."

Luca got up, drank three glasses of water and went to bed feeling the spirit of his mother circulating over him, pouring out her love.

Chapter 10

A pomaceous woman wearing a bulky yellow sweater and faded blue jeans, white sneakers scuffed with dirt and grime sat upright on the office couch, breaking in two the last bits of a candy bar. Lillian looked over her newest patient, Cassandra, her cheeks pudgy as she stuffed the last pieces in her mouth and chewed with her vacant eyes fixed on some spot on the floor. With one hand, she played with the folds of her neck and the other she ran through her stringy hair as Lillian introduced herself. Her soft blue eyes, meek with worry, she used to look over Lillian's smart suit and jacket and then at her own dress. Lillian took pity on her before knowing anything of her plight.

"I'm just so embarrassed," Cassandra said. "I've gone round and round and round about even coming here. You must think I'm pathetic."

"Cassandra, I'm happy you've come to see me," Lillian said. "I understand coming to see people like me, it's not easy. You've taken a big step and I'm already proud of you. I want to know what's happening in your life."

"It's just stupid, almost too stupid to even bring up. I'm such a baby you know. Well, I'll just spit it out, I guess. My daughter, my only daughter and child, is leaving the house to go to college and I'm going to be all alone. All alone in the house; all alone in my life. I just,

I don't think…I can't see how I can cope with it." Cassandra wailed and burst into tears. "I'm so pathetic. Oh, I can only imagine what you see—"

"It's okay, let it out. Let it all out Cassandra."

"She's the only thing in my life," Cassandra blubbered on through the tears. "I can't lose her. I even tried to get her to go to community college, but she wants the full experience. How can I argue with that? She deserves it. She doesn't know what her leaving will do to me. I'm sorry, it's too much. I'm so sorry. I must seem like a complete dolt to you."

"Cassandra, the first thing I want you to do is stop putting yourself down. I don't want to hear that here. This is a safe place. Here we will try and find out what is going on and how we can address it. That's it. There is no judgement or negativity. We *all* have made mistakes in life. Nobody is clean. Does that make sense?"

"Yes, thank you. I'll try. I just feel so terrible. I'm depressed and I don't know sometimes if I can handle it. You know what I mean? It's hard to wake up in the morning sometimes knowing what I know."

"Tell me about it. Where should we start?"

"I don't know. I don't know. It's all terrible. I've never done anything right…except my baby. I made her. She's perfect, oh she's my light, my everything. I live only for her."

"What's her name?"

"Oh, she's a beautiful name. Jadwin Stella Jones. My husband, well, that's a lie and a half, not my husband. Her father, wanted to name her Jade, but I liked how Jadwin sounded with Stella, which means star and I was strong about that name so Jadwin it ended up being."

"Jadwin Stella Jones. It's a beautiful name. Is her father in her life?"

"No, I was so stupid back then. Even now I'm stupid, but back then maybe worse. I started a relationship I guess with a man in Thailand. An online relationship. I know, it's pathetic. How low can you go? Online across the ocean? But I was lonely you know. I was thirty-six years old and I had nobody…"

Cassandra's words stung Lillian, struck her in the face and she didn't hear the rest. *She* was thirty-six years old; *she* had nobody. Luca had destroyed their relationship and while he could simply get up and move to Italy, she had nothing. She had a practice to maintain and nobody in her life.

"At least you have Jadwin," Lillian broke in. Cassandra quit mid-sentence. "I'm sorry Cassandra, can you back up? You said you were thirty-six and lonely. When you said that, a thought struck me and I missed what you said next."

"What was your thought?"

"Oh, just that in lieu of everything, you created a beautiful daughter who became your light. But we can get to that later. I want to hear all the details."

"I eventually went to Thailand and met him. I wanted to see the country, but it didn't end up like that. He was living in Bangkok and refused to leave because of his work so basically, we were just physical and I wandered around Bangkok without knowing what I was doing. I was there for three weeks in that city of sin, but what was I doing? As it turned out, I went there to let some guy use me for three weeks."

"Did it feel like that at the time?"

"Oh no. I was so desperate. I was pathetic. I was so

happy someone found me attractive and wanted to sleep with me. I hadn't felt like that, well, ever. We would be together in the morning when we woke up and in the evening when he got home from work."

"What sort of work did he do?"

"You know, I don't know. His English was a bit broken and it was hard to understand. Perhaps that's why we were physical so much."

"And then you found out you were pregnant?"

"No, that was after I came back here."

"And were you in contact with him still?"

"Yes, because we were already planning another trip for me to come back there to see him. When I told him I was pregnant, things began to change. Same old story."

"What happened?"

"At first, he seemed excited. We started talking about names we'd give the baby whether it was a girl or a boy. We started planning me coming back there, but it kept getting delayed because of his work and finally, when I was too pregnant to travel, the communication simply stopped. And, he had moved to another part of the city so I had no way to find him. It just sickens me that I did that."

"Then Jadwin Stella Jones was born and your life really changed," Lillian said.

"Yes, it was absolutely love at first sight. I can't describe it but that. I was enamored. I was so overcome with joy and emotion I thought my heart was going to burst open and I'd die, but die of pure happiness. But I knew I couldn't die, not ever, because Jadwin needed a mother who loved her."

"And you certainly love her."

"More than anything in my life. More than my life.

I only want to see Jadwin be happy. My life's been nothing but sadness except for that little angel. Well, she isn't so little anymore. And now I'm thinking she doesn't need her mother anymore either. She's become so independent."

"Cassandra, thank you for your story. I know it's not easy talking with a stranger, not at first and you did so well. So thank you. Now, when does your daughter go off to college?"

"August," Cassandra said.

"So you still have quite a few months to enjoy your time with her, right?"

"No, school takes up all her time and when she's not doing school stuff, she's off with her friends. I can't tell her how it makes me feel, but she leaves me alone all the time. I don't want to invade her life, but it just hurts. It's like I'm no longer even there. She'd rather spend all her time with her friends."

"That's normal for kids her age. I'm sure it has nothing to do with you."

"Do you have kids?"

"No, I don't."

"No offense, but whether it's normal or not, it hurts. Think about it. You've invested your whole life, love and soul into this person and then suddenly they don't want to spend time with you anymore and then suddenly they're gone. Poof. Out of your life. It's like your own soul is being ripped out of you. I feel completely empty."

\*\*\*\*

Lillian struggled to focus on her other patients for the rest of that day until she left at five to go meet up with Sarah for drinks at a place called the Dill Pickle. Sarah was already swirling a martini when Lillian walked in. The Dill Pickle had an elongated bar like an old western saloon with dark forest green walls and russet stools. The bartenders all wore old-style waiter jackets and red bowties.

"Why'd you want to come here?" Sarah whispered as Lillian hugged her from behind and then plopped down beside her.

"This place is part of Seattle heritage. Besides, I wanted to be in the hub of Seattle culture with the flying fish, the gum wall and—"

"The homeless?"

"All of it."

"Okay, well, you love to psycho-analyze everyone, including me. What about you? What's going on?"

"I've been working a lot. I needed some outside energy. I need to feel like I'm still included in the human race. I just want to be around people."

"I guess that makes sense. So what's new?"

"I have a new patient. Met her today. She really struck a nerve with me. She's a single mother who hasn't had anything going for her in her life except her one and only daughter who she had begotten from some guy in Thailand."

"Wait, she went to Thailand to steal this daughter or she got pregnant while there? Those are two different things."

"Ha, yes, she got pregnant there. Anyway, this daughter has been her whole life and she feels utterly depressed that her daughter's going to be leaving soon to go off to college. She's lonely, fearful, and she's afraid she's going to do something rash."

"Tough luck. That's why I never had kids. Nor want any," Sarah said, downing her martini.

"I feel for her. That child has brought her immense joy and now the time has come for them to part ways for a while."

"It's not like she's leaving her for good. I mean, she's going to college. I'd be happy for the little squirt."

"Oh, I'm sure she's happy for her daughter. She only wants what's good for her. But, she came to me to talk about her depression and what life is like for her and will be like for her soon. Her daughter knows nothing of how she feels."

"So what's your diagnosis? Have another kid?"

"Funny. I don't know yet. First things first, convince her not to harm herself. Or anyone else for that matter."

"You think she would?"

"I think she was hinting at feeling so depressed and overcome with grief that her daughter is leaving that she might do something terrible."

\*\*\*\*

David oscillated between a bowtie or a tie. The tie was quite formal; the bowtie was quite old fashioned. Perhaps neither. Maybe a sweater over a buttoned-up shirt and corduroys. Too professorial perhaps. His wardrobe closet was filled with browns, grays, and maroons. Must of had something colorful at one point. Why fret so much? David found a light blue button up shirt, put a pale yellow sweater over that and he wore dark brown corduroy pants. He wore a tweed jacket and a gray scally cap. He had trimmed his beard, cut his nose and ear whiskers, and wore his spectacles. He'd chosen leather shoes and he looked at himself in the mirror thinking that he looked pretty good for an old man. He took a nip of whiskey out of a flask and put that in his jacket's breast pocket. He was ready to meet Diana

Rosewood and answer all her questions on the good old Ernest Hemingway.

They met at a winery overlooking Red Mountain and the russet hills beyond. The sun was setting down into the earth and the day was beginning to whisk away into the romantic desert nights of eastern Washington. Diana wore slim white jeans and a fitted transparent red blouse and David felt lecherous just by being seen with her—they shared a full-bodied red and Diana had a notebook out asking about *For Whom the Bell Tolls.*

"Do you think it was an accurate account of the Spanish Civil War? I mean, how does one get involved in that and recollect experiences like that to create such an in-depth story? I'd be scared just trying to survive let alone remember everything that happened," Diana said.

"Yes and no," David said. "Sometimes you get a sense of a place, a feeling of an experience and you can write about it from that perspective. You can remember little pieces and create a story around those feelings and those recollections. It's like the first time I went to Italy with Francesca. I can't remember everything we did or said, but I remember how I felt during that trip, the nostalgia of those feelings and I remember little details, like the first bite of carbonara or seeing the Trevi fountain lit up at night, things like that."

"You really loved her, didn't you?"

"I did. I do. I didn't mean to bring her up."

"That's okay. I've never been in love."

"You will. You have time; love takes time. Don't seek it out; let it find you. You'll have no trouble. You're young, beautiful, intelligent," David said.

"Well, you're sweet…and a flatterer. And you're not so bad yourself."

"For an old man," David said.

"For an older man. You're not old, just older. There's a difference."

"So, what're you doing these days? If I remember correctly, you wanted to be a writer."

"I did, but now I want to be an actress. I'm saving money to move to L.A. Maybe I'll do some writing down there too, but I want to act first and foremost."

"Have you been in any productions at the Richland Players?"

"Not yet. I just decided this a short time ago. Right now, I'm working at one of the wineries pouring wine."

"Oh, so they know you around here. That's good because I thought…well, I thought with me, and, oh man now I'm blundering," David said, falling over his words.

"You thought that being here with me made it look like I was an escort?"

"Oh gawd don't put it that way," David said.

"Well, I'm not. And let people think what they want. That's what I've learned lately. Why waste life wondering what other people are thinking about you? We only get one life right?"

"As far as we know," David mused.

"So, I'm tired of worrying about what other people think. That's why I've decided to go to L.A. I'll go and give it a shot. I have a friend down there who'll help me. But anyway, enough about me. What about you?"

"What about me? I'm boring. Retired and reading through my library."

"I bet you have a lot of books," Diana mused.

"Oh yes. More than I'll ever finish."

"You have Hemingway? Steinbeck? Melville?"

"Oh yes, all of those. All the classics."

"That's what I'm into right now. Can I come see it? I'd love to see it."

"My library? Sure…when?"

"Now, let's go now. The night is young," Diana exclaimed.

"For a young budding actress, yes. For a retired professor, no."

"Come on, it won't take that long. Just a quick peek."

"Well, okay, I guess we could do that," David acquiesced.

****

They drove separately away from the winery to David's house. As he drove, he wondered what exactly was going on. Being on the precipice of entering into his seventies, he didn't know what construed flirtation, or if young kids those days simply discarded all forms of formality, in friendship or otherwise. David felt old. He just wanted to go home, curl up with a book, sip some whiskey by the fire, and remember his wife.

But, he pulled into his driveway and Diana was already there waiting for him. He unlocked the door to the house and Diana flitted in, fluttering around as if she were a butterfly and all the flowers were enticing her at once. She took in the living room. An ornamental rug lay before the fireplace. She recognized what would be David's reading chair; there was a nightstand next to it with an empty rocks glass atop a book. Some furniture, and then she saw the bookcase. It took up an entire wall and was filled with books—old, leather backed books, encyclopedias, dictionaries, English grammar books, and on down to the classics.

"Hmm, interesting," Diana said. "You don't seem to

have any contemporary books."

"No, we were always just vain. This bookcase is for our collection. There's another bookcase with our smut books in another room. This one is meant to show off a little."

"Well, it certainly does. May I look through them?"

"Yes, of course. Um, you want some wine or anything?"

"You're a true gentleman and a scholar. I would love some wine."

David went into the kitchen and through to a room hidden into darkness. He turned on an overhead light and opened his wine refrigerator. He pulled out a nice red blend, opened it up in the kitchen, and poured it into a decanter. He took a large goblet glass and poured some wine in; he poured scotch into a rocks glass for himself.

He set the decanter on the table in front of the red upholstered couch and handed the glass to Diana. "It's a little cold but should warm up quickly. Here, let me get a fire going."

"Thank you," Diana said, sipping the wine. "I've never read *The Bell Jar*. It's a good one?"

"Sylvia Plath. Yes, it's poignant and funny, despite its subject."

"I've never read any of the Russian greats. You have *Anna Karenina*. That's about a tragic love affair, isn't it?"

"Yes, a long-winded tragic love affair."

Diana smiled, sipped some wine. "David, can I ask you something…were any of those rumors true?"

"Rumors? I can only assume you're talking about a supposed love affair." David didn't feel the need to expound on any of that. He had made a mistake and that was that. It had only been a kiss, but to him, a kiss of death. He never forgave himself, even, if, Francesca had. "No, the rumors are not true. There was an infatuation once, but nothing came of it and I'm thankful for that."

Diana sipped some more wine, finished her glass, and poured some more from the decanter. "I'm sure there were plenty of infatuations. I was one of them. Oh man, I had the biggest crush on you. I've always been attracted to men with intelligence. I bet you never knew. Of course you didn't know. You didn't even recognize me at the theater."

David blushed. "Well, that's not entirely true. It just took me a minute. I was caught off-guard. It's not every day a young, beautiful woman is calling my name out of nowhere."

"Do you think I'm beautiful? I was always hoping when you looked at me in class...anyway, I dressed like a bum then. Sweats and sweaters. Nothing to attract really."

"Oh, of course you're beautiful. When I was teaching, I was always so engrossed in my subject I really didn't see people for what they wore. Literature always fascinated me, and I think my head swam throughout fictionalized worlds more so than the real world. Until I met Francesca that is..."

Diana thought for a moment. "I'm sorry about your wife. You must have both really been in love."

"No, I'm sorry for bringing it up. It's still all so new to me, being alone in this house, trying to find things to do during the day. It's just—different."

Diana set her glass of wine down, leaned forward and embraced David awkwardly, laying her head against his chest. "I know it's difficult and it will be for awhile.

I'm really sorry you're going through this."

David, his glass of scotch in one hand, put his other arm around Diana as if she were the one who needed comfort. "It's okay. It's okay. It's all a part of life."

Diana released her head from David's chest and looked up at him. She moved in slowly as David froze; she felt his body tense in her arms. She kissed his grizzled cheek softly. "Thank you for a lovely evening," she whispered.

"Of, of course," David said.

Diana released him from her grasp. "I should probably get home now. Can I see you again soon? I promise to bring more questions on the greats."

"Yes, that would be lovely. I'd love that," David said. Diana left and David stood still for some time before he sat down in his chair, thinking what she could possibly mean.

Chapter 11

Luca finished dressing just as his phone rang. He buzzed the gate and a moment later, he heard knocking at his door. He opened it and was surprised to find a slender, bald, cueball-headed man wearing sunglasses, slim black jeans, and a shirt and vest standing before him. If this was Marco, the cousin to Salvatore, they didn't share a hint of DNA in common. Luca thought a teenager was knocking at his door to perhaps sell candy bars or ask for a school donation. "Hey, *ciao* Luca, *sono* Marco," he said, spreading his hands out in front of him as if he were asking for a hug.

"*Eh, ciao* Marco, *mi chiamo* Luca," Luca said, extending his hand out to shake.

"Yeah, I know, I just said that," Marco said, shrugging his shoulders and then shaking Luca's hand.

"Yeah, sorry, it's autopilot," Luca said.

"Ah, I'm just breaking your balls. It's good, practice your Italian."

"You want a coffee or something. I was just about to make an espresso."

"No," Marco said, snapping his fingers. "Let's get one on the way. I'm already late. I need to get you to the winery."

Marco whipped around the city streets in his black sports car and Luca was happy he had not already eaten breakfast that morning as it may have ended up on the dash. Once on the highway, Marco zipped in and around the slower vehicles at around one hundred sixty kilometers an hour. Luca could hardly take in the stunning surroundings as Marco gabbed on about anything and everything, maneuvering the vehicle right behind others in the left lane until they moved over. Luca could hardly breathe as Marco got inches away from a blue sedan driven by an older man hunched over his car squinting mightily to see the road—Luca thought he would still rather be in the sedan at that moment.

Suddenly, Marco slammed on his brakes as a large truck carrying what looked like barrels of cement veered out of the right lane and into the left.

"*Che cazzo*!" Marco yelled, honking the horn. The truck moved over and as Marco passed it, he flashed angry eyes and his hand away from his chin toward the driver. "Idiots. Almost ruined the day."

"Yeah, these roads are pretty hectic, huh?"

"Nah, this is nothing. Rome. Rome is crazy."

"Are you from Rome?"

"No, Calabria."

"So, Salvatore is your cousin then," Luca said.

"Yeah, much older cousin. His dad is my mom's oldest brother and Salvatore is the first born and I was the second born from my mother so we are years different."

Once off the highway, they cruised through the scenic route to Greve in Chianti. Rolling, aquamarine hills flushed with fig and olive trees, pines and the occasional cypress spread out over the fecund land endlessly. Ancient villages came and went and everywhere there were wineries. Luca had grown up on Red Mountain but had never seen anything like this. This was true wine country.

"It's breathtaking, all those vineyards," Luca mused.

Marco creased the sides of his mouth into a frown. "Wine is like blood around here. Our hills are full of it."

Greve lay in a valley surrounded by vines, olive and fig trees, and farmhouses. Cypress trees lined the roadways leading through the vineyards and to the wineries. Luca wanted to tear up from the beauty, but held them in as he looked at Marco seemingly unfazed by all the splendor. Luca couldn't imagine living in a place such as this and ever wanting to leave. Perhaps Marco sensed this because he slowed the sports car down and they drove through Greve leisurely and Luca took in all the beautifully roofed stone, brick, and yellowed concrete houses. They were perfectly harmonious with the landscape and as the morning sun drew higher in the sky, the houses shone with brilliance.

Marco drove through the town and then suddenly swerved to park alongside a street. "You want a coffee, no?"

"Oh, yeah, I had forgotten all about it, but yes, that would be great."

"*Andiamo*," Marco said, jumping out of the car and heading across the street to a small cafe. Luca quickly followed him. The cafe had a long bar with an assortment of people drinking cappuccino and espresso. The bartender was a tall, slim, attractive man in his late twenties with just a touch of stubble attempting to be born again. "*Ciao* Fabrizio."

"*Ciao* Marco," Fabrizio said without smiling. The rest of the guests turned slightly to see who had come in, but didn't seem to want to engage in any kind of conversation. "*Due caffe*."

The man, Fabrizio, made the espresso methodically, taking his time to get the perfect flow and foam. Marco quickly downed his and threw two euro on the counter. Luca sipped the top first, enjoying the strong scent and then downing the rest. His first coffee in Italy and it was wonderful. "Damn, that's good coffee," Luca said.

"Yeah, it's Italy. Everywhere is good coffee," Marco said, shrugging his shoulders as if this was a ubiquitous fact. And perhaps it was. Luca had never been outside of the country in his forty years of life except having gone to Canada when he first turned nineteen so that he could drink with college friends. Luca realized with that coffee, in that beautiful town of Greve, that he had missed out on seeing the world, on seeing life outside of his own small little sphere. The restaurant had been everything; his working life had been everything. Work, make money, drink, and escape real life. And after forty years, he had no children, no business, no house, no wife, nothing, and he felt like he had very little time to change all that.

Marco broke into his thoughts. "*Andiamo*, let's go."

"*Grazie per il caffe*," Luca said to Fabrizio.

"*Prego*," Fabrizio said perfunctorily.

****

Castello di Nardone il Brutto, high up on a hill, overlooked the estate's surrounding vineyards—the sea of vast vines seemed to go on forever. The road up to the villa was lined with cypress trees and as they passed through the vineyards, Luca saw the sparse vines shivering in a breeze under the sun. Some workers were out in the rows pruning the buds. Marco parked down below the villa's garages. Above one of the garages was a gated area with a large pool built into the side of the hill overlooking the eastern vineyards. The villa was magnificently made of old stone with pillars rising high toward the sun. To Luca, it appeared as an ancient castle from the medieval days surrounded by a large garden walled-in by a barricade of trimmed bushes. The villa's door was made of a dark wood and painted red with two large metal ringed knockers. Marco pulled open the door with some effort.

The tasting room was a modernized take on the old. A bar made of oak had glasses lined up with bottles ready to be opened that day. A large glass showcase had familial shields and crests inside and there were two suits of armor standing as sentries guarding the bar. The walls were built with elongated holes in the sides and were filled with wine bottles. The floors were made of polished ashen stones that were speckled with blue, orange, and yellow pebbles.

A beautiful, gaunt woman came out from inside a room off the bar and greeted Marco. "*Ciao* Marco, *come va?*"

"*Eh, va bene.* This is Luca. Luca, this is Maria, Stefano's wife," Marco said.

"Nice to meet you, Maria," Luca said.

"Nice to meet you," Maria said, slowly.

"Sorry, but who is Stefano?" Luca asked.

"Stefano makes the wine here," Marco said. "Maria sells it. So, Maria, please show Luca around. I have some business to do. Luca, I'll be back later to pick you up."

"Okay, *grazie mille,*" Luca said. Marco took off and Luca was left with Maria.

"My English not so good," Maria began. "I try. You speak Italian?"

"My Italian is probably worse than your English for sure. *Il mio Italiano e' terribile*."

"Okay, English. You want meet Stefano?"

"*Si, grazie*."

Maria led Luca back through the labyrinthine corridors of the winery and into a large room filled with steel tanks. A clean-shaven man in mud-caked blue jeans and a dusty white shirt was peering at a gauge on one of the tanks. He glanced over at Maria and Luca as they approached.

"*Eh*, Maria, *chi e'*?

"*E'* Luca, *l'amico di* Marco."

"Ah, Luca, from America. Yes, welcome. When did you arrive?"

"Just yesterday. I took the train from Rome, had dinner at a trattoria and now I'm here."

"Good, good. Eh, you met my wife, Maria. I'm Stefano. I make all the wine at this estate."

"Yes, I was going to ask. What is the production for this estate each year? The vineyards seem to go on for miles."

"Well, not too much. We sell many of the grapes to other wineries so we try and keep our production small. It helps our brand. So, you want to see the winery? This is the production room. The grapes come through the doors there," Stefano said, pointing to large, garage-like doors that had conveyor belts installed through them. "The grapes come on those conveyor belts and are sorted for quality. We only use the best quality. Then, once they are sorted, they are taken to where they are pressed slightly to release juices. This will all be explained to you in more detail. You're here to learn to make wine, yes?"

"Yes, that's correct. I was in the restaurant industry,

sold my restaurant and Salvatore helped me come here. You know Salvatore?"

"No, who is?"

"*Eh*, Marco's cousin. He was the head chef at my restaurant."

"Oh good. It's important to have an Italian in the kitchen."

"Okay, I go to front now. Nice to meet you Luca. I see you at lunch," Maria said.

"*Si, grazie e spero di si.* I hope so. *Anche, il tuo inglese e' perfetto.*"

"Oh, *grazie*," Maria said, wafting away.

Stefano took Luca around the production facility, showing him the conveyor belts, the tanks, and then they went down into the cellar wherein the wood barrels were kept. There must have been a hundred barrels down there in what felt like catacombs. It was cold and dank with poor lighting; the walls were made of hard stone that jutted out from the sides. Overhead lamps lit the walkways, but most of the barrels were kept in the shadows.

"We don't usually take visitors down here and I like to keep the barrels out of the light. It affects the wine. All our vintage wine is down here. We barrel our riservas for two years."

"Oh, I was going to ask, what types of wine do you make?"

"The usual wines of course, typical of the region as-well-as some Super Tuscans, a chardonnay, some blends. I'll show you everything. We have traditional grapes and international grapes in the vineyards. *Si*, we can do a tasting before lunch to get our appetites up, no?"

"That would be phenomenal," Luca said.

\*\*\*\*

Maria lined the bottles of wine along the top of the bar. She mentioned that they received very few visitors that time of year so any wines left over could be used at lunch or Luca could take them home with him. Luca stood at the bar surveying all the wine labels, the winery, the scenery outside the winery and he thought perhaps he would never leave Tuscany. It felt like something he couldn't quite describe; it was too much for him. It felt like home, but a home he never realized he had nor missed.

The land before time, times of gods and warriors, times of wine and wild things, times of people being ruled and times of people ruling the earth. This was the land the Church was built on—this was the land of risen Christ. So much history and time and the footprints of people having walked this land. All roads lead to Rome. The land itself was stained with the blood of millions, slave and master, potter and king. The beauty that was the land wore its history upon itself in stone and sculpture, vine and wine, house and home. The people, an ancient race, an amalgamation of the world, were the very ones who spread the word of God so many years ago. Strange to think about, but God's story propagated here, in this land.

Luca turned to Maria and Stefano and blurted out, "It's so good to be here, in Italy I mean. My parents are from here, from Lucca and I can't believe this is my first time."

"Ah, Lucca? Beautiful little city," Stefano said.

"There big wall around the city," Maria said. "Walk on top of the wall and see everything. It's *una bella citta*'! Beautiful city."

"Your parents live in the US now only?" Stefano asked.

"They have both passed away. My dad when I was just a teenager and my mom just last year. Cancer."

"I'm sorry for you," Stefano said.

"What he say?" Maria asked Stefano.

"*I suoi genitori sono morti. Suo padre quando aveva piccoli anni e suo madre l'anno scorso. Cancro.*"

"Oh, I'm so sorry Luca," Maria said.

They went through and tasted the line of wines and Luca tried his best to spit as Maria and Stefano did. It seemed like such a waste of good wine, but the new Luca had to develop new habits. Still, after tasting and talking of the wines, Stefano asked if Luca wanted to revisit any and have a glass since tourists were most undoubtedly not going to show up that day. Luca had a glass of the riserva. Luca liked Stefano and his wife, Maria, very much and was happy he would be working with them.

"So, what does Marco do with the winery?" Luca asked.

"Ah, Marco," Stefano said. "He helps with organization and logistics, things like that. So, how do you feel? You want to go out into the vineyards and see the vines?"

"Absolutely."

The vineyards were situated on the rolling hills outside the villa in tight rows using a double guyot system. They were bare of fruit, but tiny buds were just about to begin to burst in the next couple of months. The morning sun drew away the dew of the early morning and the vines glistened in its bath. The earth felt hard and durable under Luca's feet and he wondered how many legs had gone up and down that very path over the years.

Stefano showed Luca the vines for the reds, the selected rows for particular reds and finally the chardonnay grapes which were facing the early morning sun but away from the afternoon heat when it was hottest.

"The chardonnay was quite good," Luca said. "I didn't really think whites from the Chianti region could produce something like that. It's crisp and fruity and leaves a nice impression on the palate."

"Yes, only stainless steel, no oak. All the fruit of the chardonnay grape are in that wine. It's complex with good acidity. I'm proud of that wine."

After the stroll through the vineyards, Stefano, Maria, and some others on the farm had a wonderful lunch with wine, cheeses, a wild boar ragu that was to die for, and some braised beef. It put Luca into a stupor and he longed for his bed.

"What time is Marco coming back for you?"

"I'm not sure," Luca said, drowsily.

"Why don't you stay for aperitivo? You can nap if you want and then we can go into town and have an aperitivo. Marco can pick you up afterward."

"I think that sounds like a lovely plan," Luca said. "What is aperitivo?"

"It's like your happy hour," Stefano said.

\*\*\*\*

Luca fell into a deep sleep, so comfortable was the bed that Stefano gave him. He slunk down into it and was absorbed instantly. He must have slept for a few hours after that long meal and when he woke up, it was already time to head out. He wished he could have dressed into something different, but that was impossible. He met Stefano and Maria in the tasting room and together they drove off down the road into town.

Greve in Chianti had a charming town square with shops and tasting rooms and restaurants. A few tourists were in the area, but it was fairly sparse. Stefano parked along a side street and the three of them walked a short distance to a bar filled with locals. They ordered three spritz cocktails and found a corner table. There was a buffet of food that had pastas and pizza and vegetables. Every now and again, someone would come up, take a plate and fill it with food. Luca was puzzled.

"So, is the food free here?"

Maria laughed and Stefano tried to calm her down with his hands. "Sorry she laughs."

Luca began laughing with her. "No, no, it's okay. This is new to me. What is this?"

"Aperitivo is you buy a drink and you get to eat the food they have. It's nothing special, but it's okay."

"Wow, what a concept. This would never work in America. The people would buy one drink and eat all the food."

Stefano laughed this time. "Yes, in Italy people are more conscious about their figures."

Luca looked around the little bar and saw that all the Italians were slender and healthy, especially the women. As he was absorbing the atmosphere in, he was drawn toward the door, and just at that moment, a woman walked in—but not just any woman. She wore red heels, red jeans, a white blouse, a neckless of shining turquoise stones, a yellow bangle around her wrist, and petite, hooped earrings, but it was nothing she wore that struck Luca, but she herself. She had just the most radiant smile and glimmeringly bright brown eyes, long, flowing curly hair like a medusa, and she locked eyes with Luca as she came in and he felt stabs of emotion prick into his heart.

He had never believed in love at first sight, but this feeling must have been what all the poets had written about.

She was walking directly toward Luca, smiling and flashing those lustrous eyes. Her hips swung side to side as the sun was shining through the windows lighting up her shadow as if she were a radiant goddess approaching mere mortals. And then, she was upon the party, standing above them as if waiting to command.

She spoke, a soft, sweet voice like a child: "*Mio fratello,* Maria, *come va*?"

"*Va bene*," Stefano said, then addressing Luca. "Luca, this is Matilda, my sister. Matilda, this is Luca, Marco's friend from the US. You have someone to practice your English with now, I think."

"Luca from America, it's a pleasure to meet you," Matilda said.

"Oh, that was better what I said," Maria said. "Matilda study in England."

"It's an absolute pleasure to meet you as well," Luca said.

"*Allora, sei italiano, no*? You're Italian, no?" Matilda said.

"My parents were born in Lucca, but I grew up in the US. Unfortunately, my Italian is terrible."

"But why?" Matilda said, searchingly. "Your parents are Italian. They must have spoken Italian in the house, no?"

"They did for a while, but my father passed away when I was just barely a teenager and my mom only spoke English after that."

"Oh, I'm sorry about your father and I'm sorry about your Italian. Well, perhaps I can help you with your

Italian and you can help me with my English."

"I think I'm getting the better half of this deal, but yes, please, that would be wonderful."

Matilda took a spritz cocktail and together, the foursome had what Luca described as an enchanting time. Lying in bed that night back at his studio, he couldn't think of anything save Matilda. She was named after the Roald Dahl character, Matilda, as she was born that same year the book was published. She was working in the Italian legal system, which boggled Luca's mind as it was too complicated to understand exactly what she was trying to accomplish. Luca couldn't get over how he felt being in her company. It was as if he were a small child and she were this magnetic star that he couldn't take his eyes off of—her voice, calling like the sirens, sweet like honey and her softly lying on a pillow. Her beauty, pure, fair, unbridled by the conventions of the day caught Luca off guard as he turned his face upon hers—her radiant smile shone like the sun beaming energy toward all that she met. Or, only to him, he hoped.

He couldn't put his finger on it, but he had never felt that way before; it was, he thought, truly love at first sight, a burning ember at each word she spoke. He thought she felt something toward him, but he didn't know Italian culture, Italian women, so well. She may have been simply a nice person. How could he tell? Ah, but she had thought about teaching him Italian and him teaching her English; that had been her idea.

If nothing else, they would see each other again. Luca lay in bed hoping that that day was nearer than the buds springing out from the vines. He thought only of her fair features and her voice as he tried to fall asleep to the twinkling stars in the cloudless and calm night sky above. Moon rays came through his window and Luca realized that he must treasure that moment, treasure those feelings he was feeling as they happened so rare in one's life. Love, powerful love, oh what a feeling!

Chapter 12

Lillian rolled over again onto her backside staring up into the dark ceiling, her arms beginning to become numb, her thoughts on the myriad patients she had acquired and what they were going through. She felt dazed, knowing that almost everyone, no, *everyone* was going through it in some fashion—if they were alive and they had feeling, they were going through something. She tried to understand Luca, she really did. He seemed to be so unfeeling, incapable of feeling; or, perhaps he felt, but neglected what it was that came out of him, escaped from addressing anything through alcohol—the numbing, poisonous slow killer of feelings. The death of his mother, a divorce, a DUI—how could he go on like normal? Italy was just another escape, but it wouldn't cure him. How had she been so blind to his disease? She knew where he was going if he didn't get help; it was a slow, painful way to die.

As she closed her eyes, a myriad of thoughts free-floated their way into her mind; it was impossible to sleep once they began to crowd together against the barrier she tried to put up. She decided to instead get up and get in the shower. She had work to do anyway. Her patient, Nick, had trashed his mother's basement wherein he was living. He had gotten angry that his mother had said some name he didn't recognize, thinking she had created a character in her mind without heed of the repercussions and then she refused to tell him about it so he couldn't save the character from the Veldt. He subsequently destroyed lamps and picture frames and books and sliced up a couch and punched a wall.

The shower only momentarily stymied the stream of thoughts coming to her in rapid fire. She tried her breathing exercises she tried to get her patients to adopt, but they weren't working that morning. Lillian shut off the water and dried herself off. "Damn you Luca for simply absconding away to Italy," she said as she wiped the mirror of the mist, revealing her watery, distorted face. What about her? Where could she go to escape? No, too many people relied on her daily reflections; she had work to do and people who needed her. Did they need her or was she just one of many out there collecting insurance monies? Lillian got dressed and tried to put her brooding thoughts behind her—it was time to go to work.

****

"Nick, I understand something happened at your home? Can you tell me about it?" Nick slumped down inside the couch with his arms folded in between his legs. He stared straight ahead as if he didn't hear or want to hear the question. "Nick, did you hear me?"

"If you keep calling me Nick, how can I answer the question? Any questions? It's totally disrespectful. I deserve respect. You don't understand that; my mom doesn't understand that. Nobody seems to understand that basic need. My mother certainly doesn't. She has no idea what I'm trying to do, not really. I tell her and she just says I'm doing good for some people, but she doesn't really care or even understand. It's ridiculous to even try with her. And then she totally makes up a character and spits out a name and suddenly the character is there and then she can't even tell me what it looks like, sounds like, how it talks and I'm supposed to find it and save it without any information? I told her not to think of characters. It's not her job, especially because she doesn't understand what she's doing."

"And you felt angry because you felt helpless in wanting to save this character," Lillian prompted.

"Yes, and I broke a few things, big deal. It's *she* who must understand what she did."

"You mentioned that the characters must be drawn or at least sketched in some capacity right? For them to become real? Did your mom make a sketch or anything?"

"I don't know. She won't tell me what she did. She doesn't even know. That's why it's so frustrating. The not knowing is probably the hardest part."

Lillian thought for a moment. "Dr. Nick, perhaps you can explain to me a little more about this character hell. What makes it so terrible?"

Nick looked at Lillian cockeyed, as if deciphering any devilry or deception. "Imagine a place where there is nothing except yourself and you are all alone and it's for forever. Empty space, nothing, all alone, forever. You're created for a purpose and then cast aside into nothingness. *That* is character hell. *That* is the Veldt."

\*\*\*\*

Lillian desperately needed a coffee after seeing Nick and as she waited in line, her thoughts moved to Cassandra having to soon give up her daughter to university. She, too, must be feeling the weight of aloneness coming soon as a storm front that engulfs everything in its path. Nick, alone with his delusions that his mother cannot understand; Cassandra, losing, so to speak, the one thing that she lives for. "And what about you, Lillian? Where're you in this fray?" She knew that she missed Luca, but not like she thought she would miss him. His drinking had destroyed something within her, a part of her soul or a part of her loving heart. As a psychologist, she knew that deep down, that part of her being could be repaired; she could find Lillian again, the true Lillian who is a singular person, not tied to another's life. But, that loving part of her heart that longed for and loved Luca she knew to be gone. And, she knew that that was okay. That was life.

The loneliness felt like a millstone tugging at her neck; she felt she could barely keep her head up. She knew, academically, that this too would pass. But, in the midst of the feeling, it was difficult to engage the rational mind to understand anything but the feelings of her immediate world. And, currently Lillian felt lonely. Thank the stars she had her work and a single friend, Sarah.

\*\*\*\*

"I met someone," Sarah said, later that evening when she met Lillian for drinks.

"Huh? What do mean you met someone? Like romantically?" Lillian asked.

"Yes, like possibly romantically. Not yet, but I think it'll go that route," Sarah said.

"Where? How?"

Sarah laughed loudly. "It's possible to meet people in this city…sometimes. But, if you must know and yes, you must know, he came to me for divorce proceedings. He's getting divorced from a horrendous woman who deceived him with all sorts of tragic tales of woe that weren't true."

"And you think you want to begin a relationship with this guy?"

"We shall see. We shall see. He's quite handsome and quite charming."

"Well, I suppose I have to be happy for you," Lillian said.

****

But Lillian was not happy. Sarah, who always seemed to keep men at bay and dated casually, but not seriously, was now going to leave the country with a man she hardly knew and go to France and Spain and Montenegro. And she was leaving Lillian all alone. She had nobody she could tell anything to—her parents, yes, but they lived in Milwaukee and wouldn't understand what was going on anyway. They had never wanted her to move out of the Midwest for one thing. They couldn't understand why she would want to leave the blisteringly hot and humid summers and the blisteringly cold and frigid winters. The mosquito was the state bird and that was funny in their eyes.

"Mom, I'm moving because I don't like beer," she had said, jocosely.

"Well, dear, there are other things than beer here," she had said, seriously, snapping her fingers. "What about that vodka. You like that vodka don't you?"

But, at the moment, Lillian wished she was in one of those beerhalls in the frigid cold smoking a cigarette with a friend, rubbing her hands together as the airy mist sparkled all around her. She didn't even smoke anymore, but she felt like she could use one at the moment. She was in her office waiting for her next patient of that day, hoping beyond hope that they simply wouldn't show up. She didn't know if she had it in her. How could she

181

possibly offer help if she was in such a dire need of it herself?

\*\*\*\*

David fixed himself a whiskey and soda, checked his watch. He wore his usual costume, but this time, he added a red handkerchief in his breast pocket. He thought Diana might get a kick out of that. They were going to go to a newly opened restaurant for wine and appetizers. When David picked her up, he saw to his amazement that she was dressed in a long, black, slightly transparent sequin dress, black high heels, and a long black leather coat. David immediately felt a bit drab in his urbane costume, but got out to open the door for his date.

"You look marvelous," David said. "You'll put on quite an impression down there in Los Angeles when you go."

"Well, thank you kind sir," Diana said. "As usual, you are quite dapper."

"I'm feeling a bit old-fashioned and overused," he admitted.

"You wear you well," Diana said, giving David a kiss on the cheek before getting into David's old green roadster racer. "This is nice, haven't seen one of these before."

David put the roadster into gear. "I rarely drive it. I figured this was a nice occasion to get some miles on it."

He found parking, and they were seated and quickly ordered two glasses of sparkling wine.

"This isn't bad," Diana said, looking around. "For Richland at least."

The restaurant had a slate-like theme to it with gray tiled flooring, black stone pillars and smooth stone tabletops. The kitchen was open and they could see the flames of dishes being prepared. There was a large crescentic fish tank in the center of the restaurant with all sorts of smaller fishes swimming as-well-as a few hermit crabs scraping the bottom of the tank. A server brought the sparkling wine and Diana ordered some pork belly.

"We'll just start with that," Diana told the server. "We want to take our time."

They clinked glasses and Diana looked over at David from the top of her glass. He smiled; he didn't really know what to say. "So, when you get to Los Angeles, what's your plan? You have auditions lined up, an agent, something like this?"

"I have a friend in the business," Diana said. "I'm hoping he can help me get started with auditions, but realistically, it's not the easiest thing to do."

David thought about what that must be like, moving to L.A. with nothing but some clothes in a suitcase, hoping to land some auditions, some callbacks, and then hopefully a role of some sort. He imagined that's what thousands of people just like Diana were doing every day. It sounded terrifying. He couldn't fathom really putting oneself out there like that with the greatest threat of absolutely nothing happening, but he supposed that's what people did who wanted to be in the business.

"I'm sure you're going to do extremely well," David said.

"Yes, just need to get down there first."

"How's the wine sales job going?"

"Oh, it's okay, not much money, but it's okay. It's fun. You meet a lot of people. It's slow right now, though, as you can imagine. But, that gives me plenty of time to read."

"I'll have to stop by the winery and throw in some

support. Probably could use a few more bottles at my place anyway."

"I'd like that," Diana said. "Ah, here's the pork belly."

They ate the pork belly with their sparkling and then ordered a bottle of red.

"Have you always been so sophisticated with your drink?" Diana said.

"Oh, I wouldn't say that. Francesca didn't drink much so we never really had anything in the house. If I'm going to admit something, though, I'd have to say I'm partaking more now than I was before. Quite a bit more."

"I can imagine," Diana said.

They finished their dinner, had dessert, and David paid the bill. They got into David's roadster and took off.

"The night is young yet," Diana said. "You want to share some wine at your place and see what sort of bookish mischief we can get into?"

"Oh, well, that would be lovely," David said.

David lit a fire and opened one of his nicer bottles. He went to sit in his usual chair, but Diana motioned for him to sit next to her on the couch. She brought out a book from her purse and giggled as she showed David the title: *Fox in Socks* by Dr. Seuss. "Let's drink until we're silly and try and read this book as quickly as possible. Let me tell you, it's a tongue twister."

"I think we're already silly, but okay, let's get sillier." David clinked Diana's glass and they took long pulls of the wine.

Diana began reading the first few pages out loud.

"You're going to have to go faster than that," David said.

"Oh just wait, it gets hard quick. Anyway, I just want to see you do it," Diana said, laughing.

They went through the book, their tongues seemingly rolling and blabbering meaningless words strung together in a haphazard way, but if they said them fast enough, the mistakes could be glossed over. Anyway, they were laughing too hard to notice. More wine was poured and once the book was finished and the bottle was finished, Diana snuggled into David's side, her hand finding David's thigh and David felt for the first time with Diana, fear and desire.

Eyes closed, Diana smiled and lay her head on David's chest like a child. "Is this okay?" she mumbled sleepily.

"Ye, yes," David said. "Yes."

She was sound asleep within moments and David didn't know what to do. Her head was on his chest and her hand was on his thigh and he wanted to wake her up and carry her into the bedroom and pour out all the trepidation and desire he felt, but he knew that was wrong and silly. Why would a young woman moving to L.A. to become a famous actress have any desire toward an old man near the end of his life. No, he was a fool and she was simply comforting him during his grief.

David slowly stood up and Diana nestled into the couch. There was no way she was going to be able to drive home. He picked her up with the little strength he had and carried her into his bedroom, set her down on the bed and pulled the covers over her. He kissed her gently on the cheek. He looked at her with just a hint of hesitation sleeping where he slept alone with his memories and then he left the room to go to his only comfort—the scotch by the fire.

****

Luca woke up feeling morose. The excitement from the night before troubled him in his dreams as they were filled with his mother's ghost drifting in and out of his periphery. He never saw her, but he knew she was there. Warning him? Angry that he had forgotten her so quickly? He hadn't thought about his mother much lately. He couldn't. It was too hard to think of her as his mother in his youth, the nostalgic memories driving him to drink. And he couldn't think of her memory in the last ten years with the restaurant because he had chosen to *be* the restaurant and neglect everything else. He only saw her face filled with sadness, but she had never said anything. Did she know though? Did she know that one day he would be all alone and forever regretful that he had wasted so much of his life and time and neglected his mother because of his work? Why didn't she ever say anything? Would he have listened?

And now he had met someone, someone so enchanting he felt he was going to burst with too much feeling. Even if she never wanted anything to do with him, he knew that the feeling he was feeling at that time was beautiful and wonderful and nobody could take it away. Of course, if he were scorned by her, he would be devastated, but it must never be so. He felt their energy together; it was meant to be somehow. That's why he was there in Italy. All the terrible things that he had done took him to that fateful moment of meeting Matilda. He would give up drinking for her. He had too; she must never discover that person he loathed.

Luca took a shower, got dressed and went to a nearby cafe for a quick brioche and coffee. He doubted he would ever cook his own breakfast in Italy as it was just too easy and cheap to get one at the many cafes that were on any given street.

"*L'occhio del bue*," the man behind the counter said.

"*Che cos'e'*?"

"*Questo cornetto, si chiama l'occhio del bue*—the eye of the bull," he said.

"*Allora, e' delizioso. Grazie.*"

Luca had no plans for that day until his phone buzzed with a message.

Matilda— I'*m in Florence for the day. Meet me for coffee or lunch?*—

Luca finished his coffee and brioche quickly and then jubilantly danced out to the street. It *was* meant to be; it was *meant* to be.

He met Matilda at a hole in the wall restaurant along Via Guelfa. They were sat and immediately Luca was struck by the melancholic fashion he saw in sophisticated Italian women—Matilda wore all black: high heels, jeans, blouse, jacket, gloves, and sunglasses. Only her skin betrayed the lack of color as it had a slight rouge and earthiness tone. But Luca thought her lovely. He pretended to look over the menu while thinking of something to say to her. He knew that she knew a growing, throbbing ember was there. That was obvious from their first meeting, but he wondered if it was now written in Italian and English all over his forehead.

"You've been here before? You have any suggestions?" Luca asked her after a moment. "How about these spaghetti and meatballs?" Luca was surprised and delighted when she laughed, a soft, not overbearing laugh, but genuine. He smiled. "I'm kidding, I'm kidding, *e' uno scherzo*. I'm not going for the meatballs like every American even if they do sound delicious."

"*Il mio polpetto*," she said. "You're my meatball now. Okay, meatball, I suggest the carbonara. It's fantastic, almost like they do in Rome."

"No, no, no, you can't call me meatball. That's a terrible nickname."

"You will be meatball until you become something else," Matilda said. "What wine shall we have with lunch?"

"I'll take direction from the master, which is you," Luca said.

"Okay, I'll take the clams so if you have the carbonara, we'll get some white wine. Let's start with the *cozze e vongole* and the octopus soup. Yes?"

"Yes, I have to agree because you're the master and know all the rules here."

"Good, you learn quick for an American, but I guess that's because you've Italian in you."

Matilda ordered the clams and mussels, the soup and two glasses of white wine, the carbonara, and the vongole. When they finished the meal, Luca was about to order another glass of wine.

"No, no, you don't want another glass. There isn't any more food," Matilda said.

"Oh, but the wine is so good," Luca said.

"Yes, it's so good because it compliments the food. The wine is part of the meal, but since we are finished with the meal, we have to move on."

"Move on?"

"Yes, to *caffe*." The server came over. "*Due caffe', per favore*."

"*Si, un cappuccino per me*," Luca said.

"*Cappuccino*? No, no, no, *aspetta*, wait. *Due*

*espressi*," Matilda said to the server.

"Not even a cappuccino?"

"No, it's after noon. Meatball, you can't have cappuccino except in the morning. Listen, when we start English lessons?"

"I think I'm free any time. Since not much is happening at the winery, I'm open. I think Stefano is taking me on a trip to Bolgheri tomorrow, but after that we can start any time."

"Okay, okay. Bolgheri is beautiful. Go to the beach. Okay, I have *compiti*, homework for you. Go to the beach and feel the sand, feel the rocks, and smell the air. Come back and tell me about it. Okay?"

"Okay, I guess I can do that."

The two espressos came and they quickly downed them. Matilda paid the bill.

Chapter 13

The drive to the coast was laden with puffy green hills speckled with olive and fig trees, farmhouses, wineries, and vast vineyards. As Luca and Stefano approached the coast, the land became flatter and sparser, but the fluffy clouds were roving and the sun was shining, revealing disparate shades of greenery. Luca leaned back comfortably against the seat of Stefano's car, his driving not nearly as wild as Marco, and enjoyed the passing pleasures to the eye.

The town of Bolgheri loomed above them as they drove in and Luca saw the magnificent thirteenth century castle that rose ever higher into the sky. All around were rows upon rows of cypress trees and Luca truly felt he had entered into another realm, another time. Bolgheri was beyond beautiful; he had wondered why Matilda wanted him to visit the beach and complete his homework, but now he thought he understood. This place was magical and she wanted him to bring back some of that magic to her. Stefano continued driving around the town and eventually, they reached a winery called Guado al Melo.

"I must speak to the winemaker here about some things going on in the vineyard," Stefano said. "If you want to walk around the town or even take the car to the beach, it's okay. Just drive normal; don't get caught by police. Be back by lunchtime, okay?"

"Great, I'll do that. Your sister gave me homework anyway that I need to do." Stefano looked thoughtfully at Luca wondering what he could mean. "She asked me to explore the beach and tell her my thoughts on it."

"Hmm, my sister always has been a little peculiar. I think that's the right word, no?"

"Yes, I thought it a strange request as well, but nonetheless, I need to complete my homework. Otherwise…" He shrugged.

"Oh, for sure," Stefano said. "You don't want to get on her bad side."

The seaside was just about ten kilometers from the village of Bolgheri so Luca drove slowly through the streets and out onto the pleasantly sparse roads toward the Mediterranean. The seas were emerald green that time of year and Luca found himself walking alone alongside ebullient waters. He took off his shoes and walked in the sand, feeling the smooth dampness under his feet. The water slowly receded and then crashed back along the shore and Luca stood transfixed listening to the wild waves. The air smelled of salt and Luca taking in a deep breath, felt so free, alone as if he were the only mortal still standing in that heavenly sphere of gods. It was impossible to comprehend how old and ancient this land was and yet, here he stood, giving himself to it, even if he was insignificant to the desires of that living sea.

Luca looked out to the sea, torn between thoughts of three women.

His mother, now a whisper on his lips, having moved onto that next great adventure, was never to be in his life again—he wasn't ready to comprehend that, wasn't ready to combat that kind of pain. He refused to think of her. He knew his mind was too weak to think about all that she had sacrificed for him and how much he had let her down, even if she never expected much. How much worse did that make it? She was the epitome of love and had loved him unconditionally. And he had been so much into his own head that he didn't give anything really back to her, just grief.

Lillian, his first love—how he had hurt her. He drank away all his best years with her and left her with nothing. What was she doing now? He only hoped that she could move on and find happiness. She deserved it. She didn't deserve the life that Luca had forged for her. She was a beautiful, smart woman who worked hard and had loved him despite all his defects, which were many.

And now, Luca couldn't believe the fortune that he still possessed; perhaps he had a chance to redeem himself. There was a love burning in his life that he couldn't imagine nor believe he deserved. He couldn't comprehend his fate.

"Don't get ahead of yourself," Luca whispered into the salty breeze. It's true she may not feel the same fatalistic energy as he did. She could be exactly what she said she was—a woman who wanted to learn English. And perhaps that's all she wanted from Luca, but, at least, he had the means to find out. He would teach her English, and he would see if something could be there.

He didn't deserve her love. No, in fact, he deserved to be in pain, hurting for love. He had ruined the love of two amazing women. How arrogant was he to think he deserved happiness? Wasn't life about making mistakes, learning, reflecting, and trying to find that elusive happiness, though? Only for those who did what was right. Take nothing for granted; take nobody for granted. He had to quit his old ways; they were finished. He would have to kill them with the sword for good.

Luca picked up a rock on the beach, kissed it. "For good luck," he screamed and threw the rock as far as he could into the sea. "Ah, love! Sweet love! I love love!" Luca looked and saw a couple down the way holding hands, walking toward him. When he began screaming, they stopped. He yelled again, "I love! I'm falling in love! *Mi piace amare*! *Amo la donna migliore*!" He heard their faint laughter on the wind and then he looked back out to sea. How many times has that wondrous, beautiful sea heard the cries of love?

Luca headed back to the car and drove to Bolgheri to meet Stefano for lunch. The trattoria overlooked a large line of cypress trees and vineyards, but the day had turned gray and rain began to pelt down. Stefano seemed agitated and ordered quickly something to eat. Luca assumed he was just hungry and needed something quick. They shared an insipid meal with some Bolgheri red wine.

"This is powerful stuff," Luca said.

"Yes, but very smooth. Excellent with wild boar or any heavier pasta, meats. How did you like the beach?"

"Oh, beautiful. Amazing. And it's wintertime. I can only imagine what it'll be like come spring and summer."

"Eh, the eyes never tire of gazing upon them," Stefano said. "And how did your homework go?"

"Yes, your sister said that I must visit the sea and take in everything. The sights, the smells, the sounds, everything."

"*Eh,* she really said that, huh? Maybe she likes you."

Luca perked up immediately. "Yeah, you think so?"

Stefano shook his hands out in front of him.

"*Mamma mia*, you like her."

"So, she is…single then?"

"Eh, yes and no."

"Oh, that doesn't sound good."

"No, she's single, but she has a history. She was with a man for a long time. Not now, but it's complicated. She needs to explain to you."

Luca ate the rest of the meal in wonderment. He wanted to rush back and see Matilda and find out what sort of complications she was in—or who her complications entailed. But how to bring it up? He couldn't simply tell her he had been talking with Stefano and she and her complicated relationship came up.

****

Luca and Stefano headed back to Florence after lunch and Stefano dropped Luca off at his studio. Luca waved as he left. Now what to do? He wanted to see Matilda. Where did she even live? He thought to try and text her.

Luca—*Ciao! Got back from Bolgheri just now. It was fenomenale. Will have to tell you all about it!*—

He didn't receive an immediate reply, but he couldn't wait around his apartment all day fidgeting. So he decided to walk the Florentine streets and get familiar with his neighborhood. He found the best way to get to know a city was to get lost in it—but sober preferably.

Luca began by going southeast of his apartment toward the stadium of his favorite football team, La Viola, the Fiorentini. This area of Florence was crowded primarily with studio apartments and small familial shops. He eventually came to some rail tracks and a heavily graffitied covered bridge. He crossed over and came to a large park with a track around it, saw that many

194

people were strolling and conversing with each other around the park. He made a mental note to come back there to begin his running regime.

He kept going until he came to the stadium. The towering walls housed his boyhood team and he wondered when he would be able to catch a match despite the Fiorentini always letting down their fan base. And then, suddenly, Luca wondered what he was doing there at all, in Florence, in Italy. He had left his work, he left his wife (or, rather, she left him), he had left his country. He was gallivanting around in his parent's country looking to learn how to become a winemaker. Did he even really want to make wine? Weren't there already enough producers in the world? He was there only to escape—from real life. Again. One grand James Bond adventure complete with a beautiful, foreign landscape, a beautiful, mysterious woman and what else—only thing he was missing was some dangerous element like espionage or a mafioso hit contract. This wasn't real life.

It didn't feel good to wander without purpose, knowing that real life was elsewhere and waiting and would eventually have to be confronted. This pseudo-reality was only stalling the inevitable, the inevitable being the rejoining of this world, but for now he wanted to push those thoughts aside and focus on the magical nature of love and the bliss those ephemeral feelings brought to a soul. His phone dinged; he opened it quickly.

Matilda—*Aperitivo alle sette staserà? Alla Scimmia vicino il ponte vecchio—*

*La Scimmia*, the monkey. Was it a date?

Luca—*Sei una scimmia :) Si, I'll be there!—*

He hit send and was immediately regretful. Would she appreciate stupid American jokes? 'You're a monkey'? Why would he send that? He doesn't know her; she's not American.

His phone dinged again.

Matilda—*You're a monkey? I love it! That's my nickname from since I was very little. You found it out :) See you at 7—*

It was love! It was meant to be. The stars were aligning as they should and would and could and he felt the elation of one who had gone through the fire of loss and into the blissful clouds of love. Her nickname? It was meant to be. Luca subsequently forgot all his perceived degringolade the moment before. It was five in the afternoon so he had two hours to get back to the apartment, shower, change, and walk to the famous Ponte Vecchio.

****

La Scimmia was a wacky little bar with a large wooden monkey painted and attached to the roof of what could have been a thirteenth century wine cellar: completely made of stone, large stones, dark and portentous. When he laid his eyes upon Matilda, he was taken aback. She was dressed in a short red skirt with long black boots, a thin, sheer black top, red bangles around her wrists, red and white candy cane earrings and her hair, down, almost went to the small of her back. Her sensualness was too much for him; he could hardly gaze upon her without wanting to spill all his secret feelings. One look and she would be able to read his mind.

He offered a weak "*ciao*" instead.

"*Ciao*," Matilda said. "You seem, what's the word, no speech."

"Speechless, yes. You look, amazing, *fenomenale*."

Matilda laughed, heartily. Such a beautiful, singsong laugh. She laughed so hard, she reached out and put her hand on Luca's wrist and Luca instantly felt her energy, her warmth. It was powerful, so incredibly powerful. He wanted more of that touch, that energy.

"You have not been here too long," Matilda said, once she was finished with her laughing fit. "All the women dress like this."

"No, there is something special about you though. You have something that all the other women don't have."

"Oh, what is it? Tell me, I must know!"

"I don't know how to call it. It's, your, energy, your power."

"Ooooh, I like this. Tell me more over aperitivo. Tell me about my power over you."

They ordered each a negroni and took small plates of food back to their table. Luca told her about his life in eastern Washington growing up, about the Red Mountain wine region, his time in school studying English and wanting to be an actor, getting into the restaurant business, meeting Lillian, and the death of his mother.

"That's terrible. How have you been with it?"

"Truthfully, I don't think about it too much. I guess I'm avoiding thinking about her because I'm afraid maybe."

"Afraid of what?"

"Maybe I can't handle the fact that she's no longer here. I used to drink a lot. I had the restaurant and I had all the excuses I could drink for. That's what I told myself."

"Oh, Luca. Not good. You know drinking only makes it worse."

"I know that now. I got a DUI. You know what that is?"

"Oh yes. I'm a lawyer. It doesn't happen as much here in Italy. We are very strict and it's not part of the culture to over drink."

"I think in America, we drink to oblivion to avoid all the terrible things that happen in our lives and in our country. It's definitely part of our culture. But I'm learning to quit all that."

"Yes, good. Here we drink as a means to add pleasure to a meal. Like right now, we have a drink and we are eating and talking. That's how we drink in Italy."

"It's much better your way," Luca said. "Anyway, tell me about you. I've been gabbing this whole time about myself."

"Gabbing. You say such cute words." Matilda told Luca how she was born and raised in Sicily, in an eastern town called Catania near Mt. Etna, how she grew up in the sea and loved swimming. She loved horses as she used to ride when she was much younger. She moved to Milan to study law and to get some more worldly experience; she worked in London for quite some time before coming to Florence to help her brother as an advocate in the wine business.

"And now here you are," Luca said.

"And here you are," Matilda said.

"I went to Bolgheri. Why did you want me to experience Bolgheri?"

"Hmm, Bolgheri is a special place. Give me your hands and close your eyes."

Luca reached out his hands and Matilda took them

softly, caressing the tops. He tried to control his breathing, but his chest began to swell and it became more difficult to breathe through his nose. Her energy was so powerful.

"Now, tell me what you saw, tell me what you heard and smelled and touched. Tell me everything about your experience."

Luca thought for a moment. He tried to still his mind, to stay calm. "Okay," he began. "When I first arrived, I saw the expanse of the sea, its greens and blues and turquoise glimmering in the light of the sun, which was bright and high in the sky. It was a gray day, but hints of blue shone through the clouds. The air smelled of salty brine, perhaps some fish had landed at a nearby port. There was a soft breeze and I smelled light flowers drift through the air. The waves were crashing against the rocks and beach, a rushing sound. I was all alone and I felt like I was the only soul alive listening to the billowing of the sea. I took off my shoes and socks and felt the sands sift through my toes, wet and grasping at my skin. I felt the water cover my feet, washing away the sand and all the guilt I have felt recently. I thought of my mother, I thought of Lillian and how I've hurt her. I thought of Matilda."

Matilda continued caressing Luca's hands and if his eyes were open, he would have seen how she raised her eyebrows and smiled, her dimples bursting through the sides of her face. But she quickly set her face back to stone before he attempted to open his eyes. "Continue, please," she said.

"I yelled into the wind just as two lovers came hand in hand along the beach. They smiled and knew I was a foreigner coming to the land of…"

"Land of *che*'?" Matilda whispered.

"Land of wine, land of Christ, and most importantly, the land of love."

Luca opened his eyes to the clear, translucent beautiful eyes of Matilda staring back at him, still caressing his hands, and she was silent for a moment.

"I knew it," she said.

What did she know? That he was falling in love with her? That he had known her for only a moment's time and yet he felt, knew, that she was integrally a part of him now? It had to be so completely obvious. What would she say? Did she feel anything toward him?

"What do you know?" Luca asked, hesitantly.

"I know you are a man of feeling, of passions," Matilda said. "And now you know more about me, about who I am. I grew up on the sea and you have now felt, seen, smelled, heard the things I've felt, seen, smelled, and heard. Now, you are a part of me."

Luca couldn't exactly explain what drove him to reach across the table and pull Matilda to him, but he did and their lips touched and he suddenly was lost in that moment—their tongues met and Luca couldn't tell which was his or hers or where he even was or if people were looking at them or if she was embraced, it all just seemed right and everything was perfect and wonderful. When they finally withdrew from each other, Luca looked at Matilda from across the table, giddy and full of feeling, but also hopeful that what he did was not wrong. He didn't know in this country; it was all new to him.

"I'm sorry. It just came over me. I—"

"It was perfect," Matilda whispered. "I felt everything."

"I haven't felt this way in, well a long time…I don't

know when. You are…I can't describe it."

"Maybe it's just Italy," Matilda said.

"No, it's not just Italy. I felt something as soon as I saw you and as soon as I heard your voice. It was like a bubble popped in my head that was blocking all my emotions and feelings. I met you and I became alive again. Your energy, your feeling. It boggles my mind."

"Luca, let's walk along the river," Matilda suggested. They left La Scimmia and walked along the stony road by the river Arno holding hands, which felt new and yet completely normal. To any bystander, they appeared to be an Italian couple in love, not knowing their hands had just barely began touching and that they had just shared their first kisses. "I have to tell you something about myself," Matilda said.

"I hope you can eventually tell me everything," Luca said.

"This might be not good. Maybe you will not want to see me again after I tell you this."

"No matter what it is, I'll always want to see you."

"Okay, then I'll just tell you," Matilda said, letting go of Luca's hand and stopping just before a bridge. "I have an ex. A recent ex. And, he's not a nice man. He's maybe, a little dangerous. And he's very jealous. Very, very jealous of me. He still thinks of me as his property."

"Okay, I was thinking you were going to tell me something far worse, like you were moving to Asia next week or that you're on the run from murdering someone. A jealous ex I can handle, I think."

"Luca, don't take this lightly please. He is dangerous. I don't know what he would do if he found out I was seeing someone."

"So, then you are seeing someone?" Luca smiled.

She kissed him then, full and sensual. And he felt everything he ever needed to feel in that kiss. He had waited forty years for a kiss like that and he couldn't believe that after all that time, all the things he had done, the bad things, the guilty things, he was experiencing it then.

"I am now seeing a beautiful *polpetto* who is crazy and foolish," Matilda said.

"*La mia scimmia con gli occhi belli,*" Luca said. "My monkey with beautiful eyes."

Chapter 14

Lillian sat still on Luca's ugly cream-colored couch staring at the flames floundering from the fireplace, lit from the night before. She had hardly moved and hardly slept. She knew, academically, what was going on with her, but diagnosing herself meant she would have to face her demons and trepidatiously try and battle against them. She was lonely, plain and simple. She had invested in a life with Luca and despite his absence much of the time because of work, it had worked for her. Now, with Luca gone, even her abysmally always single friend Sarah had found new love and had whisked off to some foreign adventure.

Lillian thought of Cassandra. Her daughter was her Luca and was soon to be leaving her behind, behind to do what?—to be what?

"Who am I?" Lillian said into the flickering flames. "What am I? I'm a lonely psychologist who only has her work, whose only interactions are with people in a great need. And now I'm talking to myself in front of a lonely, burning fire. That's what I am."

She pulled herself up, took a shower and got dressed for the day. The espresso she consumed jolted her awake. Another full schedule lay before her, but at least she had Cassandra as her last appointment, something to look forward to—and, she found herself relieved to know that Nick had cancelled.

The appointments went achingly slow, but eventually, as time seemed to do, it moved and Lillian was at the end of the day with only Cassandra left. She took a quick break for another bout of coffee and even a donut from a cafe across the street. Lillian had a love-hate relationship with the place. She loved that it was there so that she could get good coffee whenever she wanted; she hated that it was there so she could get fattening donuts whenever she wanted. And lately, that had been more and more often, but whatever she thought, she deserved them. She gulped the coffee down and slammed the donut in her mouth, the flaky, stickiness clinging to the sides of her dimples. She licked them with her tongue and felt like a beast, but she didn't care. She knew she would be feeling nauseous in a few moments, but it didn't matter because those three seconds of glazed donut bliss felt wonderful.

Cassandra was running late so Lillian had some extra time to herself, a few minutes, but those few minutes felt like eons of eternal bliss and rejuvenation. A time to check oneself and relax the mind, just breathe, breathe, in and out, focusing on the breath. Lillian had tried breathing exercises of late, getting connected with the soul, the breath of life as some yogis claimed it to be. She exhaled and then opened her eyes; she checked her notes and was about to make yet another espresso from her Italian Mocha, but Cassandra suddenly arrived in a rush.

"I'm so so so sorry I'm late," Cassandra said, flinging herself down upon the couch. "I had a problem with my daughter."

"I'm sorry to hear that. What happened?" Lillian asked.

"Well, we had planned that I would pick her up from school today and then take her shopping for some clothes, spring clothes. Her whole wardrobe is a little ratty and anyway, I wanted to spend some time with her like we planned. Well, she called and asked if she could go get some food after school with some friends instead and I know there were going to be some boys she's interested in at whatever the place is they go. And I didn't want her to go because we had a plan. Anyway, as you know, I just wanted to spend time with her. But we got in a big fight and we both said some things that weren't very nice. Finally, I told her to go with her friends because that's all she cares about."

"I'm sorry you went through that Cassandra," Lillian began slowly. "How do you feel about it now?"

"I feel terrible. All I wanted was to spend time with my daughter."

"I understand that. She's leaving for college and you want every minute you can with her. There are only so many minutes in a day and only so many moments we get with our loved ones out of those minutes."

"Yes, exactly. You understand completely. Why can't she understand that? Doesn't she want to spend time with her mother? Doesn't she realize that she's going to be leaving me and she'll have time with her friends for the next four years?"

"Are her high school friends going to the same school as her?"

"Well, no, they're all going to different schools, but she'll make new friends of course."

"Maybe she feels that since she's leaving for school, she also is leaving her high-school friends and won't get to see them much, if at all, in the next four years.

Whether she makes new friends or not, it's these friends she won't be seeing. Does that make sense?"

"Well, I suppose…but, I'm her mother. I've always been there for her. And now she can just toss me aside and spend all her time with her friends. She sees them at school enough, doesn't she?"

"You know it's not the same in the classroom. She's a teenager. She's probably at her most social part of her life as she's ever going to be except maybe in college. And, she's in that stage where she wants to have the attention of boys, I'm sure. Do you remember being a teenager?"

"No, well, yes, I remember being a teenager, but my parents were very strict and never let me go anywhere. I couldn't talk to boys at all even if they wanted to talk to me, which they didn't because I was always so plain looking and boring."

"I doubt you were either of those things Cassandra, but strict parents may persuade you to see yourself like that. Perhaps you were never let loose to fly."

"Exactly, I couldn't do anything at all. It was terrible. I wanted out of the house as fast as possible."

"And do you think your daughter may be feeling that same way, even if just a little bit?"

"Oh, well, I…don't know about that…well." And that's when Cassandra began to weep, big heaves of her chest cascading up and down like the sea breaking against the shore, Lillian thought. She let Cassandra weep, let her let it all out. The harsh realization of reality isn't always so easy to bear.

Lillian drove home in a strange mood, oddly whimsical. She had made her decision on what to do for herself.

\*\*\*\*

David met Diana down in Leslie Groves Park on the Columbia River. They strolled along on the boardwalk in the mid-afternoon sun. It was brisk as a slight breeze blew from the west, but it was sunny. The river soporifically seeped along as the pair slowly walked along the path. Anybody they passed must have thought that a father and daughter were simply enjoying a walk together in the park.

"If only they knew you were a brilliant professor and I was a budding actress," Diana said as a couple passed them and said good afternoon. "It's strange to think of all that people are oblivious to regarding other people's lives."

"Oh, yes, my how they would react if they knew I had swayed the thoughts of their children for so many years. Probably stone me to death for teaching the youth to think critically," David said.

"I don't know," Diana said. "Richland seems more progressive than the other two cities. You've done a lot of good here." Diana took ahold of David's hand as they made their way down the park pathway.

"Well, that's sweet of you," David said, trying to ascertain what the hand-holding meant. "I'm trying to catch up with it all being over. I really enjoy meeting with you and spending time with you, but it'll be short-lived, I guess, since you'll be moving soon."

"Not soon," Diana said. "Still don't have nearly enough money to move down there yet. Thank you for coming to the winery the other day though. That was a generous tip. You didn't have to do that."

Another older couple passed by and said hello. David and Diana continued walking along until they came to the end of the path. They looked out at the houses across the river, large, estate-sized homes. The river trudged along and ducks and geese sifted along with it. Out of nowhere, a large pelican broke from its resting place and glided through the sky and hovered just above the water on down the river. David and Diana watched as it scaled along the sides of the bank looking for fish.

"You know," David said. "I could help you out a little. How much do you need to get started? Although, it would mean I would lose you faster."

"No, I couldn't ask you to do that anyway. It's a lot. I've talked with my friend and he said I should wait until I had…well, a lot more than I have now."

"How much?"

"Probably to get started around ten thousand dollars."

"Oh, that is a lot," David said.

"L.A. is really expensive. Rent, driving to auditions, everything. Hopefully I can get a job as a server like everyone else trying to be an actor down there. Luckily, rent will be a little cheaper because I'll be living with a few other people, people in the business so they can help me out. I'll have my own room though so when you come visit me, you'll have a place to stay."

"You want me to come visit you?"

"Yes, of course. I'm not leaving my world behind."

\*\*\*\*

David cooked dinner that night at his place. Diana presented him a bottle of an eighteen-year scotch after they finished and David was putting the dishes in the dishwasher. She hadn't wrapped it, but presented it in a brown bag a bit unceremoniously.

"What's this?" David exclaimed.

"I know you like scotch so I went ahead and got you this. I hope it's at your level."

"Oh my, well now. You shouldn't have. Really? You can't afford this. I didn't need this, but well, just, thank you so much. That was incredibly thoughtful. Shall we open it? Do you want some?"

"Ah, no, thanks. I'll stick with wine."

Diana slept again in David's bed, he not allowing her to drive home after drinking so much. He sat awake on the couch—he felt drowsy, but couldn't sleep. David got up, poured himself a large glass of the scotch and stoked the fire, then he sat down in his favorite chair and gazed off into the flames. Fires and flames were funny like that, endlessly changing shape and allowing the endlessly changing thoughts to form and burn away, to re-form as the phoenix rebirths itself out of the ash. What a strange relationship he had with Diana, he thought. What was going on? They were friends, but seemingly intimate without being intimate. She sure drank a lot, like himself, and she had no qualms with staying over. But he knew she needed to move on with her life and he knew that he could help her with that, but that would mean losing her, despite her insistence that he could come visit any time. David thought he had made a decision when he heard the creaking of the bed. A moment later, Diana came out wearing a robe that David recognized—it was one of Francesca's robes.

"It's cold," Diana said, wrapping the robe tightly around her. "Do you mind if I wear this? I was freezing."

"Yes, of course, please do," David said, staring intently at the robe, remembering his wife. He looked back at the fire, his eyes blinking rapidly, his thoughts burning in his head. He sipped the scotch.

Diana sat on the couch. "It's late. Are you feeling okay?"

"Yes, I think so. Listen, I've made a decision. I want you to pursue your dreams and become a famous actress. I'll give you the ten thousand so that you can start your new career."

Diana was speechless. Finally, she whispered, "Are you sure? David, you don't have to do that you know. I can work here until I save enough."

"No, why waste your time here? Go, be what you're meant to be."

"I'm not wasting my time here," Diana said, coming up and crouching down besides David's knee. "I'm spending my time with you."

David looked at her, saw the robe and thought how idiotic he had been. "Diana, you are young, beautiful, intelligent. You have a path ahead of you that only needs a little push. I want to help with that push. If you really want me to come visit you, I'll come visit you, but you must follow your dreams."

Diana jumped up and hugged David tightly, squealing with delight. "Oh my god, thank you thank you thank you. Of course you will come visit me. Hopefully I'll be working by then anyway. And I'll pay you back. This isn't a gift, but a loan. Oh my god David, thank you! I can't believe it. Thank you, thank you!"

She hugged him tightly and when she pulled away, David kissed her on the lips—the kiss of death. She staggered back just a bit in shock and David's face quickly flushed. "I'm sorry, I didn't mean…I'm so sorry, I was caught up in the moment. Please forgive me."

"David," Diana said. "It's okay. It just startled me.

It's nothing, no big deal at all."

"Are you sure?"

"Yes, of course. Just don't do it again," she chided. Then she laughed. "David, we have to celebrate. I can't sleep now. You have your scotch so I'll get…no wine, I'll make a martini with vodka. Yes, that's exactly what I'll do. Oh David, you've made my whole life."

"Okay now, it's alright. Yes, have a martini," David said, sipping his scotch slowly as she pounced away into the kitchen. He put another log onto the fire as the flames had died down.

****

Matilda had some legal business to attend to in London; she invited Luca along since he had never been. It was a short, two-hour flight from Florence and Luca was amazed at how quickly Europeans could visit new places and that those new places seemed and were completely different than whatever place had just been left. In some spots in the US, that was true. If he were to fly from Pasco to Seattle, which was a less-than-an-hour flight, the landscape would be completely different— high desert would climb into towering mountains and forest and then down to the sea. But, Luca thought, for the most part, two hours didn't mean too much in the US and, what was more, was that one would almost certainly be in the same country as one departed. The people could be slightly different, their accents, their ways, but it was the same country—even Canada didn't seem to feel any different than the US, at least not to Luca. But, as he was flying on the Alitalia Airlines flight, he flew over Switzerland, France, Belgium, and into the U.K. Amazing.

They took the train from Heathrow to London,

211

getting off at the Golders Green station. After a short walk through a quaint, but well-to-do neighborhood, Matilda showed Luca to a beautiful red brick flat with white window frames and small balconies populated with potted plants—Luca thought of the novel *Keep the Apidistra Flying.* A chimney at the top was sending smoke signals to the other inhabitants of the neighborhood. The flat looked lovely just as Luca imagined London dwellings to be.

Matilda opened the door with her keys. "When I come to London, I always stay here. I rent it by the month since I'm here much of the time." The door opened to a smallish, but comfortable room furnished with old, but sturdy furniture, paintings of the English countryside, a bookcase filled with old books, which Luca wanted to rush over and peruse, but held himself—this was not his flat, but hers he remembered. The kitchen was small, but cozy enough for some wine, cheese, and whatever else they would make there.

They settled in and decided firmly that they were famished and would go somewhere first to eat. They settled on Thai food. Matilda knew a close spot. They walked there and were at a table within fifteen minutes. Luca ordered a bottle of riesling for the two of them.

"Wine with Thai food?" Matilda asked, incredulously.

"Yes, riesling is known to be wonderful with Thai food, with the spice. Remember, the wine is part of the meal," Luca laughed.

"Oh boy, I've created a monster, a monster *polpetto.*"

"A monster meatball. I like that. Monster Meatball and *La Scimmia Piccola*, the little monkey. No, I have a nickname for you." Luca looked into Matilda's luminous, large brown eyes. "You, are Occhi Belli. Beautiful Eyes. The most beautiful eyes my eyes have ever laid eyes upon."

"Hmm, I don't understand all what you say, but I like this much more than little monkey," Matilda said.

After dinner, they went back to the flat. Matilda opened a bottle of red wine and poured two glasses.

"I will respectively pass," Luca said. "My new leaf has me only drinking when there is food involved."

"Ah, I learned this one," Matilda said. "Here is your food for thought. I am your food for your thinking of your thoughts."

"Yes, whatever you just said, you are," Luca said, taking Matilda into his arms, kissing her fully on the lips.

He gazed into those brown eyes of hers and thought to himself that whatever may be in the future, this moment, this very exact moment he would try and remember forever as it was. She was his soulmate; he hoped he was hers. He was falling in love and she was falling in love. The most magnificent thing in the world was two people falling in love with each other. He had never felt anything like this and their energy, their touch, everything felt so right and natural and nothing was ever going to prevent them from being what they were at that moment. He loved her; he couldn't tell her, but he loved her.

"Follow me," she whispered.

The bedroom was small, a bed covered in a rough quilt. They kept the lights off. Luca felt nervous despite feeling everything else, but Matilda kissed him, and touched him and slowly took his clothes off—she didn't rush anything, but he felt her desire with her lips, her tongue, her whispers and caresses. He was shaking when he took her shirt off, when he unzipped her jeans. They were so tight that he struggled to pull them down, but she laughed and shimmied out of them. Then, standing naked together, their bodies touching, Luca felt her soft skin against his and he looked at her, looked at those beautiful eyes and thought only that everything he had ever done had led to this point and it was perfect. He kissed her and together they lay down upon the bed and made love slowly as if they wanted only to keep the night from ever ending.

They lay in each other's arms and Luca listened to Matilda's soft breathing. She stirred and whispered, "If ever you come here, for whatever reason, and I'm not here, ask the neighbor next door. He's a gentle old man who will help you." At that, she promptly fell asleep and Luca lay awake to savor the memories of that evening.

\*\*\*\*

"I want a baby," Lillian said to Sarah over the phone.

"Hold on," Sarah said. "What happened?"

"Nothing happened. I wanted one with Luca until I realized he was never going to be in a position to be a father. I made peace with that. Now I'm not with Luca anymore."

"Honey, I understand you're going through a lot right now. I'm almost home from France. Let's talk when I get back okay?"

"Sure, we can talk. I want to see you anyway, but I've made up my mind with this."

"Who's going to be the father? Do you have a guy in mind?"

Lillian laughed. "Oh babe, you've really never

thought about kids, have you? I can do a sperm donor. I can check my eggs to see if they are viable. I can do in vitro if need be. I don't need a man directly involved."

"Isn't it more fun that way?"

"Just get back here. I want to hear about your trip anyway."

Chapter 15

In early April, the buds began to break open to reveal their dormant shoots. Luca and Stefano went through the vineyards row by row instructing Stefano's head gardener what needed to be done to keep the vines vibrant. A flock of sheep were allowed to graze among the vines as they didn't eat the fruit nor the stalks, but rather the weeds around them. Stefano was checking the soon-to-be clusters and made mental notes on how much he was going to clip to keep the grape clusters small. Luca made mental notes as much as he could, but his mind kept meandering to when he would be able to see Matilda again. She had been down south now for a week and possibly would be there for the next few days as well. Without her nearby, the time seemed to flow drastically slower, the work in the vineyards and winery seemed drastically duller.

Luca tried to remember why he left his home, left his family, left his job to go and learn to make wine in Italy; he was there to become a better version of himself. Matilda blossoming into his life was a godsend, but he must not forget the fundamental nature of his soul. Love was a drug and Luca, thinking of Matilda, only wanted her in his arms, to kiss her, to touch her, to run his hands through her medusa hair, to gaze and get lost into those nebulous eyes—Occhi Belli—he could imagine them transfixed upon him. He shivered with anticipation. He felt as if he were going to crack open and oozing red, bubbling, loving blood would seep into the earth, into the vines, and the wine would be so incredibly intoxicating that the whole of Italy would fall under its spell. Soon, soon, it must be soon.

"So, the buds do look really good and if the weather keeps getting warmer, we should see some bud bursts come this week," Stefano said.

Luca looked at the vines, at the imminent bud bursting and tried to comprehend what Stefano was saying, but the meaning seemed foreign even in English.

"You've been seeing my sister quite a bit," Stefano continued.

"Stefano, I have to tell you. She is just, amazing. She's beautiful, intelligent, her energy, her passion—"

"Yes, yes, she's Italian. She has you under a spell. But, yes, she is my sister and I know these things. She's a good woman."

"If, if we were to date, would you be okay with that?"

"Are you dating as you say?"

"Yes, I believe we are," Luca said, looking down into the muddy tracks.

Stefano laughed. "Well, if she's happy then I'm happy."

"Thanks, Stefano."

"Don't hurt her," Stefano said, without jest. "She's had some bad ones."

"I would rather die than hurt her," Luca said.

"Good," Stefano said. "I'd rather you die than hurt her too." Then he laughed and slapped Luca on the shoulder. "Come on, let's eat."

****

David tried calling Diana, but her phone went to voicemail after a few rings. He then tried calling Luca and that went instantly to voicemail as well. He forgot Luca probably wouldn't be able to receive phone calls. Luca had told him to use some sort of app on the phone. He'd try again the next day.

David paced his living room with a glass of scotch. Yes, he had given the money to Diana and she had flown down to Los Angeles and started her new life and he was happy for her since she was so young and it was impossible for her and him to really have anything remotely resembling a relationship, but—it still felt lonely. He felt lonely.

He tried reading. David found he couldn't focus very well on the words. With Francesca, he could sit by the fire and read for hours knowing that his loving wife was in the house somewhere. Now, all alone, he found it was hard for him to do anything in the house. Too many memories. And now that Diana was gone and the loneliness creeped in, he felt he had desecrated the one space he had access to memories of Francesca—the couch, their bed, her robe—their entire home. What had he been thinking? She was so young and he was so old and he supposed he just felt lonely and needed human comfort. And now here he was again, lonely in a deconsecrated house, without even pure memories of his loving wife. But, they hadn't really done anything; Diana had provided a friendship, comfort in a time of despair. Francesca would have wanted him to move on eventually. But with a younger woman?—an old student? Nothing happened; only the desire was there. Did that make it wrong?

He tried calling Diana again. After a few rings,

someone picked up.

"Hello," David said. "Diana?"

"Oh, one sec. I'll get her," the voice said.

David heard a bunch of commotion in the background, or perhaps it was music and people just talking loudly—it was difficult to tell which. After some time, David heard a voice.

"David! Hi, how are you?"

"Diana! Good to hear your voice. Sort of, it's quite loud there. Everything okay?"

"Yes, yes, just my roommates are having a bunch of people over for a music thing. What's new? Everything okay?"

"Oh yes, everything is fine. I wanted to find out how your move has been. Any luck with work yet?"

"Still looking. It's been hectic. Trying to meet the right people to get my start. I think I might have some auditions coming up though."

"That's good, that's real good." David stared off into the fire and sipped his scotch. He thought of the times when Diana was at his house, drinking wine, seemingly seducing him, but really what had she done? Nothing. It happened all so fast and it was all gone so quickly. Just like his life with Francesca. "How's the money holding out?"

"Ug, it's so expensive here. I'm almost out of money, but I'll make do. I'll find something."

"Do you need some more just to keep you afloat?"

"No, David, I couldn't. I don't know when I'd be able to pay you back."

"Don't worry about it. This will be a gift. I can send you another couple thousand."

"David, you're so good to me. Thank you so much.

I mean it. And once I get my feet on the ground, I'll have you come visit. Does that sound good?"

"That sounds…" David was cut off from someone coming up to Diana in the background.

"What's that David?"

"Yes, that sounds lovely. I'll send you the money."

"Thank you, David. I wish I was there with you now. Those times were fun."

"I was also thinking that," David said.

"Goodnight, David. Talk soon."

"Goodnight." He hung up. The flames reached ever higher into the chimney, creating a play of shadows against the couch where Diana used to sit, where Francesca used to sit. "I'm so sorry, Francesca," he said aloud to the still air. "I'm just a dotard. I hope I didn't betray you, my dear…I guess we never talked about what would come next."

He poured himself another glassful and sat, hoping the flames of the fire would reveal something profound. Nothing came out to him. He wondered if profound insights occurred to men of his age. Did he have anything left to live for? He would try and go see Diana soon anyhow once she was established.

David fell asleep in his chair with the glass of scotch lingering at his fingertips. It fell to the floor, spilling out onto the rug. David did not stir. The fire continued burning and he slept, dreaming of times with Francesca, dreaming of times long gone.

****

Sarah had returned from France and finally had some time to meet up with Lillian. She had wanted to go to the chic Italian place, but Lillian vetoed that just in case Antonio was there with his blonde Russian girlfriend. Instead, they chose a place across the street and clandestinely spied into the bar to see if he was working. Lillian felt foolish, but Sarah insisted.

They ordered martinis. "Okay, you first, I need to know all about how this happened?" Sarah said.

"It was always something I had thought about. I always wanted kids with Luca and before that too. But, you know, Luca had his restaurant and I was working and it just never happened. I don't think I wanted kids at that point because Luca was always gone anyway and I didn't see that changing. I don't really know if he ever really wanted kids. He hinted at it at times, but really he never put himself in a place I think mentally where he could realistically be a father. A present father that is. And of course, the drinking."

"Okay, so now you want kids. And who is going to be the father?"

"There doesn't have to be a father," Lillian said. "I have a patient who has a wonderful daughter who means the world to her and that woman does it all herself. You should see how she talks about her child. That child is her whole world."

"Listen, babe," Sarah said. "I know it's been hard on you. You've been working a bunch, taking on more and more patients, and I can see it's wearing you down. But babe, a child? Now?"

"What do you mean now?"

"I'm just saying, it hasn't been that long since the divorce. I know people tend to make rash decisions when they are feeling the repercussions of a divorce. I've seen it a bunch of times."

"Sarah, I love you and you give sound advice, but what I really need from you is for you to come with me to the donor."

"What? Have you already picked one out?"

"Maybe…"

\*\*\*\*

The fertility clinic was sterile yet welcoming. It had to be—Lillian was almost walking out as she was walking in. Something was triggered within her; maybe this was a mistake. She really should think more about it. But, Sarah was now taking her hand and pushing her through the door. A petite receptionist welcomed them in and had them take a seat to fill out some paperwork.

"I don't know if I can do this," Lillian said, shoving the paperwork aside.

"Babe, I'm here for you. If you don't want to do this, you certainly don't have to. I'll only say that if anyone would make an amazing mother, it's you. There, that's my piece."

"Weren't you against it before?"

"No, not really. I just wished you had done it the old-fashioned way. A one-night stand with a hunk who you didn't have to call again, but you had one night of flaming lovemaking that you could tell your daughter about some day."

"You know, if it were to happen now, I'd take Antonio and show him a little psychological warfare in the bedroom."

"Ooh, that sounds juicy. I like it. You know, these bartenders never stay with the same woman for a long time. Maybe you'll still get your shot. Anyway, who's the dad going to be for this one? He's hot at least?"

"He's a looker for sure."

"Unless they lie to you," Sarah said, musing.

"You think they'd do that?"

"I'm kidding."

A young nurse came out. "Miss Waters, we're ready for you."

"Go make a baby," Sarah said.

****

By May, the buds were blooming and the days were longer and sunnier. Stefano had to maneuver through a bit of rain at the end of April, but neither mold nor rot had surfaced and the extra water was good for the vines. Now they could struggle and get strong, reaching ever farther down into the earth to find that supply stream to just barely quench the thirst.

Luca loved looking at the vines, spending time with them, their gnarly wooden roots and perfectly trellised shoots. He especially loved walking amongst the vines in the early morning. Out there, he felt he could feel his mother's presence. He felt her wafting in and out of the breeze, landing here and there, sometimes playing the butterfly, sometimes playing the songbird. She spoke to him out there, and Luca could finally sense her presence and feel her and hear what she whispered. He felt her sadness and she cried much amongst the vines, tears for wanting to be there when her son began his path of healing.

In one of the vineyards on a slope looking eastward was a large rock that had never been excavated. A row had been planted just beside it and it made for a perfect place to stop and rest, to sit and gaze upon the rolling hills filled with oaks and chestnut trees, interspersed with rogue olive and fig trees.

It was there that Luca sat and thought about what his mother would think of what he was doing in Italy. He envisioned her looking down upon him from heaven, watching his every move and keeping score on a blackboard. Or perhaps she really was present in the vineyard and she could walk with him. She had told him that she had always wanted to return in the form of a duck and each morning, ducks flew overhead to take refuge in a nearby pond. But Luca feared duck hunters and the delicious duck recipes crafted each day in Tuscany; even, some that he had eaten already. He refused to think of his mother as a duck. A butterfly or a songbird—that was nice.

His mother would have liked Matilda—she was Italian, someone that his mother could connect with—an Italian in the mother country. Luca was finally doing it right.

As he sat on the rock, he saw some movement amongst the vines and suddenly Stefano materialized in front of him. "Luca, hey, you come out here too in the mornings?"

"Yes, when I stay over. I find it calming and peaceful," Luca said, noticing that Stefano was pacing up and down the row with his hand to his chin as if in deep thought. He suddenly reached out with his right arm as if to grab a vine and shake it but instead shook it at the farmhouse in agitation. "Are you okay?"

"Ah, it's nothing. *I frodi* are supposed to come today, but it's okay."

"Who are *i frodi*?"

"Officials that check the vine, *bastardi,* but it's okay. Every year we talk with them. It's part of the process."

At that moment, Luca and Stefano heard the rumbling of trucks coming up the road toward the villa. Stefano reared his head up to see who was coming toward them and then Luca saw the terrible grimace on his face. Stefano muttered terrible curses and then stalked off without another word, but once he made some headway toward the house, he turned around and asked Luca if he could come help unload some grapes.

Luca thought it strange that grapes were arriving as it was only May, but Stefano was in such a mood, he decided not to ask any questions. He went with him up to the trucks that were pulling in. Then Luca saw a car torpedoing along the narrow roadway—Marco's black sports car rapidly swerved onto the dirt road up to the villa. Luca thought it crazy how that man drove, that one day he would make a mistake. Marco and another passenger popped up out of the car almost before it had completely stopped.

"*Ciao* Stefano," Marco said, then seeing Luca. "Oh, *ciao* Luca, *come stai*?"

"*Bene, bene, e tu*?"

"*Eh,* it's okay."

The other man stood near the car without addressing anyone, but Luca saw that Stefano curtly gave him a nod. The man was completely bald, a bit stout, but obviously an athlete, perhaps a wrestler or boxer. Luca looked at him and saw cold, gray eyes, and then quickly looked away—something about those eyes disturbed him. The man leaned against the car with his arms crossed, evidently not willing to help in any way.

The trucks one by one backed up to the conveyor belts and Stefano, Luca, and some vineyard workers had begun to unload the grapes so that they could be de-stemmed and sorted. The grapes were mushy and already dispensing juice, some eaten by insects and some scarred by an unknown agent. Marco watched the process and the man by the car was now on his telephone. After the grapes went through the de-stemming machine, the entire load went into one particular steel vat. When the process was completed, Marco talked with Stefano for a moment alone. Luca saw them shake hands and then Marco got back into his car with the gray-eyed man and drove off in a rush, careering around the curves as if the roads were a personal racetrack.

"What are these grapes for?" Luca asked Stefano.

"Ah, they are for a house wine I make," Stefano said.

"Where did they come from?"

"Oh, just from a friend's farm," Stefano said. "I make special wine for him."

When the wine officials, *i frodi*, arrived, Stefano was even more agitated. Luca couldn't follow the conversation from the other side of the room (trying to appear busy doing miscellaneous tasks), but the officials were animated and Stefano kept trying to calm them down, but the speech was rapid and full of words Luca had never heard before. At one point, Stefano looked over at Luca with a mysterious air about him and the next, he and the officials left and went into the villa. Luca had no idea what was going on, but if it involved officials and any sort of production of anything, he assumed there were bribes involved. Perhaps they were negotiating the price of the bribe—prices go up, bribes go up too.

After the officials left, Stefano figured it was time for lunch, even, though it was a bit early, but Luca didn't complain. It had been a strange day and he wanted to see if Stefano would open up about the morning. Stefano didn't speak at all about the officials and Luca didn't think it was his place to ask, but he was interested in who the gray-eyed man with Marco was.

"That guy with Marco seemed like a nice guy," Luca said, laughing. "Who was that?"

Stefano grunted. "His name is Vincenzo. He helps run some of the wineries."

And that was all Stefano would say on him.

\*\*\*\*

Luca called David hoping to connect with him since it had been a while. He thought David sounded a little strange upon answering the phone. His voice was slurred, and he sounded groggy as if he had just woken up.

"*Ciao* David, sorry if I woke you. Is it still too early over there?" It was seven in the morning where David was, but he usually woke up around six anyway.

"No, no, I've been up for a while," David said. "Just having my morning pick me up."

"So, I got your message the other day. Everything okay?"

"Well, yeah, I called. Is now a good time to talk?" David said, hiccupping into the phone.

"Yeah, now's good. Hey, are you okay?"

"Well, yeah, I wanted to tell you since you're my family and you're all I've got. But, anyway, I've been seeing someone sort of the past couple of months, sort of."

An initial rush of breath stopped Luca's heart for a moment. He took some shallow breaths and tried breathing through his nose and then his mouth. He hadn't been prepared for that. He had never thought about David dating someone ever again. "Wow, that is news. Who is she?"

"Well, that's what I wanted to talk to you about,"

David said, hiccupping. "She's a bit younger than me."

"David, are you okay? You keep hiccupping."

"Yeah, I'm fine, just swallowed something down the wrong pipe."

"So, she's younger than you. How much younger?"

"Well, this is a bit embarrassing, but she used to be a student of mine and not too long ago. She's twenty-eight, maybe twenty-six, I can't remember now."

"Oh, my, David, seriously? That's too young for me even to date. How did you meet her?"

"I went to a play with one of my colleagues and she was there and recognized me. I didn't even recognize her at first. Anyway, she had some questions on Hemingway and so we set up a time to meet and discuss his books and short stories. But Luca, I'm just a fool. Nothing's happened. I just wanted something to happen."

"So, you're not dating?"

"No, we're not dating. We're not anything. I'm just an old dotard, a fool of a man. She caught me at a bad time, a rough time, and she's a very nice girl. Very smart and sweet."

"Okay, what's all this mean then? You have a crush?"

"Well, no, not really. I mean, everything's at its end. See, she wants to be an actress so I helped her get set up down in Los Angeles. And eventually I may go down and see her—but no, I think nothing's ever going to happen. Any possible relationship has run its course—I mean, how could it possibly even happen, right?"

"David, I just want to make sure you're okay. Are you okay? You might go see her in Los Angeles? I mean, what for?"

"Luca, I miss Francesca. I miss your mom more than

anything. I'm having a rough time right now. I don't know how I feel about Diana—her name's Diana. I gave her some money and then I gave her some more."

"How much money did you give her, David?"

"Oh, not much, only enough to get started, but Los Angeles is expensive and it's not so easy to become a working actress."

"David, does she ask you for money?"

"Oh, no, I offered it. It's okay Luca, it's only a little bit."

"David, I love you, bud. I don't know what's going on, but I think I understand. Listen, if you go down to L.A., get a feel for the situation. I think you'll know how she feels about you when you visit her. A new place, a foreign place usually shows the true feelings of a person. You know what I mean? A fish out of water type of deal."

"Yeah, I think I do. Yeah, maybe I'll go down and visit her soon."

****

Luca met Matilda for dinner that night in a restaurant aptly called *le Rovine*, the Ruins, on the other side of the Arno. A stone structure that had been built into the side of another building during Roman times and probably had been a restaurant even then. Thick stone columns held up the ancient ceiling with large-scaled murals depicting Etruscan bucolic scenes and battles, perhaps against the Romans, perhaps against the gods. The owners were there that night and treating every table to grappa and limoncello, homemade of course. Luca drank his wine and assured Matilda she could have all the limoncello and grappa she wanted, but he was abstaining as he knew exactly where that would lead him.

For the first time since meeting Matilda, he felt that she was tense around him. She talked aimlessly about nothing and kept looking toward the door as if she wanted to leave. She poured more and more limoncello into her glass and it wasn't like her to overdo it: she, always practicing restraint. Luca hoped her feelings weren't subsiding. Perhaps she needed that extra liquid courage to tell him they were finished; that would devastate him, but, if they were, he had to know. He couldn't pretend that all was well if something was troubling her.

"Are you okay tonight?" he asked, peering over hesitantly into her distracted face.

She looked at him suddenly and laughed, took his hand, and smiled. "I'm sorry," she said. "Yes, I'm so happy with you. Yes, I seem agitated, it's true. I am. I heard you met Vincenzo today. That's true, yes?"

"Yes, sort of. He didn't say one word to me, but he was there today with Marco. They talked with Stefano briefly and then left. That guy, Vincenzo, didn't seem so friendly."

"No, he wouldn't. Vincenzo is my ex. He is not a nice man. And…I told you he's a little dangerous."

"Hmm, that would explain why he wasn't friendly today," Luca mused.

"No, no. He's just not friendly. He doesn't know about us. Not yet. My brother would not have mentioned it. So how could he?"

"You think he'll be angry if he does know about us?"

"Angry, yes. We did not end good. He still wants to be with me, but I would never go back to him. He's *pazzo*, crazy."

"Would he hurt you in any way if he found out you think?"

"He's *pazzo*. I don't know what he would do."

**\*\*\*\***

That night with Matilda lying next to him, Luca couldn't sleep, but only think about what Vincenzo would do when he found out about them. Hot blooded was not just a cliche, Luca thought. And what did Matilda mean by dangerous? Luca looked over at Matilda sleeping soundly next to him and it just seemed too perfect. Of course, there had to be some deviant blocking their utmost happiness. There always was with life. What would Luca do if he were confronted? What could he do in a country that wasn't his? He definitely didn't want to end up in an Italian jail, or worse.

He knew these moments of pure happiness could be contained if he thought about every movement, every word, every instant, but eventually, things move onward, things change. So, instead of falling back asleep, he stayed awake and listened to the beating of Matilda's heart, her soft breathing. He felt her smooth legs entwined with his, her small hand that lay gently on his stomach. He didn't want to move so that he could be encased within that scene for as long as he could.

But, as things moved onward, Luca had to get up to use the bathroom. Matilda stirred awake and yawned. "Hey," she said. "You making me breakfast, yes?"

"Yes, that's exactly right. I wanted to surprise you," Luca said, laughing. "I hope you like eggs and bacon."

"Oh yes, make me big American breakfast so that I can have stomach ache all day."

"Oh yes, coming right up my dear. What's your plan

for today anyway?"

"My day plan? Um, I have to meet Marco. I have to talk to him about winery stuff."

"Hmm, okay, well maybe I'll brush my teeth and take advantage of you before you go."

"Maybe I take advantage of you instead," Matilda said.

"Yes, maybe you should. Good idea. That's what I love about you, always thinking."

"Then hurry and brush your teeth," Matilda laughed.

"I wish every day could be like this," Luca said, philosophically. "Just you and me together like this."

Chapter 16

The days passed by quickly as May and June came and went. Tuscany was hot and humid in July. The growing season looked wonderful for the grapes, but a few drops of rain wouldn't hurt. Stefano was getting a little worried that the heat was going to cook the grapes to mush; Luca was worried that the mosquitos were going to suck all his blood out before he even saw the grapes being harvested. Large *zanzare*, mosquitos, came up from north Africa—the ones with blue backs were the most dangerous, carrying malaria and zika, and seeming to leave the itchiest stab wounds. Luca was constantly slapping himself in the face as he heard the buzzing swirling around his head. Nothing was more maddening than the incessant buzz.

Luca and Stefano went up and down the vineyard rows, looking at the dried earth and the withering grapes.

"You don't use irrigation water at all, huh?" Luca asked.

"No, we can't. Part of the rules. Only when the drought and heat become very extreme can we use water that is not rain," Stefano said, wiping his brow with the back of his hand.

Not a cloud was in the sky and the sun bore its heat down upon Luca, Stefano, and the vines. Luca swiped his brow of sweat and swatted at the swarm of mosquitos hovering nearby waiting to strike. "The rules here are much different than where I'm from. There, you can use irrigation, but it makes sense because it doesn't rain much at all."

"I had a Washington wine one time," Stefano said. "I couldn't stand it. It was like drinking a can of fruit juice."

"Yes, they can be quite bold," Luca agreed. "But it's the style. We get a lot of sun. Actually, just like what you're getting now."

"Hmm, our Sangiovese-based wines shouldn't be so fruity. We need some rain. Too much heat makes a flabby wine."

Stefano got his wish, as that night, the rain began to pour down, a storm to end all storms. It came from the sea and it first pounded Bolgheri and the coast and then moved eastward. The dark clouds came in, followed by thunder and lightning. Luca feared for the vines, for the villa, and for himself, but Stefano was out dancing in the vineyards like a crazy man. *Che pazzo!*

That next morning as the storm was passing, Marco came to take Luca around to nearby wineries to get an idea of how different producers controlled their productions. After visiting Villa Calcinaia, Fontodi, Istine, Ricasoli, and Fattoria di Petroio, Marco received a call that he took in secret outside the car. When he climbed back in, he said he would have to take Luca back to the winery straight away. Marco got the car onto the road and furiously drove to Tenuta Nardone il Brutto.

Marco whipped around the curves and after tasting a plethora of wine that day, Luca felt like he was going to be sick in the car. Marco looked straight ahead without noticing, though, passing cars going too slow in the right-hand side of the lanes. Luca thought it strange that he didn't even slow down for the speed traps, which were many and marked—something must be truly pressing, but Luca wasn't about to ask.

"Dead man's curve," Marco said.

"What's that?"

"This curve coming up is called dead man's curve," Marco said, speeding toward a curve in the road that crossed a narrow metal bridge with a deep ravine below. The bridge was shielded by a row of thick trees and the roadway went down to a single lane—Marco tailed a slower driver just as he headed into the curve. He switched gears, gunned the gas and pushed the sports car into the left-hand side of the roadway. Luca knew anything could be behind those trees at that moment. Marco careened around the driver and just as they went into the curve and the roadway became the single lane, a large truck carrying tomatoes honked its horn and tried to brake—Marco gunned the gas harder and slid right in just before hitting the truck, coming out ahead of the scared driver they had passed.

"*Che cazzo, porco di merda*!" Marco yelled and pounded the steering wheel with his fist.

Luca was breathing heavily, just happy to be alive, that he forgot all about his stomach issues. Marco finally drove up the lane to the winery and Luca hopped out. Marco left without saying goodbye and Luca wondered if that was just how he was or if something had happened, or if Marco didn't like him anymore because he had also found out about his relationship with Matilda. Either way, Luca never wanted to drive with Marco ever again.

There seemed to be a lot of commotion at the winery that day. Luca began walking toward the room with all the steel tanks because he saw quite a few farm workers going in and out of the building. As Luca approached, he saw Stefano giving directions to some of the workers, but then suddenly, the man known as Vincenzo appeared out from nowhere. Luca hung back.

He watched as Vincenzo indicated to some of the tanks and Stefano looked like he was explaining something to him. Then, a line of workers carrying large drums set them underneath the last tank in the building and began to fill them up. Luca was quite sure that that was the tank with the grapes that had been brought from the south. They then hoisted the drums up the ladders of the other tanks in the line and dumped the juice in with the wine from last year's crop. Other workers were swirling the mixed juice with long paddles at the tops of the tanks.

Stefano spotted Luca as Vincenzo was surveying the work and Stefano secretly gave Luca a wave—a wave to go away. Luca didn't want to be seen by Vincenzo so he scampered off into the vineyard where he assumed Vincenzo would not go. Luca walked amongst the vines and thought about what he saw. If they were mixing the juice from the south with the wine of the vineyard, that meant it was an illegal wine to sell, at least as the typical wines of the region. Luca put his hands to his face; he didn't want to think about the ramifications of what he saw. He would talk with Matilda about it first.

At lunch, Stefano didn't seem to even acknowledge Luca's existence and Luca thought it best not to ask about what had happened that morning. Perhaps, it was better for him not to know anything anyway.

****

Luca met Matilda later that night at his studio

apartment; he was making dinner. They began with mussels and clams in a white wine and lemon broth with parsley, garlic, and some red pepper flakes with bread from the baker down the street to mop up the broth—s*carpetta.*

"I wouldn't dream of serving you any bread I made when the best is just around the corner," Luca said.

"Thank you. You learn quickly," Matilda said, mopping up every last ounce of broth with the fresh bread. "And I didn't realize you knew how to make bread."

"I don't."

A buzzer went off and Luca put Brussels sprouts into the oven with quartered potatoes seasoned with rosemary and thyme. He then put the *Bistecca alla Fiorentina*, a large, two-inch thick porterhouse coming from the Chianina cow, onto the grill.

"Be careful," Matilda said. "You better watch that and not focus on me so much. It cooks quickly."

"Yes *tesoro*," Luca said.

"Don't be a *polpetto* tonight."

"Yes *tesoro*."

"Don't be a *scimmia*."

"Yes *tesoro*, my beautiful Occhi Belli."

"You're being a *polpetto*."

"Yes *tesoro*."

They ate their meal with the best bottle Bolgheri could brandish.

"Why such a nice wine on a weeknight?" Matilda asked.

"I don't know," Luca said. "Something feels right about it. Except, I do want to ask you something."

"*Si, scimmia, che cosa?*"

"I saw Stefano today getting instructions from Vincenzo," Luca said. Seeing Matilda's face turn pale, he knew something wasn't right. "Yes, that Vincenzo. And they were mixing wine from the winery with the grapes from the south. Why?"

Matilda slowly finished the bite of potato she was chewing on. She sipped some of her wine, but her throat felt parched so she took a big gulp of water. She looked at Luca, waiting for an answer he probably didn't really want, but she felt it was time to tell him, at least what she could.

"*Tesoro*, listen. Nardone il Brutto is a part of a larger company of wineries and Stefano only makes wine for Nardone il Brutto. He is a professional and a purest, but sometimes, even he can't control what goes on in the winery. He has bosses too."

"Occhi Belli, you're trembling." Luca took Matilda's arm, cold and layered with gooseflesh. He brought her in close. "Is it okay? Is it something that's dangerous then?"

"It can be," Matilda said.

"So, it's like the mob or something?" Luca said jocosely. Matilda remained quiet, trying to think of how she would tell him. "Wait, is it the mob? The Mafia?"

"*Si, loro sono mafiosi,*" Matilda said, straight faced.

"So who? Marco and Vincenzo? Stefano?"

"Stefano no! Not my brother. He's a good man. He just works for them. This is Italy, not America. It's not so simple here. He needed work; they had a position open. He doesn't ask questions."

"But you do. You're a lawyer. Are you *their* lawyer?"

"It's not so simple *tesoro*; I manage some of their

238

affairs."

"And that's how you met Vincenzo, yes? Your brother began working for them, got you involved, you met Vincenzo, he's a powerful man in a powerful position, you were attracted to that until he turned on you. But, now that you're involved, you can't just leave. You know too much. Is that the story?"

"Some of it, yes. I met Vincenzo first. I introduced my brother to him. We both thought it was just a small operation, but now we realize that the winery is owned by a large group of companies just like many of the other wineries. And wine is only one small part of their income. I've been trying a long time to think of a way out of it."

"And the wine? What's happening with the wine?"

"Well, Stefano is good. Usually on good years, Stefano can make the wine as is, just like the regulations state. But, on bad years, he can't. Regulations say you must make the wine with the grapes that you have, but Marco and Vincenzo do otherwise. They add grapes, juice, from some of the wineries from the south, hotter places that have more fruit to their juice. So, the wine made here is still the kind of wine they want to sell. And they sell it for much higher than they could otherwise. They sell much of it to the US."

"Strange I didn't have any at my restaurant. If Salvatore is involved with Marco, he would certainly try and have it there, but maybe he doesn't know anything about what Marco is doing—"

"Who is Salvatore?"

"Marco's cousin, in the US. He was my head chef at the restaurant."

"I'm sure he knows what Marco is involved in.

Maybe they don't import to Seattle?"

"Maybe not. It is a small market, and Washingtonians have their own wine. So, anyway, Marco and Vincenzo are adding juice from the south to the wine from up here. How don't they get caught? I thought the wine officials were very strict and always coming around?"

"Yes, but they bought the officials off, but—"

"But?"

"Only if they add a little. I think yesterday maybe they added a lot. Last year's vintage wasn't so good and the wines were a bit weak. That's what Stefano told me. They paid the officials already, but if they find out that the juice added was a lot more than what they said, there could be trouble. And I don't trust those officials."

Luca felt disgusted. What seemed like a bit of a vacation, perfect really, learning how to make wine, being on a beautiful winery in Tuscany, falling in love with Occhi Belli, and suddenly, he was sort of involved in a mafia wine scandal. And yet, he wasn't supposed to know anything; perhaps he could keep it that way, at least for appearances sake.

"So what're we going to do?" Luca asked.

"We are going to wait and see what happens and tonight we are going to forget about all that and you are going to love me…oh!"

Luca smiled and laughed. "Yes, what were you saying?"

"I'm Italian and I've had some wine. Maybe my tongue is loose and my head is feeling heavy."

"Or maybe you're right. Maybe I do."

"Maybe you do what?"

"Maybe I do love you," Luca said.

"Maybe doesn't do anyone any good. Do you?"

"I do. I love you, my Occhi Belli."

"*Ti voglio bene mio caro*," Matilda said, kissing Luca softly.

"I don't speak Italian very well," Luca said. "Maybe in English where it means something to me?"

"I love you! Being with you makes me feel that everything will always be okay. You're my meatball monkey."

"And you're my beautiful eyed monkey."

"Two monkeys sitting in a tree," Matilda said.

"Now who's being the meatball," Luca said.

"Let's stop talking." Matilda pulled Luca close to her.

****

The insemination hadn't worked, but Lillian would go again. She was at her office waiting for Cassandra to arrive—it was strange that Cassandra was late and hadn't called. Lillian looked at herself in a hand mirror. Thirty-six years old—she felt it, whatever that meant. All she knew was that she wasn't young and she wasn't old. But, she *felt* old. Old enough perhaps to not be able to get pregnant. How had it come to this? She gave her best fertile years to a man who couldn't accept them for what they were, who didn't even want to entertain the idea. But, she couldn't blame him for that; he had told her from the onset and she supposed she was in love and didn't care back then. If only she could get pregnant now. It was the one thing she needed.

Cassandra arrived a moment later breaking into Lillian's thoughts. She came in smiling, wearing a light blue dress and white shawl and appearing unusually joyful. She quickly sat down upon the couch and looked over at Lillian with an even brighter smile—she obviously couldn't wait to unleash some sort of news, but Lillian couldn't fathom what it could be. What if she somehow had gotten pregnant again? The thought was terrible.

"Dr. Waters, I'm so happy. I'm just so so so happy. I have to tell you straight away."

"Yes, please, I'm on the edge of my seat," Lillian said, sitting down at her desk.

"Well, I had a long talk with my daughter and she's decided to go to community college the first two years and then transfer to a four-year school afterward. And, she'll live at home those first two years. I'm so so so happy. I have her for two more years."

Lillian felt like she was just hit with cement and her head was shaking with confusion, shiny stars actually flickering above her like in the cartoons. What had she just heard? "Wow, that is news," she said, looking into the empty space and trying to figure out what to say next.

"You don't seem as pleased as I am," Cassandra said.

"I'm just in shock," Lillian said. "I just can't imagine how she came to that decision. I thought she was incredibly excited to go off to school."

"Well," Cassandra started. "I mean, she'll get to eventually. I think she realized the money it was going to take. Going off to school is so expensive these days."

"Yes, that's true, that's true. Can you relate to me how the conversation went?"

"You think I convinced her to stay, don't you?"

"I'm not here to judge anything," Lillian said, not really believing that, but she didn't want Cassandra to put up a wall now. "I just want to hear what happened."

"Okay. Well, we were talking over dinner. I made her favorite meal of goulash and corn on the cob and then a cherry pie. And we were talking about her leaving and I told her she was going to have to work because school was so expensive. I told her it was going to be hard to work full time and study full time too."

"How did she take that?"

"Oh, she's young and naive so of course she immediately thought she could do it. She didn't think things through of course. But kids think they can do anything, especially if they are excited about something."

"Hmm, yes."

"So, I tried to break it down for her because she doesn't even know what she wants to study yet and if she takes loans out and has thousands of dollars of debt when she leaves school and she majors in art or something that doesn't pay any money, how is she going to ever pay that off? I think that's when she finally saw my thinking."

"Hmm, why do you think so?"

"Oh, because she got quiet and really started to listen to reason. I could tell she was calculating expenses in her head and realizing that maybe what I was saying, her mother of all people, was actually sage advice."

"Hmm, okay, then what did she say?"

"Well, at first she tried to come up with some pretty lame excuses of course. You know how kids think, anything but reality. But I kept asking her how she was going to pay for this or pay for that or have time for this or have time for that. And then I told her exactly how it was going to be. She was going to work all the time, go to classes, have no time for studying or time for friends, let alone a boyfriend, but thank God for that. It just wasn't going to be realistic. I think she finally saw the big picture."

"So, then she suggested community college?"

"Well, not at first. Truth be told, she took reality a bit hard. She was crying and ran to her room and it took a bit for her to come back out, but I love her so I was patient and waiting and I just wanted to hug her and kiss her. When she did come out, she looked a mess, but I took her in my arms and just held her and kissed her forehead. I just love her so much."

Lillian sat back in her chair trying to imagine the scene. Her face, stoic and unwavering, but inside she was boiling. She wanted to reach across with long arms and strangle Cassandra or slap her until her hands hurt and Cassandra's face was bleeding profusely so that she could see exactly what she was doing, or exactly what she had done. Killing a girl's dreams for her own desires.

"Yes, you do love her," Lillian said instead. "Then what happened?"

"That's when it came to me, the idea," Cassandra said. "I suggested to her to stay home, save money, go to community college and take classes to figure out what she wants to do when she grows up. Simple right? And it just makes so much more sense."

Right. The idea just suddenly came to her. "And your daughter agreed?"

"Well, not at first, but after we shared quite a few tears together, she understood that I was just trying to make life a little easier for her and then she finally agreed. I'm just so happy. Two more years of my beautiful daughter at home with me. And she'll save money and get a good idea of what she wants to study in college. I'm hoping she'll end up going to the University of Washington since it's such a good school."

"And it's close," Lillian said.

"Exactly right, and it's close. So, a big turnaround wouldn't you say? I'm happy, feeling good. I have so many plans already for my daughter and me to do. I'm like a different person."

"Cassandra, I am happy that you are feeling happy. You should revel in this feeling and write down and explore why you think you feel this way all of a sudden—" Lillian said.

"Well, it's because," Cassandra went to interrupt.

"Wait, please, I'm not quite done. A singular moment is not going to restore a person, it's not going to fulfill a lifetime of happiness. The root of the depression, the root of the anger is still there. You have appeased your unhappiness for the moment, but at what cost?"

"What do you mean?"

"Your daughter's happiness has now been sacrificed. She had so many high hopes to go off to school and have that experience and now they are dashed. How do you think she feels about this new arrangement?"

"Well, it's nothing to do with what I want or what she wants. It's about what's possible and what's impossible and right now, going off to school is impossible. Money, work, all of that."

"Is it though? It didn't seem impossible a few weeks ago. What has seemed impossible from the beginning is you letting your daughter go. And I understand that. It must be incredibly difficult. She is your life and blood."

"Yes, it is hard and I don't see how you could understand what it's like. You don't have a daughter. Or kids at all."

"Yes," Lillian said. "You're right."

"You don't understand. She's the only thing in my life I care about. The only thing. Without her, I'd be dead. I've got nothing."

"Cassandra, this is wherein the problem lies. You are you and your life is its own entity. Your daughter is a part of your life, but your life is your own."

"No, that's what you don't understand, Dr. Waters. My life means nothing without my daughter. Anyway, I came here today to tell you how happy I was, am, and to tell you that I won't be needing any more appointments. I'm as happy as I can be now."

"Cassandra, please, we are only at the beginning of truly being happy."

"No, I'm as happy as I'm going to be, thank you very much. So, thank you and good luck and please just be happy that I'm finally happy."

After all her appointments that day were finished, Lillian left the office feeling defeated. She drove home feeling that she couldn't help anyone so how could she help herself to feel better about her own life? Here she was telling a woman that she's only temporarily happy and that her life must be her own when she herself was seeking to find something to fill a void in her own life.

A child. Would a child raise herself from her dooming unhappiness? If she were to have a child, shouldn't she have it because she wanted to simply have a child? If she were to have the child to make her happy, what if the child couldn't do that?—would that cause her to love the child less, to fling rocks and arrows at the child its whole life? She remembered reading in school the book *A Child Called It* and how devastatingly fragile a child views itself and the power that parents can lord over their kids. She wouldn't want to be that way. A child that is brought into this world just to make her happy would be an unhappy child. No, she must only have a child if the cause was because she wanted a child, no matter who that child became.

"You need to figure out your own happiness, Lillian," she said.

She parked her car in the driveway, grabbed her stuff and began walking to the front door when she felt a presence near her. She turned and saw someone standing just behind one of the yard's bushes. Lillian froze. Then, she was just about to turn and run to the front door when the presence stepped out from the bush.

"Hello Dr. Waters. It's me, Nick."

Lillian suddenly felt incredibly fearful—Nick, the delusional boy who thought he could save fictional characters an existence in character hell. He stood beside the bush with one arm behind his back as if he were holding something that he didn't want anyone to see.

"Dr. Nick! Oh, wow, you scared me," Lillian said, trying to find her keys in her purse.

"I found out where you lived because I wanted to talk with you," Nick said, moving a few steps closer to Lillian.

"Well, Dr. Nick, it's past my hours so maybe you could come to my office. How about tomorrow?"

"Oh, no that's okay. I don't need treatment anymore."

Lillian found her keys and began backing up to the door. "Well, if you just want to talk, that would be fine. Any time tomorrow would be fine."

"You don't have to be afraid doctor," Nick said. "I'm not here to hurt you."

"Oh, well, I didn't think that," Lillian stammered.

"Yes, you did. And maybe I should have come at a different time, but I just wanted to tell you that I no longer have delusions of characters and saving them and all that weird stuff."

"Oh, okay, yes, your treatment has been going really well." Lillian reached the door and unlocked it, but she felt Nick was right behind her. She turned. He stood just a few feet away.

"I just wanted to say thank you. You've really helped me," Nick said. "And I've brought you these." Nick took a bouquet of roses out from behind his back and handed them to Lillian.

Lillian didn't want to, but she reached out for the roses. She took them and was about to hurriedly close her door when something about Nick stopped her. His look, so forlorn and humble. "Thank you," she said. "They're beautiful."

"They came from my mom's garden. Don't worry. I asked her if I could bring them to you. I've been waiting for a long time actually, but I wanted to give them to you tonight."

"Are you okay? Feeling okay, Dr. Nick?"

"Yes, thank you, Dr. Waters. And I'm just Nick now. None of that Dr. Nick stuff anymore. It's going to be hard, but I'll have to find a way to live in the real world now. I'll live with my mom until I find a job, and move out then. Anyway, just wanted to say thank you again for helping me."

"Well, Nick, you're welcome. Thank you."

"Have a nice night, doctor," Nick said, turning to go. He walked along the driveway and into the street and was soon gone into the night.

Lillian closed the door, locked it and leaned against it and let out a deep breath. "*Mamma mia*," she finally said before heading upstairs to take a long shower.

Chapter 17

Luca spent the next week biting his upper lip until it bled, that perpetual nervous habit, looking at people looking at him, wondering if they knew that he knew there was a scandal going on under his nose. But, otherwise, he pretended not to know anything by going about his daily work and nobody came out and said anything to him. Even Stefano acted as if everything was as it should be.

The grapes in the vineyard were coming along nicely. The rain had really given them a boost and the sun had been tamed a bit, but Luca still felt the heat. Coming from Seattle, he wasn't used to the sweltering nature of the humidity—and the worst part, the *zanzare*, the mosquitos. They were relentless, and especially at night. Luca thought there must be a hole in his studio apartment's wall somewhere because at least one mosquito assassin found its way into his bedroom each night. He'd wake up and the hunt would be on as he slapped and scratched at his neck or face from where the blood had been sucked in exchange for poison. His vaulted ceilings didn't help either, but he got fairly adept at using his rolled-up socks as missiles to kill the mosquitos from afar.

Luca walked through the vineyards, checking the grapes and removing any large weeds out from under the vines that the sheep had passed over. He wondered how this would all end up. He didn't have to sit and ponder too long; Matilda called him after dinner just as he was about to take a shower. He heard the distress and agitation in her voice.

"Luca, I'm sorry, but I need some help," she said.

"Anything, what's wrong?"

"Luca, this isn't just anything. It's bad, in a big way. I can't—I can't even for sure want to ask you."

"What is it?"

"I'm coming over. Can you be ready to leave as soon as I get there?"

Luca ditched the shower idea and put on the clothes he had worn that day. He had no idea what was stressing Matilda out, but it must be bad. She arrived moments later; she must have been close. Luca met her in the street and they promptly drove off. He looked at her, and he saw the lines of her face, the stress lines on her forehead, a vein seemingly about to burst.

"What is it? What's wrong?"

"Listen, the officials are going to do a surprise visit tomorrow morning at the winery. I have a friend in the office and he warned me. They are cracking down on illegal wine production. The entire production that is there now will be lost and even big fines will have to be paid. Maybe even people will go to jail. Including my brother."

"But I thought the officials were technically paid off," Luca said.

"Yes, but it's bad—those officials weren't real. They were members of a different group that sometimes has fights with our group."

"You mean, a mafia family squabble?"

"What is squabble?"

"A fight, a mafia family fight," Luca said hurriedly.

"Yes, that's correct. They were fake officials and they are the ones I think who alerted the real officials of what we were doing there."

"But I thought this was all standard practice," Luca said. "Like, you've been doing this for years."

"Yes, but times are changing. They are beginning to get more and more organized. Less corruption. Which is good, but right now, it's not good for us."

"So what're we going to do?"

"*We* need to empty those tanks," Matilda said. "And make it look like somebody else did it."

"What? Are you serious?"

"Yes, it's the only way. They are coming first thing tomorrow to surprise Stefano. He'll be ruined. We *all* will be ruined."

Matilda drove quickly through the streets until she was out on the main roads and then she sped along like a light across the night sky. When they got to the winery, all was quiet. She parked alongside the roadway at the foot of the line of cypress trees. The moon overhead peeked out from some dark clouds, showering its light down upon the villa.

They got out and creeped along up to the tank room. There was a singular glow in the main villa and Luca could see Stefano's shadow through the window sitting in a chair reading and drinking some wine. Luca wished he were up by Stefano at that moment rather than down there with Matilda; the first time he would ever think that. They opened the door to the garage and stepped inside. Luca loved the smell of the tank room, the smell of juice being fermented and broken down into wine after the yeast had been added. It was his favorite smell in the whole world aside from freshly baked bread with olive oil and rosemary. But under the circumstances, there was no time to revel in its lushness.

"No lights," Matilda whispered. "Which tanks have the mixed wine?"

"I think all of them," Luca whispered back. "But anyway, we can't leave any because then it would look suspicious and not like a sabotage."

"Yes, you're right. Okay, let's start with these ones and work our way down the line. How should we do it?"

"I don't know, but let's do it fast. This place is going to fill up quick," Luca said.

Their clothes were going to be ruined, but it didn't matter. Time was pressing them onward. They twisted the wheel on the first tank, and it took a bit of strength. Luca had wondered if Matilda could have done this alone and now realized that it would have been impossible. The tanks were heavy. Finally, the wheel began to squeak and the wine began to pour out. Luca felt disgusted as the wine poured over his shoes and onto his jeans, disgusted that that beautiful liquid, that heavenly food for thought was sifting away into nothingness, never fully actualizing its purpose. But there was no time to dwell on that. They had to act fast and move on to the next tank.

They kept going down the line until all the tanks were emptied and wine was swimming and swirling down the drains. Matilda was soaked; Luca was soaked. Now what?

"Are the tanks the only ones with mixed wine?" Matilda asked.

"Yes, I believe so. That's all I saw when they were doing it. The wine in the barrels is from a different vintage or is only the riserva, I think. I don't know."

"We'll have to hope that's the case," Matilda said. "Let's go."

They creeped out of the winery and back down the driveway to Matilda's car. She started it and drove off in a hurry, only a dust cloud of guilt left behind.

Luca looked back to see Stefano standing at the window as they drove off.

\*\*\*\*

Matilda then drove to Luca's apartment. She took in a bag that had been in the back seat. Inside the apartment, she changed into spare clothes she kept from within the bag and applied makeup on her face. "I'm meeting a friend for a drink. The time won't be perfect, but she'll be my alibi. Do I have any marks or anything on my face?"

Luca looked at the beautifully stricken face of his lover. He kissed her forehead. "There's nothing I can see. What shall I do?"

"Don't tell me," Matilda said. "It's just better if I don't know. For all I know, you had dinner and stayed here all night. Now, go do whatever you want to do but don't tell me."

"I love you," Luca said.

"*Ti voglio bene amore*," Matilda said, kissing his lips and leaving quickly.

Luca decided then to take that shower. The water came down and melted away the adventure of the night and the ramifications of what they had just done. But then he began to wonder just what those ramifications were. What exactly had they done? Vandalism, yes. Sabotage, yes. But how did Italy look at those things? How would the mafia look at those things? He had been so caught up in what was happening and that Matilda was excited and scared that he hadn't really thought about what it was that they were doing. Was there any way they could get caught? What if she broke down and told someone? What if he did? Someone was certainly going to have to take the blame for the crime. It wasn't something that the winery was going to simply look past—something that the mafia would look past. And what if those who were blamed were another group of mafiosi? Someone would be punished; a war would start. Luca had no idea what kind of mafia regime this was or how seriously they took their positions. Certainly, Matilda would know the danger. He wished he could talk with her right then. He needed reassurances.

After the shower, Luca put on pajamas and cozied up in bed with a book, but he couldn't focus enough to read. He had a lamp on and closed his eyes with his wet hair on the pillow just how he liked it, dampening it enough to help him sleep. He had been doing that since he was a kid. Just as he was settling in, he thought he heard footsteps outside his front door. It was only eleven at night so that wasn't so strange, but the footsteps stopped and seemingly waited there. Perhaps it was his imagination.

Perhaps it was Matilda. But she would have knocked or texted him if she were coming over. No, it was probably his imagination. But then he heard a step, and then another. Had someone already found out about the wine? Perhaps they were seen somehow. Luca slowly put his feet down upon the floor—it creaked when he walked so he really wanted to focus on one step at a time. He stood up, put one foot forward, then another until he made his way into the hallway. He stood there and listened for a moment.

That's when he heard footsteps rapidly rush off. Luca quickly went to the door and looked out the peep hole. He couldn't see anything out there. He wasn't about to open the door though. Who could it have been? And why? To do what? Luca went to the kitchen and gulped down a glass of water. He went back to the front door, made sure it was locked and then went to his balcony to check the glass door. It was locked as well. He closed the curtains and went back to his room. He slipped into bed.

Luca closed his eyes and with all sorts of horrendous thoughts of what it all could mean, he tried to go to sleep knowing his dreams were going to be terrible, but then, bam, bam, bam. Someone was knocking at the front door. Luca jumped up and quickly ran to it, leaning against the wall just in case. He peered through the peep hole and saw Matilda standing out there. He quickly opened the door and she rushed in.

"Boy am I glad to see you!" Luca said. "Why did you come back? Why did you leave the first time actually?"

"What you mean? What first time?" Matilda asked.

"Just a few minutes ago. Weren't you just here?"

"No, I rushed over here after I left my friend. Why you ask?"

"Somebody was just here. They stood outside this door, but didn't knock or anything. I heard their footsteps and when I came to the door, they quickly ran away."

"This is not good, Luca," Matilda said.

"But why? How could anyone know anything already?"

"I don't know. I have a bad feeling about this." Matilda didn't mention that her brother had texted her and asked if she had somehow been near the winery that night. She didn't know how to respond. "I suppose I should tell you. My brother texted me and asked if I had been to the winery tonight. He must have seen my car as I drove off."

"*Che cazzo*," Luca said. "He knows. He's going to know. How can we deny it?"

"Listen, *tesoro*, please don't worry. I'll talk with my brother. No matter what, I'll leave your name out of it. Okay?"

"No, listen, I can't let you take this heat. Anyway, let's just not tell him, okay? You have an alibi, and I could have been anywhere tonight."

"He doesn't know about the tanks yet. Once he finds out, and once he finds out that the officials are coming tomorrow, he'll know what happened. He knows I have friends in the office and was probably tipped off. He'll figure it out."

"If he can figure it out, then Marco and Vincenzo can figure it out too."

"*Tesoro*, don't worry. Please, let me find a way out of this. Can we just pretend just for tonight that everything is okay and you and me can go to bed only thinking about us?"

"Since I might be dead soon, yes, let's do that," Luca said, feeling defeated.

****

Lillian met Sarah at their chic Italian restaurant because Sarah said she was already there, had already found a seat at the bar, had already opened a tab, had insisted that Antonio was not working, and because Sarah said Lillian needed to get over herself and buck up. So, Lillian put on a maroon wrap dress and made her way into the bar to her awaiting friend.

Lillian instantly stopped. Sarah was talking with Antonio who was sitting on a stool next to her. She saw Lillian and waved. Lillian couldn't back out of the restaurant now, so she put on her most disgruntled look and went over to them.

"Lillian! Hi, here, take this seat. I've been saving it for you," Antonio said.

"Thank you," Lillian said as casually as she could muster. "I didn't know you were working tonight."

"Oh, nah, not tonight. I'm just here with some friends. Enjoying the evening for once. Great seeing you. I'm sure you want to catch up with Sarah, but if you want to stop by my table," Antonio said, indicating a table close by. "I'd love to share a drink with you."

"Why don't you come up here any time you want to do a drink," Sarah said. "Easier on us."

"Lovely," Antonio said. "Okay, well, then, I'll see you both in a bit."

Lillian sat in the now vacant seat and ordered her usual martini.

"I see," Lillian said. "He's not working, that's true, but he's definitely here."

"*And*, he made a point to mention that he is here with friends. So, I asked him where his girlfriend was, and he said that they are no longer an item. He said she was too, and then he stopped and said he didn't want to air out his dirty laundry, but I insisted he tell me. So, he said she was too superficial and he ended it. And I know exactly why he wanted to tell me all these things."

"Oh posh," Lillian said. "You know nothing of the sort. He probably wants to date you."

Lillian told Sarah about her lack of fertility, about

Cassandra and her daughter, and about Nick.

"Cassandra sounds like hell. She'll be kicking herself once her daughter spirals into her own deep depression. And what's up with that guy Nick? Sounds like a serial killer in the making."

"I don't think so. Socially awkward, yes, but I think he's moving in the right direction."

"I'm sorry to hear about the baby result."

"Maybe it's not meant to be."

At that moment, Antonio came up to the bar and offered to take a drink with them. They acquiesced and each took another martini.

"So, what were you saying earlier about breaking up with your girlfriend?" Sarah asked.

"Sarah, Jesus," Lillian said.

"No, it's okay. Yes, it's true. We're no longer together and I'm happy. So, my friends are taking off, but…"

"Where're they going?" Sarah asked.

"Some club down in Sodo," Antonio said.

"Why don't you stay here with us?" Sarah said.

"Yeah? I won't be a third wheel? I'm not really feeling the club."

"What do you think, Lillian?" Sarah asked.

"Yeah, stay with us," Lillian said.

That night, Antonio invited Lillian back to his place and she decided to go. His apartment was close to the restaurant and very much a bachelor's pad. They had some wine, Antonio put on some music, and Lillian decided to just enjoy herself. Antonio kissed her and she felt she could just lean back and absorb his body. They kissed slowly; they were in no hurry. It was almost as if they had already been lovers and were reconnecting after a few years, timidly enough. Antonio took her hand and took her into his bedroom. He closed the door and Lillian decided to just enjoy the evening.

****

The sun shone brightly into Luca's room. Matilda lay sleeping soundly next to him and he seemingly forgot all about the last night's excursion. What mattered to Luca was that his lover, the beautiful, intelligent, amazing woman that lay next to him, was safe. He knew that he would never let her be in harm's way, not if he could help it. It was strange feeling that way; he couldn't even remember feeling that way with Lillian, but he wondered if his drinking had clouded his emotions so much that it had been impossible for him to feel anything real back then. He thought about how much better he felt since he laid off drinking for drinking's sake. Even the wine he drank with dinner tasted better. He could identify idiosyncrasies and aromas better, taste profiles better, and he could evaluate the wine more succinctly. All his senses seemed to harmoniously complement each other. His body felt healthy and more than anything, his mind felt clear. He could feel again. He could love again. And he did love. He loved the woman next to him and she loved him. It seemed that this was the way things were supposed to go. He had spent years of his life ruining his own and others, but there was still time, time for redemption.

There was a knock at the door, a hard knock.

Matilda sprang up, dressed only in her underwear. She quickly put her clothes on as if she knew who was behind that door. Luca felt all the fear and stress and worry bash right back into him. He got out of bed, put clothes on quickly as the pounding at the door kept on.

He heard his next door neighbor come out and address those outside the door only to receive a barrage of harsh words. The neighbor must have slunk back into her apartment as Luca heard the door softly close. At least perhaps if they were killed, the neighbor would be able to identify the murderers—if she would do it.

He couldn't possibly pretend he wasn't home. Eventually, they would be found. There was no running. Luca looked at Matilda who seemed like a completely different person, a woman frail and afraid. Luca remembered what he had thought just moments before, protecting his lover.

"You hide in the closet," Luca whispered. "I'll see who it is."

"No, *amore*, I'm staying here with you," she whispered back.

There was no changing her mind. He went to the front door and opened it. Marco stood in front of him along with two other guys Luca had never seen before. Marco investigated the small apartment and saw Matilda defiantly staring back at him.

"So, it's true," Marco said to Matilda. "You've betrayed us all."

"I saved us all," Matilda said. "The officials are at the winery even now, I'm sure."

"You cost us a fortune on a foolish whim."

"The wine is insured," Matilda retorted.

"The prestige of having wine is not. And how does it make us look? We ditch wine as soon as a sniff of officialdom comes about. We would have dealt with the officials. But, *you*, on your period probably, suddenly rush to save us all by pouring out the wine. Is she all bloody right now, Luca? Is she gushing with blood? You like that sort of thing?"

"You're disgusting," Luca said.

"Oh, no, it's you who is about to become disgusting, so disgusting that your lover is going to raise her nose at your stink. Then what will you think of her? How she easily leaves you just like she easily left the wine all over the floor. You're next my friend. You can come with us now the easy way or the hard way."

"You're really enjoying this, *eh* Marco? This is what you enjoy the most. A little man feeling big? Just like you do in your damn car racing the roadways, *eh* Marco?" Matilda said.

Marco addressed the guys next to him. "Take Luca and put him into the car."

"I'm not going anywhere without Matilda," Luca said.

"Oh, she's coming too."

Marco's goons grabbed Luca and pulled him outside onto the balcony. They pushed him forward and down the stairs and into the backseat of a black SUV. Luca decided it was probably best not to make a scene as it probably would only put the neighbors in danger and there really wasn't much he could do anyway.

Marco stood blocking the doorway. He looked at Matilda. "Vincenzo wants to see you."

"I'm sure he does," Matilda said, but her voice wavered just enough that Marco heard it.

"I'd be scared too if I were you," he said. "You've caused a lot of problems for us."

Chapter 18

The goons put a black hood over Luca's head and all went dark.

He heard the front door open and the vehicle quickly absconded away indicating that Marco was the one driving. If Matilda was in the vehicle, she kept quiet the entire ride. They jerked left and right and Luca constantly elbowed his side companions. With Marco driving and not being able to see anything, his stomach was even more queasy than usual. They never seemed to catch a straightaway before they finally arrived at whatever destination they were supposed to be at.

The goons took Luca out of the car and had him walk, tripping over rocks and roots without helping him find his way. He heard a door open, something that sounded like a cellar and he was forced to march down some steps and seemingly underground. After what seemed like a long hallway, he was shoved into a room and he heard the door close behind him and lock.

He took the hood off. He was in a cell with stone walls and an earthen floor. There weren't any windows but only a dark door to what would probably never be his freedom. He slunk against the wall and sat down.

****

Matilda was taken to another part of the estate and into a villa. She had been there many times before when she was dating Vincenzo. She knew that since Luca was there in the cellar jails, they weren't planning on simply letting him leave. Knowing Vincenzo, there was a plan and she was sure she was an integral part of it, but even she could not design what it was in his mind. Most certainly, they would just kill her and Luca and be done with it.

Inside the villa, Vincenzo sat at a grand desk looking at some papers or at least pretending to—Matilda knew he always liked to look like he was doing something, something important. Marco led Matilda to a chair in front of the desk and had her sit down.

"*Grazie* Marco. And the other?"

"In the cellar," Marco said.

"Good, thank you." Marco left the villa, got into his sports car and drove off. Vincenzo shrugged his shoulders, tried to appear calm, but inside he wanted to rip Luca's head off in front of Matilda and watch her as she watched her lover die a horrible death. Instead he folded his hands out in front of him and smiled at her. "It's been a while since I last saw you. You're as beautiful as ever."

"Where's my brother?" Matilda said.

"He's alive if that's what you mean," Vincenzo said.

This seemed to calm Matilda, but only for a moment.

"Really, you should be angry with him. He's the one who told us everything."

"What do you mean?"

"*Allora*, he saw a car leaving the winery late last night. And Marco and myself were already coming to visit him to tell him about the officials coming to see the winery in the morning. See, we already knew that. Your little stunt was stupid. You didn't think we already knew what was going to happen?

"Stefano told us everything though. It would have been a perfect crime if he hadn't seen your car driving off. See, he told us he thought he saw you leaving the winery before we found out about the tanks. But, once we checked the tanks and saw what happened, we knew exactly who did it. You see, when we arrived, apparently you had just left, and as we came in, Stefano murmured something about having thought he saw you leave and wondered if we were supposed to meet you at the winery, but you had to go off for some reason, blah, blah, blah. Actually, you can't really blame Stefano. He had no idea that you had betrayed everyone. Except, he knew you had betrayed me."

"I never betrayed you," Matilda said. "You just can't get the idea that we are not together anymore."

"Yes, except, *that* is where you are wrong."

"You never could get it."

"No, it is you who cannot get it. You see, maybe you love this American, maybe you don't. It's so hard to tell with you. But, we are going to find out."

"What are you going to do to him?"

"It's up to you," Vincenzo said, callously, calmly. "You see, killing a man is so final. You never really get to know how they feel about being dead or about who killed them. No, it's better if you can watch a man suffer knowing that the one thing he loves in life rejects him completely and never loved him. And in fact, used him for some terrible purpose. And that's how you are going to make him feel. If you truly love him, you'll make him think you never did. And if you don't love him, then he is useless and we'll just kill him. Slowly of course. You know how Marco is."

"What do you want from me? You want me to hurt my lover so you can feel good about yourself? You'll never feel good about yourself. You know why? Because you have a terrible, rotten core and you hate yourself."

"That hurts Matilda. I love myself. And I want so much more than just you hurting your lover. No, no, you don't understand at all. Go back to what I said. We are together. You and me. Always together. And you will see that you love me again and that this American was just a fascination. I can understand that. He's Italian, sort of. But, anyway, I'm happy we are together again. We shall be dining tonight at La Casa di Firenze to celebrate. Is everything clear?"

"And my brother?"

"My soon-to-be brother-in-law is doing just fine. He's excited to be a part of the family."

Matilda thought for a moment, but she saw no way out of the situation. There was only one way to save Luca and her brother. "Let's get this over with," she said.

"Oh, I should have made myself clearer. The American will be staying in the cell for a while. If you rushed there now, he wouldn't believe a word you said. No, we have to wait so that whatever you say to him, he'll know it's the truth. And we need to be married first."

"No, impossible. That's too cruel."

"Matilda, you're a brilliant woman. Of course you see that it only makes the most perfect sense. Forget about him for a while. Your only concern is us. And think of your brother of course."

"*Bastardo*," Matilda said.

"I always loved your tongue, but when we're married, it will have to change."

\*\*\*\*

David picked up his rocks glass and filled it to the brim with scotch, took a long pull and then reached for his phone. He thought for a moment and then pressed the button. The phone rang a few times and then he hung up. He sipped some more scotch and looked around the room.

He had a fire going as usual, a lamp lit so if he got the urge to read, it would be ready. He was always prepared to do his usual nighttime activities, but lately, they couldn't hold his attention. For the first time in his life, he felt that he couldn't do what he always did to calm his mind—read. No, reading didn't hold his imagination as it once did. Not since Francesca had died. And he wanted so desperately to see Diana. He knew it was stupid, but he needed her. He needed somebody in his life, even if it was a façade. He needed a distraction from the mundane and woeful life he led.

He called her again. She answered this time after four rings. David heard the chatter of what seemed like a multitude of voices. He heard music and laughter.

"Hello, hello?" Diana screamed into the phone.

"Diana, hello, how are you?"

"Sorry, can't hear very well. Who is this?" The sting of those words David wasn't prepared for. He didn't know what to say. "Hello, anyone there? Okay, I'm hanging up."

"Diana, it's me, David."

"David? Oh hi, hi, hi, how are you?"

"Oh, I'm okay. Is now not a good time to talk?"

David heard a voice in the background that sounded incredibly close. "Hey, babe, who is it? Take another hit huh?"

"Who's that?" David asked.

"Go lay down, Charlie. Give me a second," Diana said to the voice, Charlie. "David, you there? Hey David, boy what a trip it is down here. You wouldn't believe it."

"Well, I have some time. I was hoping to come visit you."

"Oh nice, nice," Diana said. "Charlie, lay off."

"You're just a tease," Charlie said.

"David, what were you saying?"

David didn't know what was going on, where Diana was or what she was doing, but it didn't sound good. He knew he didn't like this Charlie fellow. "I want to come see you," he said, loudly into the phone.

"Oh, David, now's not good. Really not good. I just started working and I'm working a lot."

"Oh? Are you in a movie? A play?"

"No, nothing like that. Acting in a way, trying to make ends meet of course."

"Just let me feel," Charlie said.

David felt as if Charlie were in his ear. Charlie was obviously trying to do something to Diana that she didn't want him to do. "Hey, maybe I need to come down there and have a few words with this guy Charlie."

"No, no, he's harmless. David, we're sort of seeing each other," Diana said.

"What do you mean? You and Charlie?"

"Yeah, sort of. You know how it is."

David didn't know how it was and that was frustrating. He had had enough scotch to know that he didn't like Charlie, but also enough to not be able to communicate very well how he felt. He knew he felt defeated and that something wrong was happening, but maybe Diana didn't want to see him anymore. "Do you want me to come down soon? I could take you away from Los Angeles for a spell and get you out of the city and into some fresh air."

"David, that's sweet. But no, I'm working now and am totally immersing myself into L.A. Look, I need to go. Take care, okay, David?"

"Oh, um, talk soon, okay?"

"Bye, David."

Diana hung up and David listened to the static of the phone or what he thought was the static of the phone for a moment. Finally, he set the phone down and took up his drink again. When empty, he poured another and once again, watched the flames into the dead of night.

****

Luca awoke again into darkness. It had been some time since Matilda walked out on him. He tried to go back to sleep; that's all he could do. To sleep and to dream, of beautiful days, but his dreams were filled with worms, spiders, and rats gnawing away at his brain and gorging on his insides. He felt he was dying and that couldn't come soon enough. Yes, to die, to sleep, an eternal sleep or a chance to be with God—either way, death seemed the better choice.

The memories of Matilda and her joy of being with him were too much against the shock of reality. She had chosen her way out, to destroy him and to destroy whatever they had, so that she could live. But what life would she live knowing her lover was wasting away in a cell in his own filth, starving to death, thinking the thoughts of a broken lover, thoughts that would kill him, kill his beating heart.

The way she had looked at him without love, without remorse, without guilt was the knife through the heart. Her eyes had been glazed over with malice even, a flare of hate, as if she were perturbed that she had to make that choice in her life—it was his fault, his fault that they had met, had fallen in love with each other, had built a beautiful thing to fruition and then just like that, the fear of a jealous lover opened up the pen and killed the fattened calf. "*Non significa niente per me.*" Those words had sealed any lasting hope for life.

He had felt destitute before, lying in his cell at the county jail with nothing to read, nothing to watch, nothing to do. He had been at his lowest point, his basest point with alcohol destroying his life. He had abandoned God for a life of hedonism, a life of pleasure seeking, a life escaping reality through the allures of an emollient liquid.

But he had never truly found happiness. The drinking always led to pain and suffering and forgetfulness. How strange it was that almost half his life he had forgotten—so many nights, so many adventures—just simply blackened memories of shadows. Shadow people, shadowy words, shadowy movements. He had felt loads of shame and embarrassment. That's what alcohol had given him. Escaped time and memories of shadows—and pain, how he had hurt Lillian, how he had abandoned his mother because his self-seeking life was always more important. And then Lillian left him; and his mother died. Both gone from his life and what did he have to replace them? Nothing but shame and loneliness. He had given up on God. What was God but an idea? God wasn't tangible enough for this world, his world.

This nascent plan to give up the false pleasures, the wrong path to get to the right path had yielded terrible results. But maybe that was his karma, his fate, his lot in life. The few months he had of giving up drinking for drinking's sake and meeting the woman he thought he was meant for, falling in love with, wanting to give up all things terrible for—all ended in a cell just like before. But this time there was no release, no hope. He was going to die there, a starved animal without anything but his renewed conversations with God—Neale Donald Walsch suddenly came to mind—and a playback track on how he had succumbed to his fate. At least he had those before his mind eventually would turn stark raving mad. What was better, to die sane and dejected or to die insane and warped?

He had gone through the events that led to his being where he was. His mother's passing, his DUI, his divorce with Lillian, even his subsequent debauchery with alcohol and his failed womanizing. A life of ruin his gravestone would read. No—there wouldn't be a gravestone. He would be burned or buried without rock or chisel. His death wouldn't be immortalized for anyone. His memory would be a passing thought in the minds of his friends and family—those who were left at least.

"Whatever happened to that Luca who went to Italy and never came back?" one would say.

"Oh, probably fell in love with an Italian enchantress and now has four babies crawling all over him," another would respond.

Even his make-believe characters in his mind didn't truly know who he was. Oh, but he supposed that would have been close. Matilda, his Italian enchantress, was real, had been real, at least she seemed real. How fickle love is! He couldn't blame her for saving herself. Both shouldn't have to die. Would it be better if she were in here with him?—absolutely not. Then they would experience the worst of humanity together. No, that would be too much. Perhaps she saved him some pain by saving herself. Yes, that's exactly right. She was saving him from the utmost pain. Yes, that's true, that's correct, that's what a lover would have done. She still loved him enough to save him from the worst pain there was— seeing his lover in a decrepit state. He couldn't think any thought other than that she had saved him from the worst kind of pain—yes, she had saved him.

Luca looked over his withering body, shivering, still in the cold of the mud. He still felt the elements, his senses still were triggered by his surroundings. He wasn't dead yet. As long as his mind was still there, he must think of things to keep him alive. His mother. Soon, perhaps he would be reunited with his mother, his father, his family that had all passed. He only remembered snippets of his father, but his mother bore the brunt of his tumultuous life's journey. What a trooper she had been! What a saint! She had loved him no matter what and he had taken her for granted until the very end. Thank God she found David. Oh the regrets, so many regrets. He hoped that if there was reincarnation, he would remember this life and what he had learned. He wanted to be reincarnated into somebody who helps people, leads a good life.

Luca closed his eyes and tried to sleep again, sleep away into death. He pondered what it would be like to die. Would a figment of a soul rise up from his body, hovering ponderously over a sleeping Luca, perhaps an out-of-body experience, then finally settling in on the fact that he was dead, would then move about as a ghost or be welcomed somehow by a host of angels…his mother came back to him with the means of locomotion, the means to move his bed or at least Luca felt the bed move and felt her presence. So, then were spirits temporarily poltergeist before moving on to the next world or the next body? Strange to think he would know this all soon enough. But, what if, just what if when he died, literally nothing happened—there was no God, there was no afterlife or after beginning…then what? He supposed it wouldn't matter to him as he just wouldn't know. It would be like going to sleep as he did every night, but this time not waking up. One could not fear that because not only would he never know if that were what happened, but it also couldn't be stopped. Why worry? What was worse, an eternity in hell or a forever sleep without consciousness or dreams? Forty years old and he still didn't know the answer to that question.

Luca opened his eyes and sat up against the wall. He had slept too long and his thoughts raced. Where was Matilda now? Hopefully she was safe and trying to get out of her own mess. That man, Vincenzo, was a devil. Luca could think of revenge, but at this point, why bother. That was hopeless; everything was hopeless.

****

Matilda frantically gathered up clothes and shoved everything into a suitcase. She quickly emptied her bathroom of makeup, a hair dryer, and anything else she might need. She could only grab a few pairs of shoes and a couple of books, a picture of her and Stefano with their parents, and some small mementos. She took both her suitcases and ran out the door and down the stairs where her car awaited her by the curb. She flung her suitcases in the back and sat down in the front. She started the car and then called Stefano as she drove off.

"Matilda? Where have you been? Vincenzo is in frenzy. He's coming to your apartment right now," Stefano said.

"Yes, I'm leaving. I left. I'm on my way out of here."

"Where are you going?"

"Stefano, I can't say yet. It's better if nobody knows. I'm changing my phone too so nobody will be able to contact me or trace me. I'll contact you when I feel safe. You need to leave as well."

"Matilda, what's going on?"

"Stefano, I need you to do something for me. Please!"

"Anything, what is it?"

\*\*\*\*

David ate a meager dinner and then took a bottle of eighteen-year scotch outside. He set up a plastic fold-up checkered chair next to the garden and poured himself a full glass. He tried calling Luca via his phone app, but once again, nothing. He hadn't been able to get ahold of Luca for a couple of months and was beyond worried. It was unlike him not to call or email. David knew that grape growing was getting into its busiest time, but still, it didn't make a whole lot of sense that Luca hadn't reached out in some capacity.

Everyone had left him in some way. He wondered if he had any more use on this earth. Why not simply go into death to see his beloved Francesca again, if that's how it worked. He hoped so. He didn't really know what to expect, but being with Francesca for so many years, her religion sort of grew on him. Believing that he would be spending time with his beloved wife again was the only way to get through this life. He sipped his scotch and watched the bees buzz in and around the tulips and daisies. The roses that grew near the fence line were in full bloom—reds, yellows, and whites. David had some vegetables growing: zucchini, carrots, and green onion. He had tomatoes within green cages set up. The garden offered glimpses of solace.

He continued sipping his scotch until it was gone. He poured another glass. He tried calling Luca again, but still nothing. He just wanted to talk, to hear Luca's voice, to hear what was going on in his life, a young man's life so full still of promise. He had emailed and emailed and no response—the sudden thought occurred that something might be wrong, that Luca was in danger. He would try calling again in the morning and if Luca didn't answer, he would contact the authorities to see what they could find. Yes, a good idea.

As the sun sank down, David felt like he couldn't move. He didn't want to move either. He took a long pull of his scotch and finished the glass; he poured another. He loved the summer evenings when the sun began to set. The desert proffered perfectly cool nights, the pride and joy really of the place. His head felt drowsy, but he wasn't ready for bed; he knew he wasn't going to read that night. Oh Francesca, how she loved these evenings out by her garden. She could sit out there for hours just talking with him. How he missed those times.

What a beautiful life he had had with his beloved, he thought. How she made his whole life meaningful and happy. He never thought he had been lonely, but once he met Francesca, he knew what true happiness was and he never wanted to be without her again. He always thought he would be the first to go. Being with her made him feel good about himself; perhaps that's why some of his students began to take an interest in him. He almost ruined his whole life back then. Don't think of that now, he thought. Only good thoughts, only good times.

David finished the bottle into his glass and sipped slowly to savor the scotch and the memories that were coming to him. All the places he and Francesca had seen together. All the conversations of books and characters—she really had been interested in English literature, which just fascinated David as she had been born and raised in Italy. But she took on her new country with a zealous pride. And she wanted to absorb anything and everything written in English, the classics at least. David laughed thinking that some of the first books she read had been her favorites of all time—*Charlotte's Web* and *Do Not Open* by Brinton Turkle. The latter he must have read to her fifteen times. Those simple nights were filled with so much pleasure.

David knew his heart was grieving and that he was tired. He finished off the scotch in his glass and closed his eyes thinking of the day he would see again his beloved Francesca.

Chapter 19

Luca sat upright with all the strength he could muster. He heard the sharp clanking of doors opening, but haphazardly and quickly. He had no idea what time it was, but it must have been time to eat something or better yet, to drink something. His throat was extremely parched—so dry he thought flakes of the skin of his tongue were being swallowed. He couldn't remember the last time he peed.

He heard the jangling of keys outside his cell and the failing attempts to open the door. That was strange, but Luca paid no mind. He just wanted, needed water. He thought without water, that day would be his last. Suddenly, he heard what he thought was someone screaming his name, a voice from the other side. Perhaps he was dying at that moment. That would be okay too. Better to die than to face his abusers again.

Then, he felt a draft and just as suddenly, he was being raised in the air, but if he thought he was going to see his body lying on the ground and his spirit being whisked off to another plane, he was wrong. He was being carried he realized by a human. He was being carried away from the cell, and then suddenly, out into the piercing light. He couldn't see; he had to keep his eyes closed it was so bright.

"Luca," the voice said. "I'm getting you out of here. Hold on, my friend."

Luca couldn't understand the words, his mind not having thought in Italian for some time and his mind not working even in English all that well, but the voice sounded frantic and yet soothing to him, as if it cared about him. He was taken some ways and then the person carrying him set him over a shoulder as a car door opened. Then, he felt he was set down and oozed into the seat of wherever he was.

Stefano jumped into the driver's seat and finally looked closely at Luca. He looked like death. His lips were completely chapped, almost worn away, his body frail and dilapidated, he stunk of human feces and body odor. Stefano only had a little water left in his bottle, but he slowly opened Luca's mouth. "Drink Luca, drink a little." Stefano poured drops of water into Luca's mouth slowly so that none would spill. "We'll get more as soon as we can."

"Thank you," Luca said to the voice.

Stefano put the car in gear and drove off quickly.

****

"*Bastardi*," Vincenzo yelled once they busted into Matilda's apartment and ransacked her rooms. Much was missing, but it seemed that she had just left. He could still smell her scent. "She's fled," he said to Marco.

"She must be going to the villa to save Luca," Marco said.

"Let's go," Vincenzo screamed.

They jumped into Marco's car and sped off. Marco drove through the streets of Siena ignoring the blocked off zones. He finally got on the highway and drove dangerously and erratically toward Montepulciano.

"Take 438," Vincenzo said. "Less traffic right now."

It was an hour drive, but Marco wanted to see if he

could get there in just over half that and he loved the curves along SP 438. He drove, passing cars quickly on the right. He was going faster than he felt like he had ever gone, at least for an extended period. They would catch Matilda and Luca and he was going to gut Luca right there in front of his witch.

Vincenzo dialed Matilda's number frantically. Oh, what he would say to her! Oh, what he would do to her! There wouldn't be a next time like before. He was going to go all out. Nobody, nobody got one over on him. The phone cut out and went straight to a number service that said the phone no longer had an operator. "*Che cazzo,*" he yelled furiously. "*Va fan culo!*" He hung up, gripped the phone in his hand as if he were going to crush it, but then dialed Stefano instead. Stefano's phone rang and rang, but no one answered. "They must be together. They're doing this together. They're dead. All of them are dead. Drive faster!"

Marco raised his brows and whistled. He was more than ready. He pushed the pedal down and swerved around a corner, just barely missing an oncoming truck.

Vincenzo counted off all the ways he was going to torture the three of them. Luca and Stefano would be first so that Matilda would have to watch. Vincenzo took pleasure in that. Then, he thought of all the various ways he would make Matilda suffer.

A dreadful gleam flashed from his eyes as Marco went to pass a string of slower moving vehicles. Marco punched the gas as he swung out from the line of vehicles and raced to try and get in front of them all. He was coming to Dead Man's Curve just as he was about to reach the last couple of cars—

But then he saw why everyone had slowed down.

A large tractor was on the right-side of the road up ahead and the cars had slowed down to pass it one at a time. Marco blew passed them and was just about to get to the head car—a large truck came barreling down the highway on the other side. In the same lane as Marco and Vincenzo.

"*Che cazzo*," Marco yelled.

The tractor, coming to the bridge, veered into the main roadway.

Marco, about to ram into the truck head on, swerved right, avoided the truck—

But his car's bumper caught the back end of the tractor as he had tried to correct his line, overcorrecting and clipping the back end. The sports car swung around into a 360-degree turn, tires squealing, smoke rising into the air.

Then the front end of the left-side of the car smashed into the road barrier over the bridge, but the force of the impact and speed at which Marco had been driving had enough inertia force to propel the car into a spin—flinging it up and over the side.

The car fell from the bridge tail first.

Both men screamed.

They fell quickly down to the river, the impact bursting the back window out. As the water burst into the car, the force of the impact felt like a crushing blow to their backs. The water crashed into their seats propelling them forward into the windshield, which shattered easily like both their necks.

Marco was killed on impact, not receiving the torture of drowning. Vincenzo, broken and bleeding out, his blood flowing downstream, only looked through murky waters up at the sun shining brightly into the

sinking car before closing his eyes and awaiting death.
\*\*\*\*

Lillian had missed her period and after a few days of waiting, she rushed to a store to get a pregnancy test. Her hands were shaking as she opened the package and read the instructions. She fulfilled the test and waited. Time seemed to stand still. When the water marks showed up, she saw but did not see. She couldn't believe it. She saw two vertical lines. She checked the box. Two vertical lines meant pregnant. How? Impossible. There was just no way…

She didn't know what to feel. She was overjoyed and scared, and scared that Antonio didn't want to be a father—but she wanted the baby. Yes, she did and she would be an amazing mother even if Antonio didn't want to be the father to the baby. But she was happy, she was so happy, she was in love already with the baby of the future. She called Sarah first.

"You have to call Antonio right away," Sarah said. "Damn, that man must have packed a punch!"

"Sarah!"

"I'm so happy for you!"

She waited to call Antonio; what would she say? She needed a shot of gin; no, she had a baby inside her. She had a baby inside her? No gin, no vodka, no nothing and she loved that that was now her choice—none or none. She called Antonio. She felt frantic. As soon as he answered, she just went into it. "Antonio, I'm sorry, it's impossible but somehow it happened and I'm so happy, but if you don't want to be there, I understand. I mean, we hardly know each other. But it's really a miracle because I never thought it would ever happen."

"Lillian, Lillian, calm down. I don't know what

you're talking about. What happened?"

"It's just a miracle. I didn't think it could happen since I'm thirty-six, but it happened. Antonio, don't be mad or sad or angry or whatever. But—I'm pregnant. I somehow got pregnant."

Silence.

And then finally, Antonio spoke. "Lillian, please tell me, are you serious? And, like, I'm the father for sure?"

"Yes, you have to be the father." Lillian laughed with tears in her eyes. "But, if you don't want to be the father, I understand. I do. I'm just so happy, I wanted to tell you."

"No, wait. Hold on. Just give me time to catch my breath. Um, wow, okay, I'm just, I'm flabbergasted. Wow, just one night. It was only one night. That's amazing."

"Amazing? You mean that? Really?"

"Yeah, I mean, yeah. I, I, I, need to see you. Can I come over?"

"Yes, yes, come over right now."

Lillian hung up the phone and began to cry. She couldn't believe it. She was going to have a baby, a beautiful, soul of a baby. Her whole world was going to change. Whether Antonio was ultimately going to be there for the baby or not, she would. She loved that baby already. That baby was now a part of her.

****

Stefano had heard about the accident the next day as he was trying to nurse Luca back to health with water, soup, and sun. They were staying at a hotel in Lucca. Stefano couldn't believe the fate of Marco and Vincenzo and what that meant for Luca, Matilda, and himself. He didn't know who else was involved necessarily in the scheme, but he knew Marco and Vincenzo had been the ring leaders. Perhaps no one else knew what was going on—or at least didn't know the full extent of the operation and they were safe. He had no idea.

Luca slept, but with ill dreams. He tossed and turned at night, but Stefano took this as a better sign, a sign that he could move again. His body had looked pretty much done when Stefano had found him, a mere corpse. A few days of good Italian eating would brighten him up though. Stefano checked to make sure Luca was sleeping and when satisfied, went out into Lucca to get a coffee and see if there was any more news.

He went to a cafe, took an espresso and a newspaper. But the television was what caught his ears. He asked the bartender to turn it up.

"A local inquisition has yielded some results," the newscaster was saying. "Without warrants, or quickly processed warrants, the carabinieri have raided the wineries of Mr. Nardone Pazzo at Montepulciano and Greve in Chianti. The results of the raid are not known at this time, but word is that much illegal activity has been found at both locations. Activity ranging possibly from drugs to illegal wine making to hostages and captives. As we learn more, this story will be updated."

Stefano finished his espresso. If Nardone Pazzo was brought before a judge, the whole operation down south could also be exposed. Stefano never asked questions about that, but he knew it was bigger down there. Montepulciano and Greve were just outposts run by goons like Marco and Vincenzo. Down in Rome and Naples, the real world of gang warfare was happening. Anyway, Stefano thought, his job was pretty much as good as dead, but that was okay. He could find work at a fully legal winery. Now, to get back to his patient.

Luca woke to his strange environment, but it felt comfortable and warm and he felt better than he had the last couple of months. His memory was foggy, but he did remember being carried out of his cell and rescued. By whom he had no idea. He sat up in bed and looked around the room—there was a dining room table, a couch, some end tables, a small kitchen. He was either in an incredibly small studio or a hotel room. He got out of bed and went to get a drink of water; he was still so parched. Luca was happy he could keep his eyes open again, but he constantly blinked from the light coming in through the curtained window.

He looked down at his body and realized he wasn't wearing any clothes and that he didn't have any clothes to put on. That's when he heard someone outside the front door. Luca quickly jumped back into bed just as Stefano opened the door and came in. Stefano laughed at Luca's predicament.

"Ah, you're awake! And you realize you are naked," Stefano said.

"Stefano! *Mamma mia*, it's you? Are you the one who saved me?"

"Saved you? Yes, in a way. I came on the rescue mission, but on orders."

"Orders? From who?"

"You know who. She called me hysterically and begged me to go and get you. Don't worry, she didn't have to beg too much. I would have anyway."

"So, she didn't abandon me completely—"

"She didn't abandon you at all," Stefano insisted. "We all had to think and figure out what to do, but things were moving quickly, and Vincenzo had a close eye on everyone."

"Where is Matilda? Is she safe?"

"Safe, yes. Very safe as far as I know, but I don't know where she is. She got rid of her phone after calling me to go and get you and doesn't have one now. And she left. I have no idea where she is. She will have to contact us."

"Those bastards. They'll be after us. They'll find us. We can't run forever. I can run back to the United States, but what about you guys?"

At that moment, they both heard a knock at the door. Luca quickly sat up in bed, his eyes widening, the fear welling up inside him once again. Stefano only smiled and opened the door. Maria burst into the room, hugging first Stefano and then rushing over to the confused Luca.

"You're okay, you're okay. I can't believe it," Maria shouted. "Stefano told me all the plans and it just seemed impossible to escape."

"But I was just asking Stefano," Luca said, nappy to see Maria was safe as well, at least for the moment. "I can run, but you?"

"Maybe we won't have to run," Stefano said. "I guess you wouldn't know. Marco and Vincenzo are dead."

"What? How?"

"Fate," Stefano said. "A car accident on their way to get you, me, and Matilda. And you know what they would have done if they had found us."

"I can imagine," Luca said. "Wow, dead. Unbelievable. But how?"

"They hit a tractor and fell off a bridge. Dead Man's Curve."

"I know that place. Dead Man's Curve. Of course.

Is it over then?"

"The head boss, Nardone Pazzo, is getting indicted on all sorts of charges I believe. So, maybe for now, it's over."

"Does Matilda know all this?"

"I don't think so. Otherwise, she would have contacted us by now."

**\*\*\*\***

The next few days were terrible, waiting and waiting and waiting for Matilda to contact Stefano. She must not have heard about Vincenzo and Marco. But there was a nagging thought that maybe she didn't want to get found even if she did know. Perhaps she had escaped and would stay hidden. How much did Luca really know about her?

They were in Stefano's apartment in Greve. Luca paced the living room wondering what to do next. Stefano was out asking around about work. The scandal surely would tarnish his reputation, but perhaps he would find something. Where could Matilda be? Somewhere in Italy? Or...? Yes, of course, why not? Luca got on the internet and booked a flight. He called Stefano and asked if he could get a ride to the airport later that evening.

Stefano came home from a day without results, but he heard Luca's enthusiasm so he felt happy nonetheless.

"You think she's there?" Stefano asked.

"I think it's our best shot," Luca said.

Luca said goodbye to Stefano, said that he would be seeing Maria and him soon and that he would call either way. He boarded the plane and was whisked off shortly after. Upon landing, he took a train into the city and then walked the rest of the way. It was rather late by the time he found the flat, but he brightened up when he saw that a light was coming out of the living room. The front door was locked so he knocked. Nothing. Nobody came to the door, nor could he see anyone moving around through the window.

Then he heard a door open the next flat over. An elderly woman came out onto her stoop and looked at Luca. "What do you want?"

"Matilda, do you know Matilda? Is she here?"

"Ah, your accent; you're American. You must be the man she's waiting for. No, she's not here now."

Luca's face fell, gloomy and crestfallen, and he looked downward toward the ground. He had such hopes that she would be at their special place, the one place that she said if they ever got separated, they would meet at.

The woman must have seen Luca's disappointment. "No, no, I mean she's not here now. She went to the store to fetch some onions and garlic. I didn't have any here at my place. See, she's cooking something. She should be back any moment."

And at that moment, Matilda appeared around a corner with a shopping bag in her hand. She saw Luca and stopped short. Her eyes, large olive ovals, couldn't believe that he was there. Luca found himself running toward his lover as the old woman looked on with a smile. They embraced and kissed and both started talking at the same time. Finally, Luca said, "No, no you first. Are you okay? Did you hear what happened?"

"I know nothing," she said. "I've been so scared I haven't contacted anyone, but I told you to meet me here so long ago and I just had a feeling you would know—and now you're here. I can't believe it. I called Stefano to go get you, before. I'm so happy he got to you before they did. I know they would come for you."

"Yes, they did come for all of us, but never again."

"What do you mean?"

"That's right. You don't know—how could you unless you read all the papers in Italy? Vincenzo and Marco died in a car accident when they were coming after us."

"*Morti*? Oh…oh, it's true? Oh, how strange."

"What do you mean?"

"I just mean how strange. Vincenzo was a bad man, a very bad man, but it's just strange after having been in a relationship with him and he's gone, permanently gone."

"I see," Luca said.

"No Luca, don't be jealous. I'm so happy he can't hurt us anymore. But it's just a strange feeling to know that he is gone."

"Yeah, yeah I do understand."

"Come inside. I'm making dinner and we have so much to catch up on."

"Yes, I'll be in in one minute. Everything has been a whirlwind and I haven't talked with David in months. He's probably worried sick about me."

"Yes, call your family. I'll finish up in here."

Matilda headed into the house and Luca tried calling David, but no one answered. He tried again, but once again, nothing. He tried calling Lillian. She answered straight away.

"Oh my gosh Luca, where have you been? It's been so hectic and no one could reach you!"

"Hey, it's okay, calm down. It's a long, long story. Everything okay?"

"No Luca, everything's not okay."

Lillian explained in detail what happened. Luca

listened and told Lillian he would have to call her back the next day. He hung up and stood still for a moment. Then he headed into the flat.

Matilda was in the kitchen preparing the final steps of dinner. She was sipping on a glass of wine and turned when Luca came in. "Hey, you okay? You look different. What happened?"

"My dad, my stepdad, David…he passed away a few nights ago."

"No, what happened? Oh, I'm so sorry. Come here," Matilda said, coming to Luca. She embraced him and pulled him close. "Oh Luca, I'm sorry. You were very close weren't you?"

"Yes, we were. He was my dad. He's the only family I really had. I can't believe it."

"Oh *amore*, what happened?"

"I guess he went peacefully. He was outside sitting in a chair by the garden and I guess he had a heart attack and died right there. Probably no pain at all they think. A neighbor spotted him and called the paramedics, but it had already been some time I guess."

"*Tesoro*, I'm sorry. What can I do? Anything."

"Just be with me; just be here with me."

****

Luca and Matilda took a car out to Cornwall and after a quick breakfast in Truro, they drove east to Penzance along the coast. They parked and took a walk out to the beach and sat in the sand on a blanket as the sun began to set. Luca held Matilda close. They didn't speak as the sun quickly began its descent into the sea. With the sun gone and leaving only the remnants of its light, it began to get cold as a sea wind picked up.

"Shall we go *amore*," Matilda said.

"Just a bit longer," Luca said. "It's funny, the sun. Every day it rises and lingers and then at the end, it disappears into the sea, but really, it's only gone from our eyes as it's lighting up another part of the world. I believe that's what happens when we die. We're only gone from the eyes of the world, but we're lighting up someone, somewhere else. David, now, is lighting up my mom's life again. I can feel it."

"*Si, amore, si.*"

"I'm alone now, but I have you. We have each other."

"Yes, we do. Somehow, we managed to survive."

"No matter what happens, I'm forever thankful that we can have these moments," Luca said. "My new life has begun."

"*Our* new life has begun *amore*. What should we do first?"

"Well…I still haven't had carbonara in Rome or seen la Fiorentina beat Juventus."

Matilda leaned into Luca's body, kissed his cheek and whispered into his ear. "But what should we do first?"

He took his gaze out away from the darkening sea as the moon began to light up the waters and turned it onto the luminescent eyes of his lover, his Occhi Belli. The sea was calm, but their love was anything but.

The End

## A word about the author...

Tim McDonald was born and raised in Kennewick, Washington. He studied Creative Writing at Pacific Lutheran University and completed a wine studies program in Italy. He has worked in copy editing, has taught English in South Korea, and has owned and operated an Italian restaurant in north Seattle. He currently lives in Washington State.
timrossmcdonald.com

Thank you for purchasing
this publication of The Wild Rose Press, Inc.

For questions or more information
contact us at
info@thewildrosepress.com.

The Wild Rose Press, Inc.
www.thewildrosepress.com

www.ingramcontent.com/pod-product-compliance
Lightning Source LLC
Chambersburg PA
CBHW052008020726
47501CB00004B/1060